How To Get A Promotion When Your Boss Is Trying To Kill You

Accurate Accounts of Office Work: Book 1
A Novel

Joseph Patrick Pascale

Published by Waldorf Publishing
2140 Hall Johnson Road
#102-345
Grapevine, Texas 76051
www.WaldorfPublishing.com

How To Get A Promotion
When Your Boss Is Trying To Kill You
Accurate Accounts of Office Work: Book 1

ISBN: 978-1-64136-844-5
Library of Congress Control Number: 2018933216

In a month of ridiculously busy days, this day had already been the busiest—as well as the most important—and the young clerk was standing in the entrance to the conference room, trembling slightly as his eyes darted between groups of people. He'd already had to do a huge amount of preliminary legwork on this project—represented by the big stack of papers in the folder he was holding—and here he was at the first meeting that would determine the route of this top-priority project. He had no idea who the project manager would be, which made him more confused about the dynamics in the room, and he was frozen in place because he had an extremely important decision to make.

He needed to figure out who he should sit with.

With his first step, he'd decided to sit next to his boss—his manager—but as soon as his foot stepped into the gray industrial carpet, he changed his mind. Sitting next to his manager might make people think that he was artificially inflating his rank, presuming to be more important and "in the know" than he really was, which would make the others look down on him and irritate his manager. No, that wasn't the best move here. He needed to think this over.

Other office workers shuffled past him as they made their way into the large conference area. Sweat had broken out on the clerk's brow, and he rubbed his chin. The group he most wanted to sit with was a handful of clerical assistants in one corner. He was friendly with them because he used to work in their department, but he knew that his manager would consider affiliating with them a poor choice. He'd heard her complain that they never did anything correctly and wouldn't return calls, leaving her department to do double the work, so he knew they were out. One of them waved when she saw him looking in their direction, but his brain was cranking too intensely to process the action of waving back.

The safest place to sit was probably with the other clerks from his department, but he could see his rival over there gesticulating excitedly, he could hear his rival's nasal laugh, and after the morning the clerk had already had, enduring his greasy rival was the last thing he wanted to do.

One of his manager's part-time assistants burst into the room and shoved past the clerk.

"The meeting is about to begin," someone announced at the front of the room. "Everyone please take your seats."

The clerk began to shake more intensely as he looked at different groups of people, considering their ranks and personalities and how he could justify sitting with them.

The assistant had whispered something into his manager's ear, and she jumped up from her seat and rushed toward the door. "You come with us," she said as they walked past the clerk.

"But, but—" the clerk stuttered. They were already down the hallway, and he had no choice except to follow behind.

The clerk walked down the hallway and into the area of cubicles where he followed their mazelike path to his manager's office on the far wall. She went in and slammed the door behind her, leaving her assistant waiting outside with his hands folded at his waist.

"What was all that?" the clerk asked.

"Phone call. The director wanted her," the assistant responded.

"The director?" the clerk whispered, the word dripping with fear.

Before the clerk could think much about it, the door swung open and his manager stormed out.

"You're meeting with the director," she said, thrusting

her finger in the clerk's direction.

"Me? The director?" the clerk muttered. "But, but—I'm supposed to be at this big meeting. I have this report. It's top priority."

"This is your top priority now. You know the director's much more important than anything going on at this meeting."

"Director," the clerk responded, as though it was a word he'd never heard before. "But this report—"

"Forget the report!" his manager snapped. "Leave it at your desk. You don't want to keep the director waiting. You're meeting him at the main office in the bigger city, so get going."

The clerk hurried back to his cubicle. He threw the folder of papers into one of the desk drawers. He'd left out all sorts of documents that he'd intended to work on after lunch. Before he realized what he was doing, he started furiously scribbling some notes to himself on where to pick up when he returned, but he stopped because he knew he had to hurry up. He started gathering a few things into his satchel when the assistant appeared in the cubicle doorway.

"She wants to know if you finished that document for 2nd Street."

"Yes, it's done."

"Well then she wants you to deliver it while you're down there rather than inter-office it. After you finish with the director, of course."

"Of course," the clerk muttered, rifling through his files to find the document.

* * * *

Under gray skies in cold air, the clerk sat on the bus, gazing out the window at the quiet afternoon of a city at work. The window was letting in the chill and the clerk could feel it through his jacket. It wasn't his warmest jacket, but it was his fanciest, which gave him slight reassurance about meeting with the director—unlike his scuffed shoes. He checked his silver wristwatch and wished that the bus would move faster. Presently, it was stopped, and two round ladies were approaching a seat near him. As one of them sat down, the whole seat lurched backward. They exclaimed and laughed, moving to the seat next to the clerk.

He couldn't understand what they were saying. They were immigrants, as was almost everyone in the small city, and in turn this made the clerk an immigrant of sorts. He was from this province, but from far away beyond the mountains and distant forests. He could speak, read, and write the official language fluently, which had been a boon in securing him his government job, but almost everyone in the small city spoke the island language. Because of this, most employees in the small city branch spoke both languages. He often wondered if this made him unqualified for the job, even though the island language was not officially recognized in government documents.

He reached into his satchel and took out a thermos. Unscrewing the lid, he took a sip. On such a chilly day, the warmth of the coffee was like an angel's kiss, and he could envision the golden heat flowing down his throat and spreading through his core. As he was replacing his thermos, he noticed the large manila envelope in his satchel. It was filled with the paperwork he was supposed to hand-deliver. Although he'd previously triple-checked it before leaving his cubicle, he took out the papers and began reviewing them once more. It was easy to concentrate amid the noise of the bus, since he was used to being surrounded by people speaking in a language he didn't understand, but every so often, he'd get distracted by an island word he knew, like the word for "next stop." He noted an extremely minor punctuation mistake in the paperwork that had been overlooked and left a mental sticky note for himself to fix it when he was in a more stable environment.

Putting the papers away, he leaned back in his seat and gazed out the window, feeling the nervousness build in his stomach when he realized he had crossed the border into the bigger city and would soon be facing the director in person. The clerk felt nervous to face his own boss, but his anxiety doubled in intensity as he thought of facing his boss's boss.

The bus pulled away as the clerk walked down the sidewalk in air so cold that it muted the sounds of the bustling city around him. What the cold did to sounds, it also did to vision: The vibrancy was taken from colors of the world, leaving too much gray behind. Even the colorful flags fluttering in front of the government building appeared to be the same gray as the swirling clouds overhead.

"Well, this is it," the clerk said, taking a deep breath as he started up the stone stairs of the building. As he opened the door, he saw a security checkpoint, and off to the side, a separate entrance marked "Active War Military Personnel."

Before he could take a step inside, he was accosted by the security guards: "Who are you?" the female guard said.

"We haven't seen you around here before," the male guard said.

The clerk was frozen with fear. He had been thinking that he might be treated poorly because of his appearance. He did his best to look as business conservative as possible, but there was just one small problem. He wore his hair in the traditional style of his people from out in the country. He liked it that way, but it was very different from the ultra-short hairstyle that was expected of formally dressed men in this region. This left him self-conscious about his hair, sensing that people judged him negatively on account of his differing appearance. He could change his hair to match theirs, but— well, he wasn't sure why he refrained from doing so.

"I think he doesn't belong," the female said.

"Remove yourself from the premises before we remove you—with force!" the male said.

"No, no! You've got it all wrong, I, I—" the clerk stuttered.

"Insolence! You would dare to say we are wrong?" the female guard said.

The clerk began to reach in his pocket to extract his government identification.

"He's reaching for a weapon!" the male security guard said.

The female guard had already lunged at him, tackling the frail clerk to the ground. He cried out in pain as he landed on the floor, his identification card slipping from his fingers and sliding across the polished marble tiles.

"What's this?" the male security guard said, leaning down to pick up the fallen card. "It's a government identification card."

"Does that mean I should let him go?" the female asked, still digging one knee into the clerk's back and holding his arms up in the air behind his head. Tears were welling in the corners of the clerk's eyes.

"I don't know," the male said. "It doesn't have a high enough security clearance to enter this building."

"Ah-ha! He was trying to sneak in!" the female said, strengthening her grip. A tiny squeal escaped from beneath the clerk's clenched teeth.

"Let's say we give him the benefit of the doubt and check his name in the system," the male said.

"Okay then, to the interrogation room in the meantime!"

the female replied, jumping up and pulling the clerk to his feet by his trapped arms.

Before the clerk fully processed what was happening, he was strapped to a wall. His arms and legs were spread beyond what was comfortable and he couldn't move them at all.

"Why is a lowly clerk trying to sneak into this building?" someone in a suit and a black mask shouted at him, prodding him with something hard.

"I'm not trying to sneak in!"

"Lies!" the masked person said, poking him harder. "What business could a lowly clerk have here?"

"I have a meeting with the Director of Communication Security!" the clerk cried.

"Impossible! The director would never meet with such a lowly clerk. Tell me the truth!"

"Actually, he is telling the truth," said a woman in a maroon suit with matching lipstick, holding up an official-looking document as she spoke. "I have a temporary clearance card for him." She threw it down in front of the clerk.

The shackles instantly loosened and the clerk stumbled to the ground. He picked up the card from the ground and rose to his feet. He turned the shiny plastic card in his hands, waiting. The woman and the masked person stared at him, and the woman eventually let out a sigh and said, "Well then? Aren't you going to head to your meeting with the director?"

"Oh, right. I'm free to go." He said this as a mixture of question and statement. The clerk took a few steps forward before he softly asked, "Where can I meet the director?"

The woman sighed and rolled her eyes. "On the 72nd floor." She implied the words "of course."

"Oh, right," the clerk muttered as he shuffled out of the room and into the hallway. The walls were made of glass and he could see stairs that reached and wound high above him. There were also two elevators, so he opted to use one of those instead of ascending the seemingly endless stairs. However, the clerk was perplexed when he couldn't find a button to call the elevator. He felt around on the wall where he thought it should be, wondering if perhaps it was nearly invisible. On the opposite side of where he expected it, he discovered a small slit in the wall. The shiny card still being in his hand, he immediately thought to stick it in there. The slot sucked the card right in. Then nothing happened. The clerk looked up the glass wall, wondering if maybe he could see the lift in its shaft, but he was unable to discern anything. He checked his watch. "Well, there are many floors. Maybe the lift is slow."

Five minutes passed. Then ten.

Not knowing what else to do, the clerk shuffled back into the room he'd come from. The shackles remained open on the wall, but he didn't see the two people.

"Um. Is anybody here?" the clerk muttered.

"You again?" came the voice of the masked person.

"Ugh, what is it?" the woman said, her head appearing above a desk in the corner. The clerk noticed her lipstick was gone.

"I um. Well you see, the thing is—funny story really—I couldn't quite get the lift to work, and then I sort of lost the card you gave me."

"What?!" the lady shouted. "Just get out of here for a minute. Give us some privacy, would you? I'll come out and help you in a minute."

"Oh, okay. Uh, thanks," the clerk muttered.

As the woman disappeared back behind the desk and the clerk was exiting, he could hear her saying, "His level of incompetence is astounding. This is precisely why we don't let these low ranking officials in this building."

She didn't come help the clerk in one minute: It was six minutes, to be exact. The clerk had been sitting against the wall in the hallway, leaning his wrist on his knees right where he could stare at his watch.

"Now what's the problem?" the woman said as she appeared in the hallway, tugging the wrinkles out of her skirt.

"I couldn't get the lift to come, and I lost the card you gave me," the clerk said as he got to his feet.

The woman sighed as she walked toward the elevators. The clerk followed.

"What happened to the card?" she asked, placing her palm between the two elevators. It glowed to life and scanned her handprint, causing one set of doors to open.

"I put it in there," the clerk said, pointing at the spot where he'd lost it.

"In there?!" the woman exclaimed. "What's the matter with you? You just go around sticking your valuables in any opening you find?"

"No, well I—"

"C'mon. I'll have to get you *another one* on the 59th floor."

"Oh okay. I'm a—well, I don't mean to be any trouble."

"Of course you don't," the woman said with a biting smile as she entered the lift and motioned for the clerk to do the same.

Momentarily, they were entering the hallway on the 59th floor. Something about it reminded the clerk of a gymnasium, and that made the clerk uncomfortable, as physical education had been his least favorite subject in school. As they walked down the hallway, the clerk could hear slapping sounds on the other side of the gray walls, with occasional grunts and shouts mixed in. He imagined people playing sports all around him and shuddered.

The woman stopped at a little alcove containing a few chairs, a water-cooler, a vending machine, and a potted plant. "You sit here and *don't move*. I'm going to attempt to get you a replacement card, but it could be a while. You know what they say about the workers on the 59th floor." She made a face.

"Actually, I don't."

"Of course you don't," she said rolling her eyes and walking away.

The clerk sat on one of the chairs with his satchel on his lap. He considered checking over his paperwork again, but found the slapping noises distracting.

Movement on the vending machine caught his eye and he saw a tiny black mouse on top of it. Then another mouse appeared next to that one, and another, and another. Some of them were nibbling on the corners of the vending machine.

"Aw, they must smell the food inside," he whispered as he stood up.

The mice squeaked and disappeared back behind the vending machine.

"No! It's okay. I won't hurt you little guys."

As if they could understand him, the tiny mice heads reappeared at the edge of the vending machine, peering down at the clerk.

"You guys are hungry? I think I have some money."

The mice were watching with interest as the clerk dug around in the pocket of his trousers. "Ah, here we go. So let's see. What do you guys like? We've got cookies, crisps, all different kinds of sweets, crackers—"

One of the mice squeaked.

"You like crackers? Crackers it is then. Let's see? A5. Here we go." The metal arm grabbed the crackers and threw them down the slot. The clerk grabbed them and tore the bag open. He extracted a cracker and broke it in four. "Let's see, one for you." The first black mouse snatched the cracker quickly from between the clerk's fingers with its teeth and scurried to the back of the vending machine. "No, don't nick it from him guys, I've got plenty for everyone. See? One for you, one for you, one for you. Hold on, let me get some more." He took out another cracker and broke it into pieces. "And one for you and you. There we go. Everyone's got a cracker now."

The clerk couldn't see where the mice had run off to nibble on their crackers, so he retook his seat and checked his silver wristwatch. After a minute, a tiny, black, triangle-shaped face appeared at the top of the vending machine. It was looking straight down at the clerk. Then another face appeared. Then another and another. All the mice stared at the clerk for a moment before the first started to nimbly climb down the side corner of the vending machine. It was quick, with its tiny, thin tail following behind the black triangle of its body. The other mice followed suit, and they all ran straight toward the clerk. They stopped a foot in front of the clerk and sat in a half-circle before him, peering at him. One let out a squeak.

"You little guys want more crackers?" the clerk asked. He reached into his pocket for the bag of crackers. He broke one up into little pieces and held them out for the mice. They were cautious, but each scampered forward and grabbed their bit of cracker. When they finished those and continued to stare at the clerk, he broke up more crackers, but this time he left them on the palm of his hand. The mice were worried about it, but finally one of them found the gumption to climb up his fingers, grab one, and run back away. Before he knew it, the mice were all in his lap, begging for crackers.

* * * *

"Cor blimey! Vermin! What's going on here?!" the woman in the maroon suit exclaimed as she reappeared in the hallway. She saw the clerk laying down on the floor. He was rolling around on his back and giggling as the ticklish mice scampered all over him. When they heard the woman they began to squeak in terror and flee. She tried to stomp on one of them that was nearby, but it was too fast for her. "Did they hurt you?" she asked the clerk as he pulled himself off the floor. All the mice had disappeared.

"What? No, of course not."

"Ugh. Disgusting. Those exterminators aren't doing their jobs.

"Anyway, I was able to get you another clearance card. Don't lose this one!" she shouted as she handed it to him. "If you lose this one, you're on your own." Without another word, the woman stalked down the hallway past him.

The clerk grabbed his satchel and went down the hallway in the opposite direction, back toward the elevators. This time, he knew to hold his palm out to open the doors and he punched in the button for the 72nd floor. There was fear in the clerk's gut as the elevator took him toward his destination, but suddenly he was distracted from it by a tickling sensation. He lifted his jacket and saw two shiny, tiny, black eyes staring up at him from his breast pocket. "You stayed in there little guy? Well that's okay, but you better stay hidden. They don't seem very kind to your kind around here."

The clerk walked out of the elevator and was greeted by a station of three ladies in green aprons. "May we help you sir? Do you have a table reservation?"

"Uh. I'm supposed to meet with the Director of Communication Security," the clerk muttered.

"I know exactly which table you are," one of the girls

said.

The clerk was thinking that he didn't know that he *was* a table when one of the other girls said, "Can I take your bag to the coat check?"

He was hesitant, as he still had to turn in that important paperwork, but the girl's hand was wrapped around the shoulder strap of his satchel. "Uh, sure," he muttered. She was already walking away with it.

"Let's just wait for her to come back with your slip. Then I'll take you in."

"Here you go, sir," the other girl said as she reappeared, handing him a tiny square with a number written on it.

"If you'll follow me right this way, sir," the girl who'd originally spoken said, picking up a long, laminated rectangle and heading toward double doors. She pushed them open and the clerk followed behind her, entering into what appeared to be a massive, fancy, ballroom-style restaurant. Waiters and waitresses were bustling around the tables, and the clerk could hear chatter and utensils clanging as people ate all around him. The girl stopped at an empty, round table. She pulled a chair out and invited the clerk to take the seat, which he did. "Here is your menu, sir," she said handing it to him. "The wine list is here."

"Okay, thank you," the clerk said. It came out as more of a question than a statement.

He opened the menu and began eliminating things he wouldn't eat: "Chicken, Cow, Pig, Fish, Crustacean." These words were vocalized as a sigh.

A waiter appeared next to the clerk. "Can I get you something to drink, sir?"

"Just water is fine," the clerk said.

"I'll get that for you right away sir."

"Let me ask you something," the clerk said to the waiter

when he returned with the tall glass of ice water. "Do you serve anything that wasn't prepared with animals?"

"I'm sorry?" the waiter said.

"All these meals. They have animal meat in them."

"Oh, you want something *vegetarian?*" the waiter said.

"Well, not *vegetarian*," the clerk muttered. "I just don't want any sort of dead animal involved with it."

"I'll have to check with the head chef."

"Okay. Thank you." The clerk thought he heard the faintest squeak of approval from within his pocket. "You stay quiet little guy," the clerk whispered to the mouse under the guise of taking a sip of his water. "I don't know why there's a restaurant in here, but I'm sure they would be extra-upset if they knew you were in it!"

The clerk sat alone, glancing around at the other diners. He assumed they were other government workers. They were wearing suits and business attire—generally a fancy-looking bunch. So much time passed as he sat there that the clerk started to wonder if he was in the wrong place—or worse—what if he'd already missed his meeting with the director? He was delayed for a long time after he'd arrived inside the building, and his manager had emphasized the need for haste.

"Oh, I'm going to be in so much trouble if I missed my appointment with the director! My boss is going to be mad. The director's going to be mad! Oh dear."

"Sir," the waiter said, returning. "The head chef said that he could prepare a dish of stir-fried arugula, spinach, and mushrooms. Will this be suitable?"

"Oh yeah, that'd be great," the clerk said.

"Excellent, then. I shall wait until the rest of your party arrives before putting in your order."

"Oh, my party's arriving? That's a relief."

After a time, a woman and man were led to the table and offered seats. The clerk tried to introduce himself, but the woman interrupted him. "I think it's best we wait until the director arrives before conversing."

"Oh. Okay then," the clerk muttered.

The waiter took their drink orders, and they each ordered water, which took some stress away from the clerk, as he had been worried he would be expected to drink alcohol. He didn't believe in drinking alcohol as it impaired his brain, and he wanted his brain to function at full capacity—even if that meant being more stressed out than was comfortable. When the waiter returned with drinks, he also returned with bread and butter. The three of them sat there silently, buttering bread and eating it. The clerk was inspecting the pair without appearing to be scrutinizing them. One was older and the other was younger. The younger woman had her hair wrapped up behind her head in an elaborate bun, and the older man had his hair close-cropped and ultrashort. He thought of his own hair and wondered if that was the reason they didn't want to talk to him. No one seemed to much care how women wore their hair in this region. They wore it in a variety of styles. He expected the director's hair would be the ultra-short cut that was standard for males.

A tall, thickly built man in a black suit appeared next to the table. There wasn't the slightest trace of a hair anywhere on him. His head gleamed in the reflected light of the crystal chandelier. His skin was yellowed like the pages of a book left out in the sun, and investigating him as best he could, the clerk couldn't discern a single hair even on the man's brow—just the shadow of dark hair that had been recently shaved.

"Greetings fellow co-workers. It was really swell of you to join me for this working lunch meeting."

"The pleasure's all mine, Director," the woman said.

"I'm flattered you'd have me, Director," the man said.

A moment of silence fell. The clerk felt eyes on him. He had to say something. Something polite and smooth. The clerk remembered back when he'd been in his cubicle this morning. In general, he did his best not to think of his cubicle as a constricting cage, and right now, the thought of it seemed quite pleasant. He could sit alone and work quietly on paperwork, sipping coffee from his thermos. He wouldn't have to worry about being in the wrong place or saying the right thing. He remembered one day in the break room, pouring coffee, one of his fellow clerks had been warning him how political it was in the bigger city's government offices. She warned the clerk to watch his tongue if he ever had to attend a meeting there. Now he was watching it too intently.

The director's eyes bore into the clerk. The director looked as though he might speak but didn't want to.

The clerk stuttered. "Really glad to a—really glad to be—meet you here, sir."

The director's stare turned into a huge toothy grin and he took a seat right next to the clerk. "This is just fantastic," he said. "All of us here from different departments—some even from different branches!" Here he was looking at the clerk, "to get some work done and eat some fantastic food. I tell you, the food here is excellent. Best restaurant in the building, by far."

"Sir, the head chef sends this, compliments of the house," the waiter said, appearing with a large clear bottle of vodka held in his hands, wrapped in a green cloth.

"Ah, excellent!" the director exclaimed.

"I'll be right back with some glasses."

The clerk was eyeing the huge bottle of alcohol suspiciously when he noticed that the director had a giant stack of papers in front of him. He gulped as he realized the others each had a stack of papers in front of them too. *"Curses!"* he thought. *"I should have never let them take my satchel! All my important paperwork was in there. For all I know they tossed it into an incinerator. If I was a true clerk, my dedication would have been such that I would have never let the paperwork leave my sight!"* Of course the clerk should have known that the elegant, higher-up government workers would take *working* luncheons. He didn't know how he could be so foolish. The pain in his neck grew stronger, causing his whole brain to ache. His stress all seemed to build up there, and it seemed that each day he worked, the stress grew. He imagined he was a puppet, and the strings that connected his neck to his arms and the rest of his body were being twisted by his puppet masters, each twist making his neck tighter and more painful.

But he noticed that they weren't yet looking at their papers and took solace. The workers were staring at their menus, and the director had just finished buttering his bread with his meaty fingers and was now staring at his menu as he chomped on the bread. The clerk pretended to scrutinize his menu.

"This bread is fantastic," the director said. "It's simply the best bread in the building. Take some more bread, won't you?" He was holding out the basket toward everyone. The others each took a piece, so the clerk did as well.

"It's good," the clerk managed politely.

"I have bread every morning during my break," the man said. "I have enough powdered bread packets in my desk for each working day of the year."

"Powdered bread? What's that?" the woman asked.

"Well, they're in little silver packets. They're very small—don't take up much room. You tear open a packet and pour the powder out into a tiny bowl. It's a powder with the consistency of flour, but more of a golden brown in color. Next, you have to add water. I put some in from the water cooler. I've done it so many times that I can eyeball the right amount, but if you're a novice, you'll definitely need to measure out the proper amount. It's not the kind of thing you want to over- or under-water. If you over-water it, you'll have a mouthful of slime. If you under-water it you're eating sand. Then I take a small teaspoon and mix together the powder and the water. You want to do it in a quick whisking motion. Once it stops making a crunching sound, it's probably done. Now it looks something like a chocolate mousse, so you'll just want to leave it alone and let it air dry for a few minutes. Once it's ready, you can just dump it out of the bowl, and you'll have a nice half-circle of perfect bread. It's delicious! It's the best bread I've ever tasted! All fresh and nice every time—and guess what? This bread is better than it!"

"Wow, this bread is better?" the director said. "On the one hand, I'm not surprised as this bread is fantastic, but on the other hand, I'm so fascinated by the delicious sound of your powdered bread that I *am* surprised."

The clerk had no input on this bread conversation and didn't see anything special about the bread he was currently eating, so he just kept nibbling on his bread and let them witter on. He was trying to be neat, but a few little crumbs were falling into his lap. He realized too late that he should have unfolded his serviette and put it in his lap like the director had done, but to do it now—the blunder would be too obvious. He would wait until he needed to extract his forks from the serviette for dining, and then he would naturally slide it down to his lap.

Suddenly, the clerk was fighting laughter.

The director must have been scrutinizing the clerk in his peripheral vision, because he immediately said, "What's funny? Did I miss something?"

The clerk was horrified, but he was still suppressing laughter. He had to answer. "Well, I, um—thought of a joke—is all."

"A joke?" the director inquired.

Then, because he realized it was impolite to have not been paying attention, the clerk quickly added, "A joke about bread."

Just below his left nipple, tiny feet with even tinier, pointy fingernails were skittering around. The little black mouse was crawling down toward the clerk's belly.

The clerk knew what the director was going to say even before he said it. The clerk became cognizant of the fact that he'd dug himself into a bad position and saw his dreams of a promotion burning before him—his dreams of obtaining the space he and his betrothed so dreamed of were dissolving like powder into bread.

"What's the joke?" the director asked.

Now the clerk was really toasted. He considered saying the joke was too off-color to tell at work, but to say that would be held against him. They'd consider his mind perverted and inappropriate, thinking of profanity during a business lunch. No, that excuse wouldn't work. No excuse would work. He had to tell a joke.

Adding to the clerk's horror, he noticed movement in his crotch and realized that the tiny black mouse was sitting there, picking up breadcrumbs in both hands and nibbling on them as though they were corn-on-the-cob. The one thing he was thankful for in this moment was that he was wearing black trousers. The black mouse would blend in with the black trousers and not be immediately noticeable.

Through all this, the clerk also became aware that he'd forgotten every joke he'd ever heard. The silence was stretching on. The director was staring at him. He had to make up one right now. On the spot.

The clerk started the way all jokes start: "Once upon a time there was a—" The clerk immediately realized that he had begun his joke the way all *fairy stories* begin, but not the way a single *joke* starts. He tried to fix his blunder seamlessly: "—knock-knock joke." He realized this non-sequitur could be construed as funny—as part of the joke!—so he let nervous laughter escape from his lips, which was a relief because the mouse was scurrying to another breadcrumb, tickling his crotch and triggering his laugh-mechanism.

The others smiled politely, waiting for the clerk to continue.

"Um." The clerk didn't know how to continue. Then he had the epiphany that all knock-knock jokes follow a certain format. "Knock-knock."

"Who's there?" the director asked.

"Bread!" the clerk exclaimed, having remembered that the joke had to be about bread. But now he was in a real bind. How was he going to come up with a punchline involving bread arriving at a door? He thought he could hear the slightest sound of the mouse chewing in his lap.

At that moment, the waiter arrived and began distributing glasses to the table, which took the others' attention. As the waiter was opening the vodka and beginning to pour a glass for each person, the clerk was struggling to think of a punchline to his joke. *"Let's see,"* he thought, *"Bread rhymes with red, shed, med—"*

"Well then," the director said, "before we toast, I must ask, 'Bread who?'"

"Bread you didn't know the baker baked me this

morning!" the clerk cried out, and then, to really sell it, he doubled over in laughter, and while he pretended it was so funny he had to wrap his arms around his tummy, he snatched up the mouse and tried to discreetly stuff it back into his pocket. He returned his hand with a tissue that had been in his jacket pocket, which he used to wipe pretend-tears from his eyes.

The others hadn't laughed.

"Onto the toast," the director continued.

Everyone lifted their glasses.

"To success!" the director said, and then came a round of glasses clinking.

The clerk could envision a promotion slipping away from him like a melting piece of ice popping out of fist. He managed a small sip of the vodka, which smelled like rubbing alcohol and tasted like drinking liquid fire. He stifled a cough into his tissue.

"This is a delicious vintage," the director said, swirling it around in his mouth. Everyone at the table agreed.

"Are you all ready to order?" the waiter asked. The people at the table nodded to each other and then the woman began to order. When the waiter got to the clerk, he said the spinach arugula dish sounded good, and the waiter moved on.

"Well, it'll probably be a little while before the appetizers come, so let's get down to business," the director said, and with that he extracted a thin, black pen from his pocket. With a determined look in his eye, the director shifted the big stack of papers in front of him and hunched over them, circling something on the paper before long. Without missing a beat, the others started to work on their paperwork as well, the man quickly covering several lines in whiteout.

"Oh this is bad; this is bad," the clerk thought, wringing

his hands and subconsciously ripping up the tissue. He spoke quickly, "I um, I have a ton of work to catch up on too," he lied, "but I really must visit the lavatory first."

The director absent-mindedly looked up from his paperwork to the clerk and nodded, grabbing his glass and taking a big gulp of vodka.

The clerk began weaving between tables where people chatted, ate, and—of course—filled out paperwork. As the clerk walked, he had no idea where he was going. On the one hand, he wanted to rush to the girls in the front and beg them to give him his satchel from the coatroom—on the other hand, he said he was going to the restroom, and he didn't want to appear to be a liar. He looked around, searching for the restroom, wondering where it could be. He didn't locate it, so he kept heading toward the front, hoping no waiter stopped him to point him in the right direction. Sweat was beading down his forehead.

"Excuse me sir, can I help you with something?" a waitress said, accosting him.

"Just heading for the, uh—" it suddenly occurred to the clerk that he didn't have to use the lie of going to the bathroom, "maître'ds to ask them something."

"Oh okay," she said with a smile as she rushed off toward the kitchen.

"Yes!" the clerk thought. *"Finally, some luck."*

He found the three girls filing each others' nails in a triangle formation.

"Oh, can we help you sir?" one of them said.

"Yes, I wanted to get my satchel from the coat check room."

"Ah, that will be no problem, if you can just present us with the slip we gave you?"

"Oh, right. The slip." He reached into his jacket pocket

and felt something warm—the little black mouse. It started smelling his fingers and grabbed one of them with both of its tiny hands. He tried to shake the mouse off his finger and feel around for the slip, but this caused the mouse to grab onto the slip with its teeth for some reason. He started tugging on the slip, but the mouse wouldn't let go.

"Is there a problem, sir?" the girl asked as she watched him struggling with his pocket.

"If you'll just excuse me for one moment," he said, spinning around so that his back faced the girls. He opened one side of his jacket and leaned his head down inside of it, close to the pocket. "Please let go little guy! This is important!" The clerk gave a final tug on the slip and it came free. "Ah ha! Got it!" he said triumphantly, spinning around.

The girl had a perplexed look on her face, and it grew more concerned as she noticed that the paper slip appeared to have been chewed up by tiny teeth, but as she spun the paper around and noticed the number, her face became downright upset. "This is all the way in the back!" she said.

"In the back?" one of the other girls said. "That area's supposed to be closed off."

"But well," the clerk stuttered, trying to keep his cool. "Did you put it back there?"

"Who, me?" one of the girls asked, poking herself in the chest.

The clerk looked at the three of them. They were all wearing the same green outfit, and as he tried to stare at the features of their faces, they seemed to blur into one another. At first, he thought the girl on the far left had the smallest nose of the three, but then when he looked at the girl on the far right, the tiny nose appeared to have shifted to her. Their features were going in and out of focus, causing it to hurt his eyes to look upon them any longer.

"I'm not sure," he admitted at last. "I gave it to one of you."

The girls looked nervous now, biting on their lips. "How badly do you need your coat?" one of them hazarded.

"Oh quite badly indeed, I'm afraid," the clerk said. "It's not a coat I entrusted you, but a satchel with my important paperwork."

"Oh my. That is bad," one of the girls said, and she appeared to be fighting with herself internally as her eyebrows twisted inward. "I'll take you. C'mon, let's check. Maybe it's right in the very front of the back."

"Oh, thank you very much. I appreciate it immensely!" the clerk said.

She started to walk down the hallway, and then she stopped and faced the clerk once more. "You're coming, aren't you? I don't want to go in there all alone."

"Oh, me? Well, okay then, if it means getting back my satchel."

The clerk followed behind the girl as they passed through a door and into a labyrinth of coats and jackets. The girl weaved in and out of them, this way and that, seemingly at random, but the clerk trusted she knew where she was going and tried to keep up.

"Okay, it's through there," the girl said, motioning a doorway covered by hanging strips of plastic.

The clerk looked at it as though it were a pit of lava.

"Well, go on then, after you, sir," the girl said.

"Right then," the clerk said, rubbing the breast of his jacket as a way of subtly petting the mouse for comfort.

As the plastic slips fell over his shoulders, the clerk stepped into the cement floor of the back room. A flashing red light engulfed his eyesight and a blaring alarm siren violated his ears. His feet began to slip and he lost his balance and fell to the ground, sliding toward some unseen point at the other edge of the warehouse-like room. He attempted to get to his feet, and flailed his arms around trying to grab onto something, but there was nothing. He cried out, but his voice couldn't be heard over the siren and he imagined he was being sucked into a black hole. A strong hand suddenly gripped one of his, pulling him back out of the room. He was panting on the ground of the coat-check room, looking up at the girl in green. "There was nothing in there," the girl said. "It was empty. Your slip must be wrong. One of us must have made a mistake—although I'm sure it wasn't I."

"What was going on in there?" the clerk gasped, out of breath, his heart pounding.

"Don't worry; you're fine. Now you know why we don't go back there very often. We put in a complaint to maintenance years ago."

She placed her strong arms under his armpits and forced him to his feet, turning on her heel and heading back into the maze of coats. The clerk hurried to follow behind her, knowing he'd be lost otherwise, but as he did so, he patted his jacket pocket. He cried out in horror, not feeling the tiny mouse, but it was a momentary horror, as he immediately found it wiggling around in his other pocket.

The other two girls said in unison, "What happened? Did you find it?" as the pair arrived.

"Nope, it wasn't there. We must have made a clanger! We're going to have to search for his bag."

"What does it look like?"

"I don't know. Ask him."

"What does your bag look like, sir?"

"Huh? Oh, my bag? I don't know. It's a satchel. One strap. Gray and black. There's important paperwork and a thermos of coffee in it."

"Okay, we're going to search for it, sir, but you should get back to your table. While you were absent some commotion happened."

"What happened?"

"I don't know, but I know a photographer from the building newspaper is there."

Worrying about what it could be, the clerk rushed back toward his table, noting the slickness on the flat bottoms of his fancy dress shoes and thinking that he wouldn't have fallen earlier if he'd been wearing the rugged black shoes he normally wore when he only had to sit and work in his cubicle. He'd worn these nicer shoes in anticipation of the project meeting he was supposed to attend, but he would have polished them if he knew he was meeting the director today.

As he entered the dining room, he saw that everyone was turned in their chairs and staring at the table with the director, the man, and the woman. The director was standing up, saying something to a woman in a chef's outfit. There was also another woman—the photographer that had been mentioned, evidently—taking pictures of five security guards holding the waiter up over their heads.

"Here he is now!" the director said, motioning the clerk as he approached. "The poor victim in all this."

"What, me? I'm sorry? What happened?"

"This insolent waiter attempted to get away with *not* serving you an appetizer. I think he made it up because he thought he could get away with it while you were absent, and then he has the nerve to make up this elaborate story that you didn't want one."

"Actually, I—well," the clerk stuttered, "I didn't think I got an appetizer with my meal because, well—"

"Did the waiter trick you into thinking that? The nerve!" the director shouted.

The photographer was flashing her camera in the confused clerk's face.

"Well no, it's not that sir," the clerk muttered, feeling his cheeks burn red. "It's just that I specifically asked the waiter not to bring me any food that had been prepared with animals."

"Huh?" everyone around seemed to say at once.

"And well, it seemed to me that all of the appetizers had been prepared with, well, animals."

"Not prepared with animals?" the director said in a confused tone. "How else does one prepare *food?*"

"Well sir, humans are omnivores," the clerk said matter-of-factly before becoming immediately shocked at what he'd said and who he said it to, quickly blurting out after, "As I'm sure you well know! I mean, I'm just trying to say that it's our choice to eat animals or not."

Everyone stared at the clerk for a moment.

"So you're telling me I should have these guards put the waiter down? That he hasn't done anything wrong?" the director said, sounding perplexed as he rubbed his thick, sausage-like fingers on his chin.

"That's right," the clerk responded.

"Oh okay, well then, you heard him gents," the director said, and with that they heaved the disheveled waiter down to his feet, and, in a triangle formation, the guards rushed out of the banquet hall without a word.

"Not sure if this will make the paper or not," the photographer said before doing a backflip over the table and hurrying behind the guards.

"Don't worry, son," the director said to the waiter with a wink. "I'll make sure you get a good tip."

"Thank you, sir!" the waiter said with enthusiasm before hurrying back to the kitchen.

The director retook his seat, so the clerk did the same. The others dug into their appetizers. "Here, let me top that off for you," the director said, pouring more vodka into the clerk's mostly full glass. "And since you don't have an appetizer, take the last piece of delicious bread."

"Thanks, sir," the clerk muttered.

"So, it's some cultural thing? That's what everyone's like out beyond the mountains?"

"I beg pardon?"

"Everyone's vegetarian beyond the mountains?"

"Oh, no. Not at all."

"I see," the director said, seeming dissatisfied with the answer.

The clerk realized that he really had to go to the bathroom, but he'd already lied and said he was going to the bathroom, so he couldn't just get up and go again. He tried not to wiggle in his seat too much, but he really had to go.

Before long, the main course was served and the clerk looked at his tiny plate of steamed vegetables.

"Can you pass me the salt?" the director asked.

The clerk realized he was being addressed, and started to reach for the salt, but as he did so, suddenly his vodka glass was being tipped over, and to his horror he realized that the clear liquid was spilling all over the director's papers.

"I'm so sorry!" the clerk exclaimed, scrambling for his serviette. "Did I do that?"

"Ugh! Unbelievable!" the director roared. "I must salvage this paperwork! It is of the utmost importance!"

"Here, let me help!" the clerk said, holding out the serviette, but the director was already scooping up the dripping pile of paperwork in his arms and running with it toward the entrance of the restaurant.

"Wait! Wait! Let me help!" the clerk shouted, rushing

after him with his napkin-wielding arm outstretched.

The other two scoffed and continued eating.

The clerk ran expeditiously after the director, weaving through tables and waitstaff, but the director was speedy, and disappearing out into the main hall well before the clerk.

As the clerk arrived in the main hall, the three girls in green stopped braiding each others' hair to look up at him.

"Did you guys see a huge, hairless man run through here?" the clerk asked.

"He went right through there," one of the girls pointed.

"Into the men's room," said another.

"Great! Thanks!" the clerk said, rushing in the indicated direction.

He arrived in the lavatory to see the director holding the pile of papers underneath the hand dryer that was blowing out a small hurricane of hot air.

"I'm so terribly sorry, sir!" the clerk groveled, fearing that his chances at promotion were completely destroyed now, having sailed away on a ship of paper-destroying vodka.

"Why be sorry?" the director said in a low voice that was difficult to hear over the sound of the air blowing out. "It was not you who spilled the liquid, but I."

"You did it?"

"I did it. And purposefully, too!"

"What? But your important paperwork—"

"Just as imperceptibly as I spilled your drink, I imperceptibly swapped my actual stack of important paperwork with a dummy set stashed away in my briefcase. These papers I'm drying right now aren't important at all, but no one knows that except you and I."

The clerk added in his thoughts, *"And the tiny black mouse."*

"I'm confused," the clerk said, forgetting that admitting

confusion was something one should never do in high stakes political situations. "Why would you spill my drink on your fake important paperwork?"

The director laughed in a low tone that reminded the clerk of a person discretely blowing his nose into a handkerchief. It could barely be heard over the sound of the hand-dryer. "I've created the perfect excuse for us to meet in private, and even if someone happened to be eavesdropping, they could never detect what we were speaking about over the noise in here."

Fear shot into the clerk's gut.

"You're a loyal government worker, aren't you?"

"Uh, yeah, yes, of course!" the clerk blurted, fumbling over his scant words.

"I knew the answer to that question before I asked it. That's why I'm entrusting you with such an important job. It's a job that's too important for someone with the status of a mere clerk," he spat the last word as though it were a bitter liquorice candy, "but I think you're more than that."

The clerk continued to stare at him with a perplexed expression.

"If you catch my drift," the director added with the hint of a sigh.

The clerk twisted his eyebrows.

"So tomorrow, and each workday after, when it's time for your lunch break, you are going to tell everyone that you are going out to take your lunch break at one of those island cuisine restaurants nearby. But you're not actually going to a restaurant!"

"What if one of my co-workers wants to come with me?"

"Does that usually happen?"

"No, but I usually eat my lunch at my desk."

"Well don't invite anyone then."

"But what if they invite themselves?"

"Say you're going to lunch in a tone that implies you would be angry if anyone tried to tag along with you."

"I don't know if I know how to convey all that through a tone."

A vein was starting to throb in the director's left temple. He continued to dry the sheets of paper with vigor. "Well then, if anyone asks to go to lunch with you, just make up an excuse like you have to talk to your wife on the phone while you eat because of some financial situation."

"Okay. That could work," the clerk said, "but what if they ask me to bring them back something from the restaurant?"

The director spoke through clenched teeth. "Just figure it out."

The clerk thought he might be irritating the director, so he attempted to remedy the situation. "Okay, okay. I got it. I'll figure it out. It's all under control. All taken care of. Although, if I'm not going to go to a restaurant during my lunch break, when am I going to eat?"

"It doesn't matter when you eat," the director said quickly, trying to brush the topic aside. "Eat whenever you want, wherever you want. Take another—secret—lunch break some other time to eat. During the lunch break everyone knows about, you are going to get on a bus and travel down to this very building in the bigger city. Once here, you will take the lift up to the 97th floor where the federal bowling alley is located. Go there and get a lane to yourself. A person will challenge you. Bowl against this person. It doesn't matter if you win or lose, just make sure you remember the person's bowling score. I need you to record this number in an encrypted spreadsheet file in your work computer. At the end of the match, the person will say, 'Good game,' and shake your hand, discreetly leaving you with a slip of paper detailing further directions. Then you can head back to your cubicle in the small city. Make sure you label the bowling scores as 'FAT,' and list the previous day's date."

"Fat? Like the weight?"

"Yes, like the weight. You'll receive further directions after the first bowling game."

"What if more than one person challenges me to a bowling game?"

"Why would that happen? It won't happen."

"You sure? What if it does and I get the wrong—"

"It won't happen! We can't be accounting for every little contingency here. Just listen to me."

"Okay, I'm listening. What else?"

"What do you mean, 'what else?' I told you everything!"

"You said to listen."

"I mean listen as in follow my directions!"

"Oh, right. Got it."

The director evened out the stack of papers on a sink and tucked them under an armpit, using his newly freed hand to adjust his necktie.

"Wait, if my manager catches me taking a second lunch break, can I tell her you said it was okay?"

"What? No! Of course not! This conversation never happened!" With that, the director stormed out of the restroom.

The clerk hurried after the director. They passed by the three girls who were now sticking their fingers in each other's ears. The director pushed the double-doors to the restaurant open, and as soon as the clerk stepped foot in the restaurant, he remembered how badly he had to go to the bathroom and realized he'd missed his chance.

"Were you able to salvage your papers?" the woman asked the director back at the table.

"No, sadly, no," the director said, dropping the papers on the ground. "I'm going to see if my assistant has any duplicates. Now, now, don't look at your co-worker with scorn. It was an honest mistake. He didn't mean to knock over a full glass with the unexpected clumsiness of his hand. Let's just order our dessert and forget this whole thing happened."

As the clerk was eating a baked apple stuffed with cinnamon, he noticed that one of the girls in green was running up to their table clutching his satchel. He was excited, but tried not to get his hopes up. The way his day had been going, he expected the papers would mysteriously not be inside, or they'd have found another bag that looked exactly like his but belonged to someone else. *"What a dreadful day!"* he thought. But then he remembered the covert conversation with the director in the lavatory and thought that maybe he'd been given a secret promotion. *"Promotion—"* just thinking the word made him feel weak in the chest.

"Ah, here's my assistant with the backup paperwork now," the director said. "She's so on top of things. I haven't even asked her for it yet."

The clerk's face twisted like a burning piece of paper.

"We found your bag, sir!" the girl said with cheer, holding it out to the clerk. He grabbed it and dropped it in his lap, opening it quickly and feeling relief wash over him as he saw the envelope and the thermos.

The director's hand remained outstretched and empty.

"Why were you getting his bag if you're my assistant?" the director asked the girl.

"What? I'm not your assistant," the girl said. "I work here at the restaurant. I'm one of the maître'ds."

"You're not my assistant?" the director said with confusion in his voice. "I have an assistant who looks just like you!"

"No, I'm afraid not, sir," the girl said, taking a step back from him. "I think I took your overcoat when you first came in. That's probably why I look familiar." She took another quick step back and then scampered in the direction of her post.

"That's strange," the director said, rubbing his bare scalp. "I could have sworn she was my assistant."

"Well, this looks like it's sending a clear message to me," the clerk said. "I've got to deliver this important paperwork to the 2nd Street Ave Building, and I just finished my dessert, and my important paperwork was dropped right in my lap, so thank you very much for having me to this excellent lunch, and I think I'll bid you all farewell until next time."

As the clerk started to rise from his chair, the director clapped him on the shoulder and forced him back down. "Now, now. You wouldn't leave before coffee, would you?"

"Did you say coffee?" the clerk asked. "How did you know that's my one guilty pleasure?"

"Oh, I didn't know. I just know you're a dedicated worker, and I wouldn't want you rushing back to work with a full stomach and nothing to provide you with energy."

"Coffee is a nice pick-me-up," the old man said. This reminded him of something, which prompted him to tell a long story. And then the other lady also told a long story as second cups of coffee were being poured out by the waiter, and both of the stories were so intricate, and filled with such strange departmental jargon and technical terms, which were entirely incomprehensible to the clerk, him being from a different department, that he could scarcely make any sense of what were saying. All the while, the clerk was waiting for the waiter to leave the check, but the check never came.

"Well, we should get back to work," the director said.

"No one wants to go back to work after that great nosh up, huh? Well, I'll make the first move," and as he stood up and grabbed his briefcase, the clerk thought he flashed him the slightest hint of a wink. As the four of them walked toward the entrance, the clerk thought about the fact that there had been no exchange of money.

The clerk feared the worst as he descended the elevator to the first floor, but he made it there without incident, and the security guards didn't so much as look at him as he exited the building. As he walked down the stone steps in the cold, gray air, he suddenly became aware of a figure addressing him.

"Hey buddy, can you spare some cash?"

The clerk was being addressed by a ragged fellow laying across the bottom three steps. He had a gray beard so thick and full that it covered most of his chest, and he wore a tattered brown trench coat, scuffed work boots with small holes in them, and a green winter hat.

"Oh, you need some money? Uh. I'm not sure if I have any change left. Let me check."

As the clerk dug his hands around in the pocket of his trousers, he noticed that the man was sipping the straw of a giant plastic soda cup, and in his other hand he had a mostly eaten cheeseburger, and there was a large box of fries on the stairs next to him, as well as a steaming cup of coffee.

"Wait? Why do you need my money if you already have all that food?"

"I don't need your money for food. I need it for my campaign."

"What campaign?"

"I can't tell you that. Will you just agree to give me your change if you have it?"

"Yeah sure, but I—"

"So you agree?"

"Yeah, yeah, I agree," the clerk muttered, continuing to dig his hand around in his pocket. "But I got bad news for you. It looks like I'm out. I don't have any physical money on me."

"You don't? But you've got some cash at home, right?"

"I don't know, I guess, but—"

"So then you've got to give that to me."

"What?"

"You said you'd give me your change if you have it. So you have it. It's just not here. Look, no big deal. No problem at all. I'll just come with you." He took a big bite of hamburger and tucked his fries into a pocket.

"Wait, wait. I didn't agree to that!"

"Yes you did. You just did. I specifically asked you!"

The clerk imagined his betrothed's face as he walked in the door with this suspicious-looking character. "No, no, no. There's no way that's happening tonight. I'm too busy." He imagined the delight on his betrothed's face when she saw the little black mouse he'd bring home. He reached into his jacket pocket and pet the mouse's tiny head, feeling its little circular ears.

"But you said! You made a promise to my campaign, sir! A campaign promise!"

"Alright, look, look. I'll tell you what. I've got to come back here for work tomorrow. You going to be around?"

"I think I could make myself available," the scraggly old man said, reaching into his pocket for some fries and then stuffing them into his mouth.

"Alright, I'll get the change tonight and then bring it here for you tomorrow afternoon around lunchtime. Okay? Sound good?"

"Yes! Sure thing! I appreciate you supporting my

campaign!"

The clerk walked away, wondering why he should have to support a campaign he didn't know anything about. He could feel the mouse skittering around in his pocket, perhaps upset by the cold air.

* * * *

Later that evening, the clerk was exiting a bus in the small city. The air was freezing and it had already grown pitch black outside, making it feel as if he were walking through the desiccated bowels of old man winter, even though it was only autumn. He still had to walk down several blocks to get home, so he cupped his hand around the mouse inside his pocket to keep the little guy warm. People walked in the streets all around him, some pushing grocery carts but most giving the impression of milling about aimlessly in the cold. They were all ages and sexes, including families. The high-rise apartments looming above the clerk were boxy shadow monsters with hundreds of pale yellow eyes.

Before long, the clerk was in front of his building, which was as plain as all the others. He climbed the stairs to the fifth floor, and walked down the hallway to the flat where he lived. When he opened the door, he was greeted by the sight of two large men laying in bed in the front room and staring at a picture tube. They each had their own fork, but they were slurping noodles from one large bowl.

"Hey guys, how's it going?" the clerk said as he locked the door behind him.

"Good," they said in unison, not looking over at him.

Without further conversation, the clerk slipped past them and opened the door to the room where his betrothed lay waiting. The only open floor space in the small room was directly in front of the door. The clerk stepped in and closed the door behind him with care. A large bed took up most of the room in the center, and it was surrounded by tanks and cages filled with animals, with a dresser in the corner. His betrothed lie in the bed, covered in blankets, her flowing auburn hair spread out everywhere.

"Hello dear," he said. "How was your day?"

"Oh thank goodness you're home! It was just exhausting. Absolutely terrible. It was job interviews all day."

"How many did you go to this time?"

"Oh I don't know. Upwards of sixty. I felt very confident about two of them, but they haven't called me back yet, so I'm losing my optimism."

"Oh dear," the clerk muttered. He was about to show her the cute mouse to raise her spirits when she interrupted.

"But now that you're home can you do me a huge favor, pretty please?"

"Sure, what is it?"

"Can you go to the market and get me some bread? I can't eat my sandwich without bread."

"Oh, of course you can't. Sure, I'll go. Any special kind of bread?"

"No, just whatever."

"Do you want anything to drink?"

"Nope, just the bread."

"Okay. Bread it is. One bread, coming up!" The clerk threw his satchel on the bed next to his betrothed and turned on his heel, reopening the door.

"Thanks so much!" she called from the bed as he closed the door.

"I'm just going to get something real quick," he muttered to the two blokes in bed, who hadn't even turned to look at him.

"Okay," they said in unison.

Down the elevator and back on the broken sidewalk, the

clerk headed toward the main avenue, which had the nearest market. He grabbed the mouse out of his pocket and held it with both hands, snuggling it close to his chest. "Looks like our adventures for the day aren't over, little guy."

The mouse squeaked. The clerk thought it sounded happy.

He slipped the mouse into his shirt pocket before entering the corner market. Bread was easy to find. He grabbed the first loaf he saw. "Aw, you're probably hungry too little guy. It was hours ago that I gave you those crackers!" he whispered to his pocket. "Hmm—what does a tiny black mouse eat. I know! Cheese!" He rushed to the refrigerated area and grabbed a wedge of white cheese.

As he was walking toward the counter, the aroma of hazelnut coffee turned his head toward a kiosk of coffees and teas. He knew his betrothed didn't think he should drink coffee after work because it would prevent him from getting a good night's sleep, but he'd never be able to stay awake until his bedtime if he didn't have another cup of coffee. He quickly got a small coffee, loading it with sweets.

He bought the stuff, and as he was about to leave, the cashier said something to him in the island language that he didn't understand. Feeling flustered, the clerk responded, "Thanks," in the island language, which caused the cashier's eyebrows to twist in annoyance, so the clerk fled outside into the cold air. He couldn't just return home with the coffee, so he sat in the alleyway next to the market. He put the coffee cup on the ground and opened up the wrapper around the cheese, breaking off a miniature piece. He then took out a slice of bread and ripped apart two similarly miniature pieces and put the cheese between them to make a tiny sandwich.

"Here you go: An adorably tiny sandwich for an adorably tiny mouse," he said, taking the mouse out of his pocket and plopping it into his lap. The mouse quickly climbed across his leg to the knee where the sandwich was resting. The mouse took a few sniffs of it before grabbing it with both hands and nibbling on it.

"I should have added some mayonnaise or mustard for it to be a real sandwich," the clerk mused. "Wow, you really don't have any fur on your ears. They almost look like human ears. They're even too big for you, little mouse!"

The mouse kept munching on the sandwich.

The clerk giggled as he stared at the rodent. "You're such a fun best friend, little mouse. I guess my best friend deserves a name, so what should I call you?" the clerk rubbed his chin and thought about it as he scrutinized the mouse's shiny eyes. "I can't stop thinking of you as 'little mouse.' I guess I'll just call you Ellem. Is that good? Do you mind that mouse-friend? Ellem?"

The mouse continued eating the sandwich.

"Okay, Ellem it is." The clerk put a finger on the mouse's head and started to pet it. He had a big smile on his face as he sat there, petting the mouse.

The clerk was so engrossed in petting the mouse and giggling about the little bites it took of the tiny sandwich, that he hadn't noticed a couple had stopped to stare at him in some mixture of horror and pity. When he did notice them, he became flustered. "Well, it looks like you're done with your sandwich little mouse, so let's be on our way." He made sure everything was stowed in his bag, picked up his coffee, and placed the mouse back in his pocket.

The woman screeched with disgust. "You put it in your pocket? Gross! Don't put it in your pocket!"

"Why not?"

"It'll poop in there!"

"Nah," the clerk said dismissively. But then, he held

open his pocket and peeked in. He could see some little black bits of what could have been feces. The mouse peeked its head out and tried to see what was going on, but the clerk's jacket was blocking its view. The clerk reached down and grabbed his coffee and his grocery bag.

The clerk squinted at the woman's face, feeling like he was having a tough time focusing on it. She seemed so familiar. "Hey," he said. "You're one of the girls who works at the restaurant."

"No I'm not. I don't work at a restaurant." She exchanged puzzled glances with her companion.

"Yeah, yeah! I recognize you now. In the bigger city. In the government building. Remember? It's me. You lost my satchel and then found it again."

"Are you sure it was me?"

"Well, I don't know. It was you or one of the other two girls."

"Oh, so now your story's falling apart! Suddenly you can't tell the difference between me and two other girls! I see how it is. We all look alike to you, don't we?"

"No, of course not, it's just that, well—"

The girl harrumphed, and the man said, "C'mon. Let's go darling," as they stormed into the store.

The clerk took a big gulp of coffee and started to make his way back toward the apartment.

As he opened the door, he saw that one of the large men was on all fours on the bed, and the other bloke was standing on his back, reaching toward the ceiling. They were yelling to each other about something in the island language.

The clerk muttered a greeting, and rushed on, as they seemed to be too distracted to pay attention to him.

Entering the bedroom, the clerk immediately handed the grocery bag to his betrothed.

"Thanks very much! I'm starving!" she said. "Oh, you got cheese too? But we already have cheese for sandwiches." She leaned over the bed, reaching under it, and then held up her arm when it grasped a package of pre-sliced cheese.

"Oh, I know. It's not human cheese. It's for a surprise!"

"A surprise? Oh, that reminds me, I completely forgot to ask you how your big meeting at work went. How was your day? How'd everything go?" Her eyes were open wide and she looked very eager and excited.

"Today was amazing because of—" he stuck his arm in his jacket, reaching into his shirt pocket. "—this little guy!" He held the mouse forward in his hand.

The excitement was wrung out of her face as her features crumpled in confusion. "What is that? A mouse?"

"Yeah!" he said, putting his hand down and letting the mouse run onto the bed.

His betrothed recoiled from the mouse and held up the blankets over herself like a shield. "Where'd it come from?" she shrieked.

"Well what's wrong, then? You love animals!" They were, in fact, surrounded by animals in cages and tanks. "You used to have hamsters! It's practically the same thing!"

"No. That's a mouse. Where'd it come from?"

"It followed me home. From the office."

"What do you mean it followed you home? Are you telling me that's a wild animal?"

"No, it's not a wild animal. It's really friendly! This is the farthest he's been from me all day." The mouse was scampering around on the bed in front of the clerk.

"That's only because you've been feeding it cheese all day!"

"No, I didn't give it any cheese until a little while ago," the clerk argued. Then he added after a moment of silence,

"I fed it crackers before that."

"See! Tell me where it came from."

"The bigger city."

"More details."

"What do you mean? I don't know. It was living behind a vending machine with a bunch of other mice, I guess."

"See! It *is* a wild animal! Get it out of here! Get it off the bed!"

The mouse had started to scale the mountain her foot made under the blanket, so she whisked her foot back, causing the mouse to flop around frantically.

"C'mon now, don't be like that. We've got room for one more, don't we? Can't it stay in with the hermit crabs or the turtles?"

"Absolutely not! It's a wild animal, probably full of fleas, and ticks, and diseases!"

"Nah," the clerk said, scooping the mouse back up defensively. "It's too cute for all that."

"Please listen to sense. You have to get that thing out of here. Go set it free on the sidewalk. You can even give it the wedge of cheese."

"No! Ellem's my friend! I'm not going to leave it out in the cold!"

She sighed in exasperation. "I'm too hungry for this!" Before long, she was eating a sandwich. The clerk had hung up his jacket and trousers on the coat hook and was sitting on the bed next to her, with the mouse in his lap.

"Do you want a sandwich too?" she asked after a time.

"Yeah. I'm going to make it in a minute."

"No, no. That's okay. I'll make it for you." She leaned under the bed to get the ingredients and before long, handed a sandwich to the clerk.

"Thanks very much," he said, biting into it. He didn't

mention the fact that it was too dry, with not a drop of any condiment on it.

Later on, the clerk's pre-dreams were interrupted by his betrothed saying, "You're falling asleep! Get that mouse out of here already."

"No," he muttered, his voice heavy with sleep. The mouse was lying down on the pillow next to his nose.

She sighed. "Well, don't blame me when it runs away to live in the wall while you're asleep."

The blare of an alarm clock woke the clerk before dawn. He opened his eyes and saw a huge, blurry black shape. He gasped and jumped back, but realized that it was the mouse sleeping next to his nose, exactly as it had been the night before. "Oh, it's just you, Ellem," he whispered before punching the alarm clock to turn it off.

The mouse's black eyes slowly opened. It shook its head and scampered in the direction of the clerk. He held it in his hand as he leaned over to kiss his betrothed on the forehead. She let out a faint moan but didn't wake.

He quickly got dressed and stationed the mouse in his shirt pocket. Exiting the room, he immediately heard the sound of the two large men snoring loudly. He tiptoed to the far corner of the room where the toilet and sink were, closing the curtain that divided the corner, but since the curtain did nothing to buffer sounds, he sat down for his morning urination so that the loud splashing wouldn't disturb the sleeping men. He washed his face in the sink and brushed his teeth. Opening the curtain, he slipped past the sleeping men to the corner closer to the bedroom, which was the kitchen. He took the coffee pot out of the cabinet and set it to brew. As he leaned against the counter, listening to the sound of the coffee brewing, he couldn't help but watch the two men sleep. One was on his back with his mouth wide open. He was snoring the loudest.

Out the door and into the chilly air, the clerk noticed that the sun was just beginning to rise over the distant skyscrapers. As he walked down the sidewalk holding his ceramic cup, the inside of his fingers felt warm from the hot coffee, but the front of his fingers felt cold from the winter-like air. "It's not winter yet, Ellem," the clerk muttered at some point. "It oughtn't be this cold." The clerk was wearing his warmer jacket, which wasn't as nice as the jacket he'd worn the previous day. When he was getting dressed before in the cold bedroom, the warm jacket seemed like the best idea, but now that he was more awake, he was starting to think it was a bad idea not to look his best since he had to go to the bigger city during his lunch break.

The two morning security guards at this office knew him, so they just said "Good morning" and let him through the full body scanner without asking to see his identification card.

"Hey bro, I'm not a doctor or nothing, and this machine's not a medical x-ray machine, you know, but you might want to get your heart checked out. It looks a little irregular," one of the security guards said, a concerned expression on his face.

"Oh, really?" the clerk responded. "That's disturbing. I will definitely look into it."

He took the lift to the seventh floor, which was the floor he worked on. This building only had ten floors, so the clerk found it easy to navigate. "I think we tricked 'em little guy," the clerk whispered to his left breast pocket.

When he exited the lift, he found his floor unexpectedly dark. "What's going on?" he whispered. "I'm not usually the first one here." To his shock, he was lifted up by his armpits.

"Off the ground! This is a serious drill; you're going

to get our whole department in trouble!" a woman hanging from the ceiling said.

"Oh, I'm sorry," he muttered, suspended in the air by her strong grip. "I hadn't realized." He could see the tops of all the cubicles from here.

"Unobservant as usual," she scoffed. "Well I'm not going to just hold you like this forever! Get out your climbing gear."

"Uh, well the thing is—"

"What?"

"You're not going to want to hear this—"

"What is it? Out with it!"

"I didn't think to bring my climbing gear with me today."

"What? What is the matter with you?"

"It's okay, don't worry. I have spare climbing gear in my desk."

"In your desk?!" she said as though he'd claimed it was on the sun. "Where's your cubicle? All the way on the other side of the office?"

"Yeah," he muttered, feeling like a puppet again as his limbs dangled.

"Well hold up your legs. I don't want to have to steer through this labyrinth of cubicles. I'm taking you in a straight line—the most direct path."

"I'll try."

"You don't try! You do it!"

The clerk responded by tucking in his knees and holding his shins with his hands, so his co-worker began the slow process of moving across the ceiling. There were only a few other people crawling across the ceiling. The clerk's legs felt as though they were increasing in weight. He did his best to readjust his grip, but his fingers were slipping, his legs were demanding to come free. The woman grunted slightly as she continued her slow pace. Finger by finger he was losing his grip on his legs, when suddenly he lost them all at once. His legs went swinging down into a cubicle and slammed straight into a cabinet, knocking over a big stack of papers. The papers went flying up into the air, swirling around the suspended clerk, and they started fluttering down onto the woman sitting on the cubicle desk, landing everywhere, but mostly on the floor.

"My paperwork!" the woman on the desk shouted.

"Unbelievable!" the woman holding the clerk exclaimed. "That's it! You're not my problem anymore." She dropped the clerk, and he fell onto the desk, sprawled out around the other woman. He lie there on his back for a moment, watching his disgruntled co-worker scuttle away on the ceiling.

The woman on the desk was pouting. "I'm going to have to do that all over again. It fell on the floor, and we're expected to treat these drills as though they're actual saboteur attacks, so everything on the floor has to be considered compromised by the enemy!"

The clerk was worried that the woman would start crying, and then he'd feel like he had to comfort her, but it was against policy to hug another co-worker. He was so uncomfortable that he considered just getting up, grabbing onto the top of the cubicle, and hopping over to get away from her. He jumped to his feet. "I'm sorry!" he said, and turned around, grabbing the top of the cubicle wall closest to him.

"Hey! You can't just ruin my entire week's work and run off!" She grabbed onto the end of his trousers and held on. He tried to pull himself up, but she caught a better grip of his leg and pulled him down. They flopped all over the desk for a moment as the clerk tried to free himself.

"Okay, okay! I'll help you. Just let me go!" the clerk

shouted.

"Good," she said.

"How can I help?" the clerk muttered, contemplating making another chance at escape.

"Well, first we've got to figure out how to collect it all off the floor."

"No problem. I'll just lean over and grab it. I just need to adjust something." The clerk crouched into the corner and plucked the little mouse out of his pocket, taking a moment to stare into its excited little eyes, then he swapped the mouse with the contents of a pants pocket that would be more secure. "Okay, I'm ready."

He grabbed onto one of the cabinets mounted onto the desk and flopped the top half of his body over the side of the desk, outstretching his arms to reach for the papers. However, when he expected to be closing his hand around a piece of paper, he instead found that he was still some distance from the floor, and the shock of this caused him to lose his balance, leaving most of him dangling over the desk.

He shouted out in shock and fear. "Was your desk always this tall?!" He was holding all of his weight on one arm and felt as though he wouldn't be able to keep his grip for very long.

"Yes, of course!" the woman said.

He was so far from the ground that he worried that he would seriously injure himself if he fell.

"Help! Help!" the clerk started shouting.

"What should I do?" the woman asked.

He tried to turn himself around so he could pull himself up with his other hand. His hand grasped at random all over the desk, trying to find something to grab onto, and he took a death grip over the first thing he found. It was just in time too, because he lost his grip with the other hand. Now he found himself falling, and realized that what he'd grabbed was the cord of the woman's large, office telephone.

"Let go! Let go!" the woman was shouting. "You're going to break the phone!"

"Grab onto your end so it doesn't break!" the clerk shouted back. The cord stretched all the way and snapped the clerk up a bit before it continued to swing him around in front of the desk. He felt the woman grab the cord up on top of the desk, securing him. As he dangled there for a moment, holding onto the phone cord with both hands, he could see that the phone handle itself had stopped not too far from the floor. "Do you have a tight grip on your end?" he shouted up to the woman.

"Yes, I think so."

"Okay, good. Keep holding on, I'm going to lower myself closer to the ground and grab the papers."

"Sounds great," she called down to him.

He wrapped his legs around the stretch of spiral cord that was immediately below him, and then attempted to lower himself hand by hand, in hopes of avoiding rug burn on his palms. It was a painstaking process, but before long, his feet were touching the phone handle.

"Now comes the hard part, Ellem."

The mouse squeaked from within his pocket.

He was still too far from the floor to reach the papers, but he knew that if he lowered himself a bit more, he'd be able to hold the phone with one hand and reach the papers with the other. He was in the process of lowering himself when the phone handle decided it couldn't hold his weight anymore and broke off of the cord, falling onto the papers below with a plop.

Now he was slipping, and fearing he would fall onto the ground, he quickly did his best to wrap the end of the cord around one of his hands. He managed to pull this off, and now he was dangling so close to the floor that he had to bend his knees to keep from touching it. "Well, this could be good," he muttered. He grabbed the phone, since it was on top of the papers, and stuffed it into the trouser pocket that didn't contain the little black mouse, and then, since most of the papers were in a big stack, he started grabbing the ones that had landed apart from those first, adding them to the big stack. Some of the farther away ones he had to use his foot to pull over closer to him, but when he'd gotten most of them, he scooped up the big stack into his hand. Now he noticed a new conundrum. *"How am I supposed to climb all the way back up there while holding all these papers?"* he thought, and then he shouted up to the woman, "Hey! I got the papers; pull me back up." A moment passed. "Did you hear me? Pull me back up, posthaste, please." His legs hurt from bending and his arm felt like it couldn't hold on too much longer.

"I am pulling," the woman called down. "It's not working. You're too heavy!"

"Please try!" the clerk called up in a whine, sweat breaking out on his brow.

The woman grunted to show her effort, but the clerk didn't move at all.

"It's no use! You've got to climb back up here yourself!"

"Oh dear," the clerk muttered.

The mouse squeaked.

"Thanks for your support, best friend! I won't let us touch the floor. If only there was some way to store these papers so I had both my hands free—" He tried to stick them in his jacket, but he knew they would fall out. As they were sliding in the direction of his trousers, he realized that was the place. He stuffed them in the front of his pants, on the outside of his skivvies. "Wow, surprisingly secure." With his newly-freed hand, he grasped higher up on the spiral cord, and then he used the other hand to grab up above that hand— and this hand was still wrapped and tangled in cord, but he left it that way so that in case he lost his grip, he should still be attached to the cord. "Okay, again," he muttered between labored breaths and set once more to pulling himself up a small distance. Bit by bit he made his way up the cord, getting closer and closer to the surface of the desk. His muscles felt like they would tear and burst. He knew he was going to fall at any moment, that he didn't have the strength to make it, but just when he was on the verge of complete exhaustion, a hand was reaching out to him from above.

"Take my hand!" the woman called out.

He reached up and she grasped his hand, pulling him the little bit of the way up so that he could put his hand on top of the desk and pull himself on.

She didn't say anything as he sat panting for a moment. When he caught his breath, he said, "Here you go. I got your papers back," and pulled the wad of them out of his trousers.

The woman's eyebrows curled backwards and she looked as though she'd become nauseous. "I'm not touching those! Besides, you're going to be working on them for me. You got all of them, right?"

"Yeah, of course," he muttered.

She stepped closer to the edge of the desk and leaned over a bit, searching the ground below.

"No you didn't! There's still papers down there!"

"What? That's not possible! I grabbed them all while I was dangling from the cord."

"Then what are those?"

He looked down toward the ground, and saw that there were indeed five or six scattered papers. "Well you don't really need those, do you?"

"Of course I need them! This is a sequenced report you ruined! You're going to have to compile it back in the right order. We need every page or it won't make sense!"

"Oh dear," the clerk muttered. The thought of climbing back down there seemed to drain the last of his energy and he plopped onto the seat of his pants.

"Hey, c'mon! You gotta get those for me! You're the one who knocked them all down there."

"Alright, alright, I'll go. Just give me a minute. I need a glass of water or something. You have some water?"

"No, I don't have that," she said in a tone that implied it was an absurd request.

"Well could you please go to the break room and get me one?"

"I can't climb over there! I don't have any climbing gear!"

"You don't? Then how'd you even get in your cubicle in the first place."

"Same way you did."

"That lady carried you over?"

"Yeah, of course. She's the best. She always carries me around during these things."

The clerk scoffed. "She didn't seem so nice to me," he muttered under his breath.

The woman sighed loudly.

"Alright, I'm going," the clerk said, stretching his arms up and letting out a loud groan. He threw the phone handle down on the desk and said, "Let's do this, little guy," as he grabbed onto the phone cord and started to repel down the desk.

The woman's confusion at his words turned to anger as she saw the phone. "I can't believe you broke the phone on top of everything!" she shouted. "The department's not going to want to pay for a new one, but I can't work without my phone! I'm going to be in so much trouble because of you!"

"I don't think it's shafted," the clerk shouted up to her, with a grunt between each word as he descended with care. "I think it just came off the cord. We should be able to plug it back in."

"I hope you're right, or I'm nicking the phone from your desk! You take the heat for all this!"

The clerk was too exhausted to expend the extra energy to continue this conversation. As he reached the end of the cord, he realized he was still quite far from the remaining scattered papers. "How am I ever going to reach those?" He felt like he could lose his grip at any moment. He just wanted to get this over with so he could take a rest. He began to swing his legs and then shift his body weight back and forth, building up momentum on the cord. Soon he was swinging back and forth like a pendulum, but he still couldn't reach any of the papers with his hands. "Okay, I better be careful about this or I'll touch the floor," he muttered. The standard gray carpet of the office had always been extremely ominous in his mind. "Here we go!" he shouted, stretching a foot onto a piece of paper and pulling it closer to the center of his swings. "Perfect!" He repeated the process and found it very successful. When all the papers were within arm's-length, he waited to stop swinging back and forth, and then he reached down with care and scooped them up, crumpling them as he shoved them into his trousers. "Now I've just got to get back up there." He looked up and felt like crying because the surface of the desk seemed so far away. "It looks worse than it is," he told himself. "Getting up there will be the easy part." He reached one hand above him, wrapped it around the cord and pulled. He could feel his bicep muscle stretching beneath his skin. His whole body was in pain and he was drenched in sweat. "One hand at a time," he grunted, reaching the other hand above that one and pulling despite the extreme pain. "Just a little farther. You can do this!" He grunted as he tried to pull himself up the next stretch of cord, but exhaustion took over, and he shouted as he fell, plunging straight toward the ground. *This is it! I'm finished! I'll be fired! I'll never get a promotion!* he was thinking as the gray carpet rushed toward him—when suddenly he landed in something soft.

"What the heck are you doing down there?" the woman screamed from the top of the desk.

He didn't know the answer to that himself. He knew he'd landed, but he could also tell he was still moving. He looked around and realized he had landed in her desk chair and it was rolling out of the cubicle, into the hallway between cubes, but then shooting through that, and continuing into whoever's cubicle was across from the woman's. "Oh dear," the clerk muttered. The cubicle hit the chair of the co-worker across the hall, and elicited some sort of complaint, but the clerk had been moving so quickly that he ricocheted back out into the middle of the gap between cubicles.

"What happened? What did you do?" the woman shouted to him from the desktop.

"I fell, that's what," he called back. "I have the papers though."

"Great! Bring them back over here."

"How? I'm stranded out here!"

"Can't you push off of something to propel yourself back over here?"

He looked around a little. "I don't think so. Throw me over something I can use as a paddle."

There was silence for a few moments, then she called

back, "I don't see anything like that."

"I just need a stick or something."

"Why would I have a stick in my cubicle?"

The clerk sighed and realized he was going to have to get himself out of this predicament. "You okay, Ellem?" he whispered to his trousers. The mouse squirmed a bit as confirmation. "Alright, let's see here. I'm not too far from that portion of cubicle. Maybe if I shifted my weight a bit, I could roll the chair over there close enough to touch the wall, and then I could push off of it." He wiggled around back and forth, holding onto the handles of the chair, trying to get some momentum. "Oh bollocks! I'm going the wrong way," he grunted. He was rolling back into the other bloke's cubicle, but he didn't want to stop his momentum and get stuck, so he kept wiggling.

"Hey man, c'mon. Give me a break here. I'm trying to get some work done. What are you doing in here?"

"I'll just be a moment, if you can be so kind as to hold onto your desk and kick my chair back into the other cubicle," the clerk said, not stopping his wiggling.

"Oh, I'll kick your chair all right!" he said, grunting as he put his full force into a hard kick at the chair. The clerk went wheeling away, and the chair slammed right into the desk in the woman's cubicle, the handles wedging underneath.

The clerk climbed up to the desk and flopped onto it like a little kid climbing out of a swimming pool. "Alright, we did it," he said, gasping for breath. He extracted the crumpled papers from his crotch and added them to the pile of big papers. "I'm going to be on my way then," he said, abandoning the stack of papers on the desk and turning to climb over the cubicle wall.

"Not so fast!" the woman called out. "I'm not redoing all this. You are!"

"Redoing it? But I have no idea what it even is."

"C'mon, it's a doddle! Just monotonous and time-consuming. Here's a cryptogram. I just need you to retype it all, but change the words to match up with this new cryptogram."

"Retype all this? That alone will take forever without even changing anything! Don't you have a version on the computer?"

"No! Of course not! Too insecure. Now take this," she shoved the cryptogram at him, "and take this," she pushed the pile of papers forward with her foot, "and get it done by the end of the day."

"But I haven't even started on my own work yet!"

"Do you want me to notify my supervisor of all the trouble you've caused me?"

"No," the clerk whispered, sounding defeated.

"Then get moving! Let's go."

The clerk scooped up the pile of papers, then turned to face the cubicle wall, but turned around again. "Okay, earlier, I was just trying to make a quick escape before you asked me to do more exhausting things, but I don't know how to get back to my cubicle without climbing gear."

"Not my problem! Get out of here!"

The clerk turned around and discreetly took the little mouse out of his pocket. "You okay, Ellem?" he whispered. He thought it looked cute while it wiggled his nose at him. He swapped it back to his shirt pocket and stuffed the big stack of papers into his trousers. He grabbed onto the top of the cubicle wall and hoisted himself over, landing next to another office worker who was sitting on his desk cross-legged, writing up paperwork.

"Hello friend, might I ask you to give me a lift to my cubicle as I've misplaced my climbing gear?"

"I'm busy! Get out of here!"

He hopped over to the cubicle on the other side.

"Hi there, sorry to intrude, but I seem to be stranded far away from my cubicle."

"We've all got to worry about our own problems, man! This is the busy time of year."

This went on similarly for some time before the clerk stumbled upon a generous co-worker.

"You say you've got a set of climbing gear in your desk?" the co-worker said.

"Yes, that's right," the clerk responded.

"Well then, why don't you borrow my climbing gear, go get yours out of your desk, and bring mine back here?"

"Yeah, sure thing! That sounds great! Thanks so much!" the clerk said.

As the clerk dropped down from the ceiling onto his desk, his rival immediately peeked his head over the cubicle wall, revealing only his beady eyes and greasy forehead. His rival was also his cubicle neighbor, his rival was also a clerk, and his rival was his rival because he was the closest competition for the promotion, as far as the clerk could tell.

"You're in pretty late this morning. I don't think upper management appreciates tardy employees," the rival sneered.

"Ugh. I've been here since before you. I just had something else to take care of!" The clerk reached down into the top desk drawer and extracted his climbing gear, ripped the stack of papers out of his trousers and dropped them into the drawer, and then giving a glance over to his rival, he decided to lock the drawer. Stuffing his climbing gear into his trousers, the clerk re-hooked his line to the ceiling and began to climb away.

"You just got here and you're leaving already?" his rival called after him. "You're not going to get any work done today!"

"I work ten times faster than you anyway," the clerk called as he swung on his ropes. "I'll make up for lost time."

The clerk felt like an upside-down crab as he crawled in the direction of the co-worker who he'd borrowed the climbing gear from, but as he neared, he realized he had no idea which cubicle the co-worker was in. "Oh dear," he muttered. "This cubicle farm all looks the same from up here." The clerk came to the soul-destroying revelation that, despite his exhaustion, he was going to have to check every cubicle to find the right co-worker, so he spent the next stretch of time scurrying overtop cubicles, dropping down into them like a spider on a thread of web, inspecting the person's face (which in almost all cases resulted in them spewing complaints at him—he assumed everyone was in a bad mood because of the emergency sabotage attack blackout drill), realizing he had the wrong cubicle, climbing back up to the ceiling, and checking the next one.

"Are you here to deliver me coffee?" one co-worker joked.

"Nope, but that is an excellent idea," the clerk responded, and as he climbed back up to the ceiling, he decided to crabwalk over to the break room. Once there, he dropped onto the counter and drank a few cups of water, and checking over his shoulder to make certain that no one else was nearby, he let the mouse take as much water from the cup as it liked. He smiled as he watched it lap up the liquid with its tiny pink tongue.

He started fixing himself a cup of coffee when someone behind him yelled, "Hey! There you are! Enjoying yourself with a break and leaving me stranded at my desk after I'd taken such a compassionate heart to you!"

The clerk turned around to see the co-worker who'd lent

him the climbing gear in the arms of a man who was crawling across the ceiling.

"I was attempting to give it back to you!" the clerk said in his defense. "I just got tired. It's right here, take it."

"Thanks," the co-worker said in a tone filled with disdain.

The clerk finished pouring his coffee and took a big sip. He added another spoonful of sugar. Then he noticed that someone had left a bowl of nuts next to the coffee pots, so he took a handful of those, wrapped them in a napkin, and put it in his pocket.

He waited for the other two co-workers to leave and then snuck the mouse some more draughts of water before he re-equipped his climbing gear and made the journey back to his cubicle.

Sitting cross-legged on top of his desk, he decided to get started on some of his own work. "I'll finish that lady's paperwork later," he mumbled to himself. As he worked, he unfolded the napkin and laid it out next to him. "One for me," he whispered as he popped a nut into his mouth. "One for you," he whispered as he dropped one into his pocket.

Over the sound of crunching was the sound of papers shuffling.

"One for me. One for you."

His pen scratched on the paper.

"One for me. One for you."

He opened the bottle of whiteout as they crunched away.

"One for me. One for you."

He peeled a yellow sticky note and stuck it onto a paper.

"One for—"

"What's going on in here?" the rival said, his eyes appearing just over the cubicle wall.

"Don't worry about it," the clerk said.

"Wow! You're taking your lunch break already and you haven't even managed to get any work done today!" He tsked.

"I'm not taking my lunch break yet. It's only—oh dear! Is that the time?! I have to take my lunch break!" In a panic, the clerk began to gather his things.

"Unbelievable," his rival said as if talking to someone else. "The work ethic of some of the people around here. I don't know how they manage to keep their jobs."

The clerk ignored him as he swung down the hallway in the direction of the elevators.

He walked up the block to the busiest avenue in the small city, his eyes immediately searching for a bus to take him to the bigger city. He walked up to a bus stop on the corner across the street. No one else was waiting for a bus here, so he thought he might have just missed one. The busses were very frequent on this avenue though, and there was usually at least one every few minutes.

"Should I wait or not? It might be faster to just walk in the direction of the bigger city and jump on a bus when one's passing me." He leaned his weight back and forth on the balls of his feet. The traffic looked terrible right now. The traffic light at the intersection changed and the cars didn't even start moving because everything was so backed up. He looked down the street to see if a bus was coming, but there were none in sight. "I'm wasting too much time here! I need to get going or I'll be late!" he exclaimed, rushing down the sidewalk, moving much faster than all the cars. He added in his thoughts, *"I can't be late for an assignment from the director!"* He glanced over his shoulder to see if any busses were on the horizon, but he didn't see a single one. The mouse started skittering around in his pocket. "Are you getting nauseous from my quick movement, Ellem?" the clerk asked. "Here, you can look out. I'm not at work right now. It doesn't matter if anyone sees you or not." He stopped for a moment to adjust the mouse. It was very receptive to the clerk's touch, and the mouse sat with its tiny hands holding onto the edge of the pocket and his head peering out at the world ahead of him. As the clerk had been fiddling with the mouse, he failed to notice that whatever was causing the traffic backup must have been resolved, because now all the cars were moving at a fast pace. He thought he noticed just in time, because a bus was just now speeding past him. "I've got this!" he said, running forward after the bus. He pushed himself a little harder, running his fastest, and he found himself parallel to the bus. He waved his arms frantically at the driver.

The driver glanced his way and pointed up ahead, motioning that he wouldn't stop the bus until the next bus stop.

The clerk tried to keep up with the bus to make it to the next stop, but it was moving too fast for him to keep up such a pace. *"Of course I get a driver who's a stickler for the rules and will only stop at the official stops! Busses pick me up in random spots all the time!"* He tried to keep walking quickly, but the bus was already out of his sight. He looked back in the other direction to see if there was another bus, but there wasn't. Forging on, he soon found himself at the next bus stop, but the bus he'd seen was long gone. No one else was waiting at the stop, which he attributed to the bus he'd seen having stopped to pick them up. He stood at the bus stop, catching his breath for a moment, then peered out in the direction he'd come from, trying his hardest to see as far as possible in his search for a bus. He didn't see even the hint of a bus, not even a van that resembled a bus. To make matters worse, he saw that something was backing up traffic again, and the vehicles he was peering at weren't moving at all. "Maybe we can use this traffic to our advantage, Ellem!" the clerk whispered. "Hold on tight. I'm going to catch up to that bus!" The clerk began sprinting down the sidewalk, weaving through slow-moving families with baby carriages and workers taking nice, leisurely strolls during their lunch breaks. *That bus wasn't very far ahead of me. It's got to be stuck in all this traffic. I'm sure I can catch it!"* the clerk thought as he ran, his feet feeling more dexterous than usual in his determination to catch the bus and make it to the bigger city. He ran and ran, shocked that he hadn't yet encountered the bus. Suddenly all the cars began moving quickly again, and he stopped and hunched over to catch his breath as two lanes of vehicles blasted past him. "This is crazy," he wheezed between breaths.

Suddenly, a bus pulled up right next to the clerk. He began flailing his arms to get the driver's attention and rushed in as the doors were pulled apart.

"The bigger city?" he asked. He never asked bus drivers where they were going in complete sentences because most of them spoke different languages than him and he was paranoid they would become confused and take him to the wrong place.

"No. The big city. No stops in bigger city," the bus driver grunted, clearly in a hurry to keep moving and pick up more fares.

"Oh. Thanks anyway," the clerk muttered, hopping back out of the bus. "Man, what luck today, Ellem!" the clerk complained to the mouse. "These busses are always going to the bigger city!"

With his shoulders slouched and his pace slowed, the clerk continued in the direction of the bigger city. It was much too far to walk all the way, but he assumed he had to catch a bus sooner or later.

At the next bus stop, the clerk collapsed on the bench, determined to just wait as long as it took. The traffic was barely moving, and he had already wasted the entirety of his lunch break, but he was on a secret mission from the director, so he had no choice but to push on and hope he hadn't totally screwed everything up.

Eventually, a bus rolled up, and when he got on and asked, "Bigger city?" the driver gave his affirmative answer in the island language. The clerk took a seat in the very back of the bus so he could sit and whisper with the mouse in private. He put his satchel down on an empty seat next to him and took the mouse out of his pocket, cradling it in both hands and holding it so close to his face that its multitude of long whiskers tickled his nose. "Today has just been the worst, Ellem," the clerk said, giggling. "You're too ticklish, little guy! I'm going to tickle you back!" he put the mouse in his lap and started rubbing its sides and turned it over so that he was rubbing its belly. The mouse squeaked and righted itself, sprinting out of his lap and up his shirt, coming to rest on his shoulder.

The bus driver suddenly cranked up the radio, blasting a news report in the island language. Everyone on the bus seemed to be paying attention to it, so the clerk attempted to translate it for himself. *"Something about our war overseas. Something about our robot planes and dead enemies. Enemy saboteurs?"* The clerk shrugged and looked out the window.

They slowly rolled through the traffic, eventually coming to a stop in the main square of the bigger city. The clerk took a deep breath and slowly let it out. "Here we go again, little mouse," the clerk said, and as if it understood him, it scrambled into his shirt pocket as the clerk stood up.

The clerk paid the bus driver and walked up the sidewalk to the large government building. As he pushed the glass door open, the female security guard immediately said, "Who are you?"

"We haven't seen you around here before," the male security guard said.

The clerk put up his trembling hands and took a step back, pressing his back against the door. "I have my identification card; just let me get it out!"

"Not so fast!" the female security guard said. "How do I know you're not taking out a weapon?"

"I'm not taking out a weapon, I swear!"

"There's only one way to make sure you don't have a weapon on you!" the female security guard shouted in his face, spraying his cheek with spittle. "Through the scanner!" She prodded him in the arm with her finger.

The clerk slowly stepped forward.

"That's right. Go through there and let me see everything you're packing," the male security guard said from his position behind the desk.

"I'm not packing anything," the clerk muttered.

He stepped through slowly, imagining the two security guards looking at the x-ray picture of his private parts and laughing.

"What's up with his heart?" the male security guard said in his baritone voice.

"Let me see that!" the female security guard said, pushing closer. "Make sure he's not strapped with explosives!"

"Naw, it's nothing like that," the male said.

"You're right though. It does look strange. He's probably dying or something. You might want to get that checked out, kid."

"Great," the clerk muttered under his breath. He checked his watch and almost had a real heart attack just from seeing the time. He looked up at the security guards and saw they were staring at him.

"Well, your security clearance card?"

"Oh, right," the clerk muttered, thinking to himself, *"I totally forgot about that thing! I do hope I have it on me."* He took out his wallet and flipped through the various cards. "Well, here's my government-issued identification card," he muttered, flashing it at them.

"Yes, but that doesn't prove your clearance to this building," the male security guard said.

"Right," the clerk muttered. "I've got it here somewhere."

He checked his pockets and didn't locate it. "If only I'd worn my trousers from yesterday," he thought, thinking that he must've left the card in the pocket. Feeling certain that he didn't have the card on him, he made the display of checking through his satchel because he didn't know what else to do.

"You don't have it, do you?" the male security guard said.

"Unfortunately, it would appear not, *but,*" he said, emphasizing this word and holding up a finger. "You guys were here yesterday when they issued it to me. You know I'm allowed in here. Can't you just let me through, just this once?"

"I don't know you're allowed in here!" the female security guard snapped. "I don't know that I saw you yesterday!"

"It's policy," the male security guard said in his deep voice. "Even if I did remember you and wanted to let you in, I couldn't break policy and let you walk in without the proper clearance. I'd lose my job." He turned to the other security guard. "Call her in."

Some time elapsed with the male security guard standing uncomfortably close to the clerk.

"Looks like she's not coming," the female security guard said. "You're going to have to take him to her."

"Right," the male security guard said. With a quick flash

of silver, the clerk suddenly found his arms in pain as the security guard handcuffed his wrists behind his back, twisting his shoulders—the clerk felt—unnecessarily hard. Then without warning a sack was placed over his head, blinding him.

"Is this really necessary?" the clerk protested. "Honestly! I even have a government ID! You know I work here!"

"I only know what they pay me to know," the guard said in his deep voice as he shoved him forward. "Policy."

The sounds the clerk heard when he was shoved off of the elevator made him think that he was on the floor the woman in maroon had taken him to the previous day. Amidst the horrifying slapping sounds on the other side of the wall, the clerk remembered that this had been the origin of the mouse. "Oh no! I'm restrained and we're in my best friend's home! I hope it doesn't decide to leave me for its old family. I wouldn't be able to stop it even if I wanted to!"

"There you are," the guard said. "He's all yours."

A loud sigh followed. "Is this who I think it is? Again? Two days in a row? The third time?"

"Beats me," the guard said, giving a final push to the clerk's back before he walked away.

The sack was lifted as the woman in maroon—this time wearing a low-cut black top and a maroon miniskirt—peered into the clerk's eyes. "It is you! I'm going to have to speak with whoever's in charge of your performance review! This has got to stop!" She dropped the sack back over his face and started dragging him toward the elevator.

"She can't know who's in charge of my performance review," the clerk told himself in his mind, thinking that there was still hope for his promotion.

The clerk was told to wait outside the room of the masked person and he heard the lady say, "I need another favor," in a voice he would describe as "sultry." After a handful of minutes, she returned, freed him of obstructions, and shoved a shiny card into his palm. "I swear," she said, her face so close to his that he could smell the gross warmth of her breath, "That if you lose this one—that if you show up here again and are unable to gain entry to this building without disturbing me, that you are seriously going to regret it."

The threat was vague enough that the clerk felt unthreatened.

"I sincerely apologize for inconveniencing you, and I hope that you will not judge my entire work ethic upon a few mistakes made in my attempts to navigate a new environment."

The woman sighed loudly and stalked away in the direction of the elevator.

The clerk leaned against the wall and decided to wait until the woman left so that they could avoid an awkward elevator ride together.

A moment later she was shouting at him, "Aren't you coming? How long do you expect me to hold the door?"

"Oh, right," he muttered, and thus the awkward elevator ride was not avoided.

He was relieved when the woman got off at the 28th floor without another word.

As he waited to get to his floor, he tried his best to remember every detail of the covert conversation with the director. He knew that the director had been talking in a lot of coded language to give the clerk hints about what was going to happen. He'd said the word "encryption" to point the clerk in the right direction and mentioned something about "Federal Bowling Alleys" which the clerk knew had to refer to something important. *What could that mean? F.B.A. Federal Business Association? First Booking Agreement?*

Well, I'm sure I'll figure it out. I know the director wouldn't assign me a task he wasn't confident I could handle."

The clerk was picturing the 97th floor, and his instincts were telling him that it was definitely going to be the kind of place he was accustomed to working in. There would probably be wall-to-wall cubicles and flowing pots of coffee to keep his concentration steady.

He got off at the 97th floor and found himself standing in a lobby with potted plants. He heard strange noises in the background. *"Is that thunder? Something crashing?"* He pulled open the large door that was in front of him and the noises grew louder. His mouth fell agape and his pace quickened as he realized that he was standing in a massive bowling alley. "Oh dear, Ellem," he whispered. "I think I'm in over my head."

Dragging his feet, he inched his way to the counter at the front. Three girls appeared behind the counter, peering down on them. They were each wearing the same collared green shirt.

"Looking to bowl a game, sir?" one of them said.

The clerk chewed his lip as he stood peering at her face. "Fancy meeting up with you girls again," he said, addressing the three at once. They looked similar. He was almost certain they had the same color hair. It was a light brown color that turned into more of a blonde at the tips—but then as he studied the scalp of one girl, he realized that her roots were actually quite blonde, in fact, the blonde was running through all the way to the tips, but—wait no, there was certainly some sandy brown mixed in there. His eyes felt like they were bulging out of his head and he became so dizzy that he began to stumble.

"I'm sorry sir, but I don't believe we've ever met. Perhaps we've passed each other in the—Sir? Sir? Are you okay?"

It felt as though the whole room was spinning. He felt like he was standing on the top of a plate being spun by a performer at a circus. He wobbled this way and that, sometimes taking several bumbling steps in one direction, moving farther into the bowling alley where people shouted complaints at him, but he was so dizzy and disoriented that the world was a brown-stained blur.

One of the girls had hopped over the counter and attempted to catch him, but he was moving too fast for her as his feet spun him all around the room.

"Sir! Sir!" she was shouting as she chased after him. "Please stop, sir! You can't go through here without wearing the proper shoes! Sir! Sir! Stop, sir! Take a seat sir!"

Dizzily, he stumbled all over the alley, traversing the entirety of the place as he zigzagged back and forth across it. All at once he stepped on ground that was exceedingly smooth, and his feet came right out from under him, sending him flying down one of the alleys and into a group of bowling pins. He groaned in pain as the metal contraption repeatedly punched him in the head, attempting to scoop up the pins.

"Sir! Sir!" the girl was shouting. She jumped high into the air, kicked herself off one of the score-keeping screens, and flipped down onto the tiny space between lanes, her nimble feet taking her down to the end of it and reuniting her with the clerk.

"Sir, are you alright?"

"Yes, I—Oh no!" he shouted, his hand reaching for the left side of his chest. He felt wiggling in his palm and let out a sigh of relief.

His head was lolling back and forth as the girl stared at him with a concerned expression. *"Remember,"* he was thinking. *"Remember why you're here. You're on an important mission for the director. What did he say to do?"*

"I need—" the clerk muttered, trying to think of what he was supposed to do. "I need—"

"Oh, I think I know exactly what you need," the girl said.

"Oh yeah! That's it! I need to sign up for a bowling game!"

"No no no," she said, lifting him up by the armpits. "What you need is a doctor. I think I'm going to call an ambulance. You don't look so good."

"What do you mean? I'm fine!" he protested as he stumbled back on his feet.

"I don't think so. You're looking worse by the minute!"

He knew why he was looking worse by the minute. She'd mentioned the idea of calling an ambulance, and that would cost him a fortune if she did it! He was only on the lowest rung of employees at present, which meant that he only had access to the lowest, measliest, most pathetically bare-bones insurance policy. See, if he were to compare it with the director's insurance policy, the director would be wearing a nice, thick, custom-made, custom-fitted overcoat. It'd have a fur-lined collar, thick padding throughout, and buttons to hold it shut, just in case of the unexpected circumstance that the zipper should break.

By contrast, the insurance the clerk was wearing was an old cloak that had been handed down for generations, originally belonging to a poor hobo. The stitching was so shoddy that it was coming apart in all places, to the point where there weren't so much "holes" as an absence of cloak. When he held it up to the light, he could barely see it—it appeared to be only some sort of shadow or ghost, and one day when he was wearing it, a strong gust of wind kicked up, and as he attempted to wrap the cloak more tightly around himself, he found that there was no cloak; there wasn't a single trace of it. It hadn't blown away—it had just disintegrated. With an insurance policy like that, the clerk would have been better off if he'd been paid a bit of extra change to buy a snack or a cup of coffee, because the doctor or the hospital would be so expensive, that if he were naked wearing so thin a cloak, he would freeze to death whether he took it off or not.

"I'm fine, I'm fine, I assure you," the clerk said, leaning his weight on the girl's firm shoulder. "Just take me over to an open lane so I can get started."

"Sir, I really don't think someone in your condition should be bowling. Maybe you should sit this round out and at least return to your desk and take a rest."

"I said I'm bowling! You can't talk me out of it!"

"Alright, alright."

"Now take me over to that one! It's empty."

"I can't take you to that lane sir."

"Why not?"

"Because you're not properly equipped sir. Why do you think I'm supporting your weight as we journey back across the lanes?"

"I leaned on you. You didn't have much of a choice, did you?"

"Oh I have a choice every second of my life, and I chose to support you, sir. You're not wearing the proper shoes. You're not allowed back here without the proper athletic shoes."

"But I don't have proper athletic shoes! I have my dress shoes because I'm at work!"

The girl snickered before thinking better of it and clearing her throat. "Did you hit your head hard, sir? You seem very confused. Everyone knows you rent shoes at a bowling alley."

"Rent shoes? Oh right. I knew that," the clerk said, his face paling even more than it already was at the thought of sticking his feet into someone else's disgusting shoes.

"Here sir, have a cup of water," one of the other girls said as the pair returned to the counter. "It looked like you took quite a tumble."

"Oh, he took quite a tumble," the other girl said.

The clerk downed the water in one go, regretting he couldn't slip some to the little black mouse. "Shoes! I demand shoes!" the clerk slurred.

"Right away sir!" one of the girls behind the counter said. She rushed in one direction before whirling back around to face the clerk. "What size, sir?"

"Uh, that's a good question," he muttered. "Let's see here—" He tried to lift up his foot, but he started to stumble, so he found himself hopping on one foot back in the direction of the bowling lanes.

"Sir!" one of the girls was shouting. "Sir! Come back! Sir you can't be over near the lanes!"

He was stumbling back toward the lanes as if he had no control over his feet. He felt as if the whole place was on an inclined plane that sucked him in the direction of the pins with the momentum of a thrown ball.

"Sir! Sir!" the girl shouted as she neared him. She tried to grab his shoulders to stabilize him, but she was sucked into his tumbling and they fell on top of each other in a jumble.

The clerk protectively reached toward his chest and felt the mouse wiggling.

"Here sir, let me give you a hand," the girl said, lifting him up and carrying him as though he were a newlywed bride before depositing him onto a chair in an empty lane. "You just stay put. She's bringing your shoes over. Actually, here, let me help you with those." She knelt down and started to untie his shoes.

"Wait! No! What are you doing!? Don't do that!" The clerk had just realized that his bladder was on the verge of bursting. That cup of water must have put him over the edge. Thinking back over it, he realized that he hadn't gone to the bathroom all day. His day had been too crazy to even think about going to the bathroom until this point. It was too late. He could already feel his shoe sliding from his foot.

"It's okay," the girl said. "I do this for elderly people all the time."

"But you don't understand!"

Now she was removing the other shoe.

The clerk couldn't take it anymore. "I have to go to the loo!" He jumped up from his seat expecting to sprint toward the bathroom, but his socks were so slippery on the polished wood floors that instead of moving anywhere his feet flailed around underneath him for a moment before he fell down on his rear end.

"Oh no!" the girl said as he fell. "Why didn't you say so? I do that for elderly people all the time as well!" The cheer in her voice was the exact opposite of the horror in the clerk's eyes as she lifted him up like a zookeeper carrying a chimpanzee. He felt so weak that his protests only came out as puffs of air through his nostrils as she whisked him straight into the bathroom.

* * * *

He sat wide-eyed on one of the empty lane's seats once more after the trip was over. His mind was attempting to remember the policy on sexual harassment.

He was so disturbed that the person addressing him had to shout at him and shake him by the shoulders after several times of failing to get the clerk's attention.

"Huh, what?" the clerk muttered.

"I *said,*" a person in a fedora and a scarf repeated, "That you look like a talented bowler, and I would like to challenge you to a game."

The disheveled clerk sat staring at the person through half-open eyes. He was confused as he knew there was no way he could have looked like a talented bowler, and he thought that this character in the hat must have been even more confused than he was. He was just about to open his mouth in protest when he realized that this had been part of the director's plan. "Ah, right," the clerk said, winking.

The person rebounded his wink with a confused look.

The clerk was about to stand up when he remembered he would fall in his slippery socks, but as he looked down, he saw that he was wearing garish purple bowling shoes. "How'd that happen?" he muttered.

"What?" the person said.

"Hey, can you do me a favor before we get started?" the clerk asked.

"What?"

"Here, have a seat over here next to me right here."

"Okay," the person said with suspicion, taking the seat.

"I have a question to ask you."

"Okay?"

"It's more of a secret really."

"Okay? I don't know if you should be saying any—"

"Well, it's a secret with a question attached."

"Uh—"

"I've never bowled before. How does it work?"

"What?"

"I've never bowled before. How does it work?" the clerk repeated.

"Oh I heard you! I'm just surprised. How is it possible

you never bowled before? A friend never invited you to a game?"

"No."

"You never went on a class trip?"

"Nope."

"Never saw it on the telly?"

"Of course not! Look, I've been focusing on my career and trying to build a proper life for myself! I didn't have time to be dilly-dallying around with any crazy leisurely sports! Just tell me how to do it!"

"I'll tell you how to do it," the person said in a soft tone, leaning closer to him, "but you have to promise me something."

The clerk could have sworn the person licked his ear while saying the second part of the sentence, but because he didn't want to have to worry about filing two sexual harassment complaints later, he told himself it was just the moisture of hot breath at a close proximity. "What is it?" the clerk said in a tone of horror.

"You promise you'll do it?"

"Yes, yes, I promise."

"You have to beat me," the person said in a voice like a puma.

"Okay. I promise I will defeat you at this game I have never played before and know nothing about," the clerk said. "Now tell me how to do it."

"Well, I think you'll be quite good," the person went on, jumping up from the seat and whirling around, the scarf trailing not far behind. "A natural even. You seem like someone who's good at sticking parts of you in holes."

The clerk gritted his teeth as he stared ahead, the words "sexual harassment!" repeating in his mind.

"See, you just walk over to this nice display of *balls*—"

The clerk didn't like the way the person said balls.

"Aren't you *coming?*"

The clerk didn't like the way the person said "coming" either, but he got up and shuffled over.

"And you select the ball that *feels* the nicest—"

The clerk didn't like the way the person said "feels" while caressing the balls.

"And you jam your fingers in the holes," the person did so and grabbed up the ball with both hands. "Pirouette over to the lane, and—toss it straight into the pins!" Releasing the ball while spinning around, the person's face dropped as the ball flew into the gutter and rolled the rest of the way down the lane without striking any pins.

"And then you put some chalk on your hands," the clerk's challenger continued, "and grab your ball when the machine shoots it back out, and toss it directly into the pins for real this time!" The ball flew down the lane, suddenly curving and falling into the gutter. "No! This can't be! Zero points on the first turn of such an important game? How could I do this! I have so much catching up to do!"

The clerk stood staring blankly, waiting for the rage to end.

"Well? What are you gawking at? I showed you what to do—or at least the general idea of it. Your turn!"

"Oh right. Do I have to do something with this thing too?" the clerk asked, indicating the score entry system.

"No. I can take care of the score. You trust me, right?"

"Uh, I don't know. I guess."

"Keep a close eye on me if you're worried, but it'd make no difference. The system senses how many pins fall or stand."

"Oh, right," the clerk muttered. "I guess I'll find a ball then."

"Find one that's suitable!" the person said in a sing-song voice.

"These all feel too heavy," the clerk called back to his opponent. "Do I want it to feel too heavy?"

"You want it to have a good weight, but not feel *too* heavy."

"Oh, right." The clerk took another minute weighing balls, decided they were all going to be too heavy, and grabbed one. He was gritting his teeth as he inched toward the lane. He glanced to his left and right, trying to catch some of the form of the other bowlers. He frowned and attempted to hurl the ball down the lane. Instead it just fell out of his hands, rolling at an extremely slow pace into the gutter.

"Well I know I've not shown myself as someone capable of advising you in this situation, but you want to give it a little oomph."

"I know," the clerk muttered, feeling like he was back in physical education class around a bunch of overly buff farmhands. "You said you challenged me because I seemed like I knew what I was doing, didn't you?"

The person doubled over in effeminate laughter, the fedora falling on the ground. "You're right! You're right! Go for the spare then, chap!"

Mimicking his opponent, the clerk put some chalk on his hand, retrieved his ball when it rolled up, and gave a bit of a sprint as he went up to unleash his ball. The result was the same: the ball rolled into the gutter.

"Now that we've had our warm-up throws," his opponent said, "let's get down to serious business. I've got lost ground to make up for!" With a very sincere expression, the person held the ball up in the air, then leapt forward and lunged like a fencer as the ball flew down the lane. A gurgle of pain was heard when the opponent saw the ball veer into the gutter. "What am I doing wrong? This can't be!" The attempt at a spare went no better.

The clerk tried to vary his throws, but whatever he did, he couldn't sever the ball's attraction on the gutters. Despite their similarity in score, the two took their news very differently. The clerk saw each throw as something that got him just a little bit closer to achieving his goal and moving on with his day.

By contrast, with each throw, more sweat appeared on his opponent. By now the person looked as if returning indoors from a torrential downfall. "I don't get it. The only reason I'm down here is because of my excellent bowling skills. What are you, some evil talisman?"

"Huh, me?" the clerk mumbled, poking at his chest.

"This ends now! There's still time to fix this grave error!" the person shouted, leaping up. Running toward the balls, in one fluid motion, the opponent managed to grab a ball, spin around, lunge, and release the ball down the alley. To the shock of both, the ball flew straight down the alley, smashing into the center pin and sending them all flying apart like violent dominos. "Yes!" the person shouted. "Yes! I did it! I broke your evil curse, and now I can proceed according to plan!"

The clerk paid his opponent little attention and just kept chucking his ball on his turn to get this over with, ignoring the fact that his ball just rolled into the gutter every time.

"This is it. The moment of truth," the opponent said, ready to throw the ball against the last set of pins. "Come here my brave challenger. I'm serious. Come closer."

The clerk shuffled closer.

"I'm going to throw this ball at those ten pins, and I'm going to knock down eight of them."

"Okay?"

"Just watch. It will be perfect." The clerk stepped back as his opponent unleashed the ball. It flew down the lane, curving a hair toward the right side, and it collided with the pins in a mess.

The clerk realized that nine of the pins had fallen over.

His opponent let out a scream of terror so loud that everyone in the place turned to look at them. "This can't be! This can't be!" the person repeated over and over.

The clerk was shuffling over to get his ball when his opponent accosted him. "Look, we both know what's going on here," the person whispered loudly into his ear. "You need to subtract one from my score before you take it down!"

The clerk didn't move, chewing on his lip.

"Promise me!" his opponent whisper-shouted, shaking him by the arms. "Promise me you'll subtract one from my score before you write it down! Promise me!"

"Alright, alright! Just let me go," the clerk muttered.

The person breathed a deep sigh of relief, adjusted the fedora, and stalked away toward the restrooms.

The clerk took a notebook out of his satchel and jotted down the number of the person's score on a piece of paper, adding in parenthesis, "minus one?"

The clerk was ready to leave, anxious to get his own shoes back on his feet, but just as he was ready to go, he realized that their scores were still displayed on the machine, and it was flashing that it was the clerk's turn to go. Not knowing how to make it go away, he decided he'd better give his ball a final throw and hope that finished the game automatically. He reached over and grabbed his ball, and as he stuck his fingers in the hole, his ring finger refused to enter. "There's something stuck in here," he muttered. Poking around at the hole, he tried to dislodge whatever it was. "Oh, it's a piece of paper," he realized, still struggling to get it out. Just as it popped out of the ball, it fell to the ground at his feet.

He reached down to pick it up, but as he glanced downward, he realized that the entire ground was covered with scattered pieces of paper.

"What on earth is going on here?!" he complained. "All these papers weren't here before! There's no way on earth there's a rational explanation for all this!" He grabbed at the papers that were near his feet, on top of the mountain of papers that seemed to be growing all around him. They were colored strips of paper that didn't have any writing on them. "Where'd the paper from the ball go?" he muttered to himself. He kept grasping at papers and letting them fall back through his fingers as he realized they weren't the piece of paper he was looking for. These papers were bright reds, yellows, blues, and greens, but the paper he was looking for was a rolled up piece of white paper. "This is unbelievable! It's got to be here somewhere!" He was vaguely aware of loud shouting and cheering, but he was too focused on being annoyed that the paper could be lost. The clerk kept throwing handfuls of paper behind him, but there was so much paper everywhere that he had no idea if he was just searching through the same pieces of paper, making the whole thing worse. His knees were sore as he crawled around on the ground, searching desperately for the piece of paper. He collapsed onto his back as though he'd intended to make a snow angel in the cushioning of paper.

"It's hopeless, Ellem. I lost it. Who knows if it was important or not."

As he dropped his hand back near his head, his left hand felt a piece of paper that was thicker than the others. "Ah ha!" He grabbed it. It was definitely the rolled up paper, and he held it tightly before sticking it in a pants pocket and retreating back toward the counter.

"I need my shoes back please, ma'ams," he said to the girls at the counter.

"Okay sir. Can you just give us our shoes back so we can exchange them?"

"But if I don't have my shoes back first, what will I do with my feet?"

"What do you mean?"

"Do I have to put my feet on this dirty, public floor?"

"It's not public. This is a high-level security clearance area. You're wearing socks, aren't you, sir?"

"Well, yeah."

"So there you go. Your bare feet won't be on the floor."

"As if I want my socks on the floor," he grumbled as he submitted and leaned down to untie the laces. He handed one of the girls back the ugly bowling shoes and she disappeared into a back room.

"You still don't look so good, sir. How do you feel?"

"I feel fine. Just great," he muttered.

"Well, maybe you should visit a doctor all the same."

"Yeah, yeah," he grumbled. He had a headache, but he knew that was just from hitting his head, and a doctor couldn't fix it any better than an acetaminophen.

"Here are your shoes, sir," the other girl said, returning them.

He slipped into his shoes and slumped out into the lobby.

"Did you see that fellow just bowl a perfect game?" the person in the fedora hat said in a tone thick with disappointment. "He was just rubbing it in my face."

"I didn't notice," the clerk responded.

"Going down?"

"Yeah."

"Well this one's going up, so don't take it." With that, his bowling partner was gone once more.

Alone in the lobby, save for the mouse, the clerk unfurled the paper in a furtive motion and glanced at the message before tucking it back in his pocket. It had read, *Today the alley. Tomorrow 195. Continue the rotation.*

The clerk pursed his lips and stepped into the lift once it arrived. Finding it empty, he pressed the button for the first floor. On the 96th floor, several people entered, including a particularly obese man whose girth was shoving the clerk into the corner near the buttons. The elevator seemed to be stopping at every floor. One person would get off and two people would squeeze in, making things even more uncomfortable. The emergency phone underneath the buttons began to ring. After it rang twice, the obese man peered down at the clerk and said, "Answer it."

"Why? It's not for me. You answer it."

"I can't reach it from here. You're in the way. You answer it. And if it's for me, you hand it to me, but if it's for you, then they'll have reached who they're looking for."

The phone rang again, so the clerk gave in and answered it. "Hello?"

"Ah, smashing!" a familiar woman's voice said. "I thought I'd catch you."

"Oh, hello ma'am," the clerk replied as he realized it was his boss, the manager of his department.

"By the way, great work with everything, great work—you know what I'm talking about."

"Oh, thank you, ma'am," the clerk muttered. He didn't know what she was talking about, but that wasn't the kind of thing one admitted to one's boss. Not if he wanted a promotion he didn't.

"Anyway, I'm ringing you up because I need to know how those reports are coming along."

"Reports?" the clerk murmured, mostly to himself,

before he remembered the stack of paperwork that was waiting for him in his desk back in the small city. "Oh! Yes, the reports."

"Are you just about done with them?"

"Well, you see the thing is—"

"Yes, yes, don't say another word. I know where you are, clearly, the thing is, I need you to get back here on the double and finish those reports before morning; otherwise I'm really sunk for my big meeting tomorrow."

"Oh, I see," the clerk said, his shoulders dropping. "Well, I'm just on my way back now, so—"

"Excellent, my dear! I knew I could count on you." The phone clicked off. His boss was too busy to ever say "goodbye."

He wished he could have said to her, "But I had to do something for the director!" Yet he knew the director had specifically forbidden him from using this excuse, and he wondered if the director had informed his boss of the situation. On the one hand, he probably had, since his boss hadn't been concerned by his absence at all, yet on the other hand, why hadn't she assigned his work to someone else? There was much he wanted to tell her: How tired he was from all these crazy days of work in a row, not to mention the already exhausting, less crazy days that had come before. He wanted to tell her he thought it was unfair that he had to go back and do all this extra work now, when it was just about time to be heading home. He could never say any of this to his boss though. Clerks looking for promotions don't say such things.

After much longer than he would have liked, the lift arrived at the first floor. The obese gentleman had ridden with him the entire way and was now bantering with the security guards as he made his way out.

The clerk was walking down the sidewalks, shivering

slightly with his hands in his pockets, imagining what his new desk might be like if he got the promotion, when these daydreams were cruelly ripped apart by a gravelly voice shouting, "Hey! It's you!"

He stopped and turned to face a man whose beard pre-ceded him. It was the hobo-looking nutter from yesterday. "You're back! Just like you said you'd be! I'm glad. I don't know how seriously you young people take your campaign promises."

The clerk felt like it would be better to just fall asleep on the sidewalk and not be involved in this conversation. He could feel the ache of exhaustion in his legs and might have fallen asleep on his feet if the loud crunching of the man biting into a dill pickle didn't disturb him back to complete consciousness. "Uh, look, I'm going to have to catch you tomorrow."

"Catch me tomorrow?" the man said, looking up from his meal. There was a tray of food spread across his lap. "What do you mean?"

"Look, I was just so tired by the time I got home last night, and then I had to get up to go to work first thing in the morning, so, you know. I totally forgot to grab some change."

"Oh no," the man said as though he'd just been deliv-ered horrendous news. He dropped his fork and put his hands over his head.

"It's no big deal. I'll just grab it for tomorrow. I've got to come back here again anyway."

"Oh, so you think I'll just be sitting here on the sidewalk again tomorrow? I'm running a campaign here."

"Campaign," the clerk breathed as a hybrid of question, confusion, and annoyance.

"I think I see what's going on here," the man said.

"You're finding it hard to commit to a campaign that you know so little about."

"That I know nothing about," the clerk corrected.

"Well I can't go saying this too loudly—for obvious reasons—but maybe I could let you in on it."

The clerk stared at him blankly.

"If I knew you could be trusted."

The clerk twitched his eyebrows. He glanced slightly toward the end of the block, wondering if he could be rude enough to just walk away. The crosswalk was only a few steps away. He couldn't do it. Some invisible superego held him there.

"You know what? You look like an upstanding young man. I think I will entrust you with some knowledge about my campaign. You did already pledge a contribution, after all."

The clerk's eyes felt heavy. He wished he had something to lean on—a cane or a sofa.

"Have you ever thought to yourself, 'All these politicians are corrupt and untrustworthy! My taxpayer money shouldn't be spent on the Dionysian excesses of this malfunctioning, bureaucratic excuse for a government! My hard-earned cash shouldn't be spent on bombing people at random overseas! Killing poor innocents—even children! My word, think of the children!—killing poor innocent children with robots from the sky!' Surely you've thought of that before, and wept with immense, indescribable sorrow to think upon it?"

The clerk stared at him.

"Certainly you have! And then you've said, 'I'm going to have to fix this! I'm going to make some changes and run for office myself—raise myself through the ranks. I'll do it just after things at work stop being so busy, after things settle down at home.'"

A cat had appeared from an alley and was sitting not too far from the hobo on the sidewalk. The clerk wondered if he would be better off becoming a hobo. If he built up the nerve to panhandle, it might not be so bad to annoy people until they gave him enough money for food. This bloke had a feast every time the clerk happened upon him, and it was making his stomach rumble, reminding him that he hadn't even had a lunch break today. He was running on nothing more than a bit of peanuts and coffee. Two more cats appeared and sat with the other cat. They were looking directly at the clerk with their yellow and green eyes.

"But these things are always getting pushed back—getting in the way. That's why I'm here. That's where I come in: I'm you. I can take your place—get out there and right the wrongs of this political chaos—be your voice like a sword to cut the red tape of bureaucracy—slice apart the sectarian politics—bring peace to our people—keep the jobs and wealth on our shores—just like you'd do."

Taxis were honking their horns on the street because a car was blocking their way as it failed to parallel park. Four more cats had joined the group that continued to stare at the clerk. He held his hand over his chest.

"And I've figured out the whole complicated process so you don't have to. All we have to do is raise more money than everyone else running—and raising money is something I've spent my entire life mastering, mind you. I know I'll raise enough money with the support of others like yourself who truly care about the cause. Today: A Representative. Tomorrow: The Prime Minister!"

The clerk imagined grabbing a fistful of the hobo's mashed potatoes, stuffing them into his mouth, and falling asleep on the sidewalk with his tummy full. One of the tortoiseshell cats took a step forward.

"Now that I've got you all revved up about the future, I know I can count on your first contribution tomorrow!"

"Yep, you got it," the clerk said, immediately turning on his heel, rushing down the sidewalk and through the crosswalk.

It was always tough to catch a bus back to the small city around here because there wasn't technically a bus stop in that direction, but there was a spot at a five way intersection behind the courthouse where the busses would pick you up, even if it was technically illegal for them to stop there. To make matters worse, there were always much fewer busses running in the early evening than there were at earlier times in the day. A bunch of other commuters were milling about the unofficial bus stop, all looking tired and impatient. A couple of men and women were in suits and others had the look of day laborers, but the clerk had the impression that they had all just slogged through a long day of work and were headed home. He wished the same were true of himself and felt like he could double-over from hunger pangs. Across the street there was a small deli, and as the clerk squinted through the traffic, he could see that the neon *OPEN* sign was lit up in green. He glanced at his companions waiting for the bus. They looked like they'd been here a while. A bus had to be arriving any minute now. He looked back at the deli. He could get an egg and cheese on a bagel—no, that might take too long to cook. He could get a submarine sandwich with cheese and veggies covered in olive oil and vinegar. His mouth was salivating, but he knew even that could take too long to prepare. He could just run in and grab a bag of crisps. That might work. He edged down to peer at the road that led down to the front of the courthouse. There was no bus coming through the traffic that he could see. The clerk sprinted over to the crosswalk, but as soon as he got there, the traffic light changed and four lanes of traffic were blasting past him in both directions.

"C'mon. C'mon," he muttered, his anxiety causing him to keep looking over his shoulder at the road the bus would come up. The light changed again, and he started to go across, but a car honked its horn at him—scaring him half to death—and he jumped back. He hadn't realized the diagonal street of cars were going to go before the walk signal would ignite. At last the little green man appeared, giving him the go-ahead, and he sprinted to the other side of the street. Looking back to make sure he wasn't missing the bus one last time, he opened the door and burst into the deli. There was only one other customer in the deli, but the clerk immediately realized it was an old man, and he was taking his sweet, sweet time asking the deli clerk what every ingredient behind the massive glass case of sandwich fixings was.

The clerk was literally sweating as he stood there, leaning his weight back and forth from foot to foot. He looked out the glass window in the front of the store and saw that the people on the other side of the street were still waiting for the bus.

"Is that meat moldy?" the old man asked.

"No sir, it's olive loaf," the deli clerk said with a hint of exasperation in his tone.

"What's that?" the old man asked.

The clerk was losing his composure. There was a rack of crisps on top of the counter. He was going to run up there, grab a bag, and say he was terribly, apologetically apologetic for cutting in line, but could he please just pay for the bag of crisps because he was in a massive hurry? That might work.

"Do you have bangers or rashers back there?" the nonagenarian croaked.

"Rashers, yes."

"Ellem, can I pull this off?" the clerk murmured. The act of turning his head slightly to whisper at his pocket was the reason he saw the wide, white bus rolling up out of his peripheral vision. He rushed to the door and slammed into it with his full weight—he'd expected it to be a push, but it was a pull. Shaking himself off, he pulled the door open and scrambled down the sidewalk. The bus was stopped on the other side of the street now. He couldn't tell if the people were still getting on or not from this vantage point. Vehicles rushed past him in a blur. There was no way he could jump in there and make a break for the other side of the street. "I'll do it as soon as the light turns though, regardless of if I get the walk sign or not." He felt like he could have made five triple-decker sandwiches in the time it took for the traffic to stop. As soon as there wasn't a car in the intersection, he ran, and he could hear horns beeping at him, but he just kept going. His triumph of making it to the other side was immediately deflated when he saw that the bus was no longer there. He fought the urge to just collapse right there on the sidewalk, looked up the street and saw that he could still make out the back of the bus—it had an advertisement wedged between its red brake lights that said something about a divorce lawyer in the island language. Sprinting down the sidewalk, he could tell it was going faster than he was running. He kept going though, determined to get back to the small city as soon as possible.

Fortune smiled on the clerk in the form of a red stop light. The bus had to stop at it, and after another moment of running, the clerk caught up to it. He ran next to the doors and thrashed his arms about in an effort to get the bus driver's attention. When the bus driver noticed him, he didn't open the doors, he motioned that he wasn't at a stop and he couldn't let the clerk on. The clerk pleaded with his facial expressions, jumping up and down, making desperate body language. The driver looked torn. He glanced behind him, then turned his head all around and decided to open the doors, motioning for the clerk to hop on. The clerk rushed on, too out of breath to confirm with the driver that he'd be going to the small city, and the driver immediately slammed down on the gas, propelling the bus forward and sending the clerk tumbling down to the ground, rolling down the aisle on top of his satchel and not stopping until he hit his head on the seats in the back. The clerk immediately checked his pocket, then in a sigh whispered, "As if I didn't already have a headache."

He'd thought he was done falling, but before he could even climb up to a seat, the fast-moving bus hit a bump in the road—a speed bump or a pothole—and the entire back of the bus bounced up into the air. The clerk went tumbling down farther than he thought he should have been able to, and realized he'd gone into some sort of chasm.

"Hey! Hey!" some voices repeatedly began shouting.

The clerk had landed on his back, and he was looking around in a room that reminded him of the engine room of an old locomotive burning coal in a furnace with pipes and steam making all sorts of noises.

"Hey! Hey!"

He realized two middle-aged men and a middle-aged woman all wearing the same blue uniform were looking down at him. At first he'd thought they were angry for his intrusion, but now he realized they seemed excited that he had arrived, and they rushed over to another spot and grabbed picket signs off the ground.

"What's going on here? Where am I?" the clerk muttered. He was still on his back and the mouse crawled up out of his pocket, onto his neck, sniffed his chin for a moment and then gave it a lick. "Little guy! Hide yourself before these guys notice you!" As if understanding, the mouse scurried back into his pocket.

"We drive the province to work every day, so give your bus drivers a living pay!" they started chanting.

"Bus drivers? Where am I? Is this the bus?" He tried to look up from where he'd come, but it was difficult to see.

"You don't know where you are?" one of the people said. "You mean you didn't come down here on purpose?"

"You didn't read about it on our social media page? We've been posting!"

"Posting about what?" the clerk muttered as he stood up, rubbing his head.

"Our strike."

"What? Bus driver strike?"

"Yes, exactly. You haven't heard?"

"Of course he hasn't heard! They've got us crammed down next to the wheel-well where no one knows we exist!"

"Why don't you go picket someplace more visible?" the clerk asked, feeling uncomfortable and wondering how he could escape.

"Oh no! We're not falling for that. That's how our co-workers started this whole thing years ago. They protested out in front of city hall and guess what happened? A squadron of cops rolled in, beat 'em all up, tear-gassed 'em, pepper-sprayed 'em—the whole nine yards."

"Why would they do that?"

"Charged 'em all with disorderly conduct—picketing without a permit."

"So we have a permit. But the only place we're allowed to picket is crammed down in here where no one sees us."

The clerk wanted to say, *"Well this is all very dodgy and*

I'm going to be leaving now," but instead he said, "Well, now that I know about your plight, I'll be sure to let others know, but right now I think it's important that I get back up to the, uh, regular part of the bus." With that, the clerk turned around and tried to walk away, but it was cramped and dark in here, and he really didn't see any way out.

"I'm afraid it's not so easy to get out of here once you've come down," one of the bus drivers said.

"We can help you out though, friend," said another.

"Yes, yes, we'll help you out of here." The bus drivers jumped into action like a teenage cheerleading squad. Despite their age and generally wide-looking physique, they started climbing on top of one another, hoisting themselves up so that they were standing on top of one another's' shoulders.

"Quickly now, friend," the bus driver on the bottom said. "This isn't the most pleasant position to be in."

"Uh, what should I do?" the clerk said.

"Climb up us. We've made a ladder for you. And be careful not to touch any of the pipes, or really any of the metal in here. It's all quite hot."

"Okay," the clerk muttered as he stepped forward, thinking (with sarcasm), *"This isn't awkward at all."* As he approached the first man, he realized that he was much bigger than he'd seemed at a distance. He was so tall, the clerk couldn't even imagine how he'd fit on a bus. He wasn't even quite sure how he fit in this space, yet somehow, the three bus drivers all fit in this room aligned like a totem pole, and the clerk still couldn't see the way out.

"Go on, hurry," the bus driver on the bottom said, clearly feeling the weight of the other two.

The clerk had been trying to figure out how to go about this, but being prompted and seeing no other way, he grabbed onto the man's belt, his fingers actually reaching down into the waist of the man's pants, and he hoisted himself up like a trapeze artist preparing to do a trick, pulling the toes of his black shoes up and resting them on top of the man's belt, then he reached up and grabbed onto one of the shirt buttons with both hands, since there didn't seem to be anything better to hang onto, and he used the buttons as a ladder, slowly pulling himself up a few of them until he was in range of the man's shirt pocket. It was a bit far away from the buttons, but he leaned over toward it and felt himself falling, yet the frightful moment passed and his hands caught onto the top of the shirt pocket. He pulled himself up onto the rim of the pocket in a similar fashion to the way he'd done with the belt, and now he was within range of the man's shoulder, where he found the shoe of one of the other bus drivers. He grabbed onto the sole of the shoe and pulled himself up, using the laces like a rope-ladder to get up onto the man's shin.

"How do I get up these pants?" the clerk shouted up to the bus driver.

"Just grab onto them in bunches and pull yourself up!" the bus driver who was now under him responded.

The clerk tried to comply, but the dark blue pants were made out of a thick material and appeared as if they were freshly starched, so that grasping them seemed impossible, and after a few attempts, the clerk almost fell backward off the man. "It's no use!" he cried out in fear and frustration.

"It's okay, go up through the inside," the bus driver he was attempting to climb called down. "I've got plenty of leg-hair. You can grab onto those to pull yourself up."

"Uh." The clerk's nose was twitched in disgust.

"Don't worry, it won't hurt me. I have strong hair and stronger skin. It's okay, friend. We're all friends here. It doesn't matter if you're in my pants for a moment."

The clerk gritted his teeth, crouched a bit, securing his footing on the tongue of the man's shoe, which he kicked off of as he jumped up his shin, grabbing two fistfuls of leg-hair. It was dark inside the man's pants and he had to grope around to find new handholds. The clerk felt as though he wouldn't make it. There was nothing to secure his feet with, and he had to rely on his upper body strength to pull himself up.

He was already at the man's knee though, so it wasn't too far to grab a hold of the bottom of the man's boxer shorts, which he scooted up as quickly as possible, trying to avoid becoming more intimate with the man than was absolutely necessary, and then reached his arm up, gripping the waist-line of the man's pants and hoisting himself up out of the darkness and into fresher air. Now it was a similar climb up shirt buttons and onto the pocket.

As he reached the man's shoulder where the female bus driver's shoe was resting, she said, "I can get you up the rest of the way, and she kneeled down, hoisted the clerk up from underneath his armpits, and shouted, "Quick! Grab a hold and pull yourself out!" as she held him up.

He grabbed onto some sort of metal rim, pulled himself up with what felt like the last of his strength, and flopped out onto the sticky aisle of the bus. He was sweaty, panting, and tired as he lay there for a moment. "Thank you!" he shouted in the direction he'd come from, but he was over near the wheel well and only saw the slightest space. Before he could wonder how on earth he'd managed to fall down it, the bus was suddenly screeching to a halt and someone was com-plaining at him in the island language.

"Oh, sorry," he muttered, as he tried to get up out of the aisle, and then he caught himself and apologized again, this time in the island language, as he pulled himself onto a seat and sank back in it. He reached into his pocket and extracted the tiny black mouse. "You make it through all that okay, Ellem?" he asked, holding it close to his face on the palm of his hand. The mouse was smelling his hand excitedly and licked his fingertips a few times. "Glad to see you're in such good spirits, little guy. I, for one, am knackered, and I would like nothing more than to eat as much of a banquet as I could manage until my strength failed me, and I passed out in bed until morning. Unfortunately for me, I've still got work to do."

The mouse looked at him with shiny black eyes and twitched its whiskers all around.

The clerk smiled at the mouse, looked around to make sure no one was watching, and gave it a kiss on the back before depositing it into his pocket. He looked out the window and saw that they'd already crossed the border into the small city and were nearing where he lived. "You know what? Just because I still have to work doesn't mean we can't stop by, grab a quick bite to eat, and say hello to my betrothed," he whispered to his pocket. "I'm sure you're hungry too, Ellem."

He called out, "Next stop!" in the island language, and before long, the bus brakes were squeaking to a halt and the clerk was climbing out onto the sidewalk. He walked a few blocks up to the apartment building, and was soon entering through the front door.

The two large men were busying themselves in the kitchen, cooking something that smelled very spicy and un-appetizing to the clerk, despite the fact that he was starving.

"Hey guys, how's it going?" the clerk said as he closed the door behind him.

They took a moment to finish feeding each other spoon-ful tastes of whatever was in the pots that were shooting out steam into the whole room. They had their arms twined around each other's like they were in a romantic comedy.

"Everything's *delicious* with us," one of them said in his island accent, laughing.

The clerk quickly slipped past them into the bedroom where he found his betrothed leaning halfway into a cage where she was feeding all the little neon green and blue parakeets orange slices.

"Mmm oranges," the clerk said, entering the room.

"Wow, you're home late," she said, turning her head and talking to him through the bars of the cage. All the little birds were chirping.

"Yeah, well I'm not even supposed to be home now."

"What do you mean?"

"I had to go do some work in the bigger city, but they need me back in my usual office to take care of some important documents."

"This late?"

"Yeah, they need them yesterday. You know how it is."

She gave the last slice of orange to an excited parakeet, climbed out of the cage, knee-walked over the bed, and dropped down at the edge of it, joining the clerk on the sliver of floor. "My poor hardworking sweetheart." She put her hand on his cheek.

"I didn't even get a lunch break today. I'm starving. Are there more oranges?"

"Oh, nope. I'm sorry. The birds and I ate the last one."

The disappointment on the clerk's face was evident.

"I'm sure we can figure out something for you to eat. Why don't you take off your shoes and relax before you have to go back to work?"

"Okay," the clerk muttered, kneeling down to take them off while his betrothed climbed back onto the bed.

Once his shoes were off, he collapsed onto the bed, but he didn't bother to take off the rest of his clothes since he was going back to work soon anyway. He folded his hands behind his head and rested his head on the pillow. He could feel Ellem wiggling around in his pocket, but he didn't know if it was a good idea to take him out here or not. *"You're probably hungry too, little guy,"* he thought.

"Let's see here," his betrothed said, her voice muffled since her head was upside-down, peering at where their food supplies were kept under the bed. "We've got canned beans, canned spaghetti, a slice of bread—"

"A slice of bread? Can I have a sandwich?" the clerk asked.

"Sorry," she said, her head appearing back up near his. "I kind of, well, ate the rest of the sandwich supplies for my lunch."

"Oh," the clerk said.

"We really don't have too much. I guess we should go to the store soon."

"It's okay. I'll just have the can of beans. The protein should keep me going."

"You got it!" she said, excited to grab the can-opener and peel off the lid for him.

He sat up, tucked his legs together, and ate the beans cold with a spoon, wondering if they would have been better if they were warm. His betrothed was tinkering with the other animals, so he used the opportunities when her head was turned away from him to slip beans down into his pocket, which the mouse grabbed and ate with a clear eagerness.

Once his beans were through, he left the empty can and spoon on the night table next to him and lay back down. "I'm just going to rest for a moment," he called over to his betrothed, "and then I'm going to head back to work. It was nice to get to spend a little bit of time with you though."

"Aw, you're sweet," she responded.

The next thing the clerk knew, he was disturbed by something shaking his hips. It seemed to be causing his entire body to vibrate. It would stop for a second and then disturb him again, stop for a second, disturb him again. He became aware of a voice murmuring in the background and that combined with the shaking was enough to wake him from his sleep. His eyes opened to see two figures peering down at him from the edge of the bed. He realized it was his betrothed and his manager from work. This caused him to realize that he was in bed under the covers and he had fallen asleep when he needed to be at work.

"Oh no! I fell asleep!" he shouted, throwing the blankets off of himself and pouncing onto his knees. It was at this point that he realized he was completely naked.

His boss didn't seem to notice, and if she did, she didn't show that she cared. "How could you go to sleep? You knew I needed you down at the office! It's a good thing I stopped by to check up on you!"

The clerk was busy wrapping some of the blankets around his lower half. "I didn't mean to fall asleep, I swear! It's just that things were so crazy down in the bigger city that I didn't get a chance to take a lunch break and I was starving, so since I was passing by here on the way back to the office, I decided to stop by and grab some dinner."

His manager had a look on her face that he interpreted as skepticism.

"How did you know I was here?"

"I was working late in the office myself, and you hadn't showed up yet, so I thought to stop by your residence, since it was not too far out of the way on my return home." Her eyes narrowed at him. "And it's a good thing I did!"

"Don't worry," the clerk said. "I'll be on my way post-haste! I'll be able to get everything done before morning."

"I hope that's true because I left some priority documents in your inbox."

"Okay, you've got it. You can count on me."

She nodded and continued to look at the clerk. The clerk pursed his lips and decided to nod back. He glanced at his betrothed, who was standing next to his manager, but her expression was enigmatic.

A hermit crab scratched on the wall of its tank.

"Let's go then," the manager said. "You can walk me back to the main avenue."

"Oh, right, okay, that's no problem," the clerk muttered, blushing, looking around, and pulling the blankets tighter against his crotch. "It's just that, well, I need to get redressed."

"I know," the manager said matter-of-factly. "That's no problem. I'll wait." She stood there, unmoving, her gaze fixed on his.

"Oh, oh, uh, okay then," the clerk stuttered, wondering why the words, "sexual harassment" had been so prominent in his mind recently. After a moment, he realized he couldn't just remain there. "Um, uh, do you know where my clothes are, darling?"

"Right! Your clothes!" she said. "I hung them up over there." She indicated the far corner of the ceiling, near the window above the bed.

"Thanks," he muttered, crawling over there while trying to hold the blanket over himself. He tried to keep the blanket draped like a robe, but he found that it was firmly tucked into the bottom of the bed, and it wouldn't reach very far. Despite this, he tried to keep his decency with what little sliver of blanket reached up there, but his betrothed had hung his clothes up on hangers with clips, and he was having difficulty getting them undone with one hand, so he realized he had no choice but to drop the blanket. He unclipped his skivvies and tried to get them on as quickly as possible, but in his haste to lift up his leg, he lost his balance and fell on his back, bouncing onto the bed and flopping all over the place as he attempted to wiggle into his shorts. He had less trouble getting into his trousers and undershirt, but as soon as he slipped into his button-up shirt, his mouth dropped open in horror. "Where's Ellem?!"

"What?" his manager and betrothed asked at the same time.

He ignored them, beginning to look around frantically, but seeing no trace of the little black mouse.

"Here, I've got your shoes, if that's what you're looking for," his betrothed said, holding the pair of black shoes toward him.

"Oh, thanks," he grumbled, scooting down to the edge of the bed. When he let his legs hang over, there was so little room that one of his knees was pressing against his betrothed and the other was pressing against his manager. As he held the first shoe up preparing to put it on his foot, he saw two shiny black eyes looking back at him. *"There you are, Ellem! Quick! We've got to get you back into my pocket without anyone noticing!"* He held the shoe higher, turned it so that the opening was facing toward him, and he leaned it against his chest, forming a ramp for the little mouse to climb down.

"What are you doing?" his betrothed asked. Both the women had puzzled expressions.

As if the mouse could read his thoughts, it scrambled down into his pocket.

"Just putting on my shoes," the clerk said, continuing

the process. He accidentally bumped his toe into his manager's crotch. "Oh, sorry."

If she noticed, she didn't say owt.

"Okay, I'm ready," the clerk said, hopping down from the bed and finding himself pressed up against the two women.

"Spiffing. Let's go," his manager said. She twisted to open the door and knocked the clerk and his betrothed onto the bed. They inch-wormed further back on the bed so there would be room to open the door enough for her to squeeze through.

"Have a good night at work!" his betrothed said, kissing the clerk on the cheek.

The clerk stepped in front of his manager and led the way through the front room. The two large men had fallen asleep spooning in bed. One of them was snoring loudly. The clerk opened the front door and held it for the manager.

Out on the street, it was a dark blue night, as clear and cold as if it were the middle of winter. The clerk was shivering in his fancy jacket and wondering why he hadn't grabbed his real coat. Since he and his manager were alone on the quiet side-streets, he wanted to ask her about recent work-related occurrences, but he thought maybe it would be inappropriate, and he remembered the director distinctly warning him not to mention what he really wanted to talk about with his manager.

She wasn't saying anything, just walking forward at a steady pace.

The clerk thought he should try to make some small talk, but he couldn't think of much to say. "Nice night," he said into the muffled background noises of the city. "Chilly. But nice."

"Yeah. It's nice," his manager said.

"Crazy week at work, huh?" he said without thinking.

"I think it's best we not talk about work under these circumstances," his manager responded.

"Oh. Right."

"Just make sure you take care of the priority work when you get there."

"Yes, of course, ma'am."

They strolled the next few blocks in silence. It felt awkward to the clerk, but maybe it didn't to the manager.

"This is where we split up," she said as they arrived on the main avenue. "I'll check in on your progress first thing in the morning."

"Alright, see you then. Cheers!" the clerk said.

As he walked down the avenue, he weaved through all the other people who were out enjoying themselves or running errands. There were smells of traditional island food every few buildings, but that wasn't tempting him too much. What was tempting him was the thought of a cup of coffee—not just because it would warm him on this frosty night, nor because it would be a delicious treat for his tongue, but because his mind was incredulous that he was awake right now and he didn't know how long his mind would agree to staying awake once he sat down. He had been so comfortably asleep that he could have remained passed out until morning, yet here he was, trudging back to work. Well, he supposed he wasn't really trudging, just walking normally, albeit with a tired shuffle to his steps, but he knew that he was trudging through a frozen tundra mentally. On the next corner, there was a small restaurant that he thought might have decent coffee this time of night. The island style coffee was stronger than he was used to, but he could sweeten it a little extra. He slipped into the cafeteria, which was full of yellow light, yellow tiled walls, and excitedly chattering people.

The waitresses seemed friendly and were talking with many of the patrons.

As he waited in line, the clerk rubbed his neck. He hadn't realized how sore his throat felt until he anticipated sipping a hot beverage.

When the waitress behind the counter called, "Next!" in the island language, the clerk stepped up and immediately began to stumble over his words.

"I possess a hot coffee," he said in the island language with his thick provincial accent. "Wait, no!" he said in his usual tongue. He tried the island language again, "I have. No. I—I—" The clerk felt like he could start crying right on the spot, but he managed to hold back.

The waitress had already begun to get him a coffee. She said something he didn't understand, but was motioning at four different sizes of to-go cups, so he thought he knew what she was asking, and since he had no idea what the island word for "extra large" was, he pointed at the size he wanted. She said something else he didn't understand as she grabbed a cup of that size and walked back to the espresso machines.

"I want! I want!" the clerk said to himself in a scolding tone of the island language as he remembered what he should have said.

"Thank you very much," the clerk said in the island language, handing the waitress money as she handed him the steaming hot cup.

"Are you okay, sweetie?" the waitress said in the province's official language, sounding quite fluent.

"Yeah. Yeah, I'm fine. Thanks," the clerk responded in his own language, forcing a smile.

He took his cup of coffee and walked away in shame, wondering if he should have explained to her how bad it made him feel to be unable to speak more of the island language after living here so long. The worst part of it was that, from what he could tell, all of the actual immigrants could speak more than enough of the provincial language to get through life effectively, whereas the clerk, by contrast, could barely string two words of the island language together, even though everyone always told him that the provincial language was much more difficult to learn than the island language.

With his coffee sweetened and soothing his throat while simultaneously burning his tongue, the clerk was back out on the bustling sidewalk, making his way toward his cubicle. He was about halfway finished with his coffee when he glanced up to see someone pointing a gun directly at him. His eyes widened in horror, but before he could react any further, he was watching his cup fly out of his hands as if in slow motion, the creamy brown liquid flying up into the air and splashing down onto the crosswalk in front of him. As time sped back up and pain surged through his chest and shoulders, the clerk realized he had been tackled and was being pinned to the sidewalk. The person with the gun had approached closer and was standing near his head, the gun held loosely at the person's side, and the clerk could see that it was not a normal gun, but looked like some space-age gadget.

"Bugger and blast it!" the clerk cried out as he wiggled to free himself.

"Yes. The facial scan is one hundred percent accurate. This is the perpetrator," the person with the gun said.

"Let's get him into the van for questioning, then," the person on his back said. The clerk felt himself unceremoniously dragged to his feet. On the side street, there was an unmarked black van. The back doors opened and the clerk was tossed in before the other two people. As soon as he'd been let go of, he tried to move his arms and realized they were somehow bound behind his back. He was worried the mouse had been hurt in the assault. If the impact of landing on the ground had hurt the mouse, the clerk knew he'd have to find a veterinarian who'd be open at this hour to treat the poor little thing.

"Sir, we've taken you in for questioning in reference to your association with a wanted saboteur. You're going to have to explain some of these photographs."

One wall inside of this van was apparently a digital screen. It was covered in images of the clerk taken within the last couple of days.

"For example, what exactly is going on here? It seems a little unusual to sit on the ground outside of a grocery store in the middle of the night, don't you think?" The image revealed an overhead image of the clerk sitting cross-legged on pavement, leaning on a brick wall with a bag of groceries next to him. The couple who had been bothering him was also visible, but the woman's face had been blurred out.

"Explain what? I'm drinking a coffee. Just like I was trying to do tonight before you guys came and dumped it out all over the street!" The clerk hadn't expected his tone to take on rage.

"The coffee doesn't explain anything."

"How did you even *get* that picture?" the clerk asked.

"How wouldn't we get it? Do you think there's anything we don't see?"

"Well yes, I would think that there are many things you don't see, although you haven't identified yourselves, so I don't know quite who you are." They gave no response. "Are you the police?"

"You think the police have this level of technological

superiority? They wish they possessed half the technology we possess! The police have our scraps from last decade. Maybe eventually they'll have what we have now—but just think of the advanced technology *we'll* have by then!"

"You haven't answered any of my questions!" the clerk complained.

"Look. You're the one who's answering our questions here, pal. But if it will help grease the gears, fine, I'll tell you that we took this image from a surveillance bot."

"What's that? Oh, right. The robot planes. I thought only the military had those. You're from the military?"

"Bah! You think the military would have this jurisdiction? Look. We've got pictures of everything."

The screen changed to reveal a picture of a bus at a stoplight. The image zoomed in to reveal the clerk's face gazing out the window of the bus.

The clerk let out a grunt of protest, and the screen changed again to reveal an image of him on the ground in the government building being pinned down by a security guard. The next image revealed the clerk in the federal bowling alley. Once more the image changed, revealing him about to use the toilet at his apartment.

"Man! You were even taking pictures of me in my flat? What, are you guys obsessed with me or something?"

"Sir, I can assure you we've taken pictures of everything," the person said in a comforting voice. As if to prove it, the screen changed to show a picture of the director sans shirt, revealing his meaty, hairless chest as he flexed his biceps.

The clerk was visibly taken aback, but the image changed to him at the federal bowling alley, being helped to his feet by one of the girls, then a picture of one of the girls at the restaurant handing him his bag, and then back to the picture of him sitting outside the grocery store and speaking to the couple. All of the girls' faces were hazy and unclear in the images.

"Now that I've answered some of your questions, you will answer some of ours. Who is this woman?"

"How should I know?" the clerk responded.

"Clearly you know this woman. And she's not a good woman to know. She's on our most wanted list as the Ace of Spades!"

"What do you want with me? Why don't you use your sophisticated equipment to track her down?"

"Ah ha! So you know how she does it, don't you?"

"What are you talking about?"

"Don't play dumb with us! Tell us who she is. Tell us everything!"

"Alright. I'll tell you everything. Although it would seem you already have photographs to tell you everything I know—anyway, it was like this. I had a hectic day at work, and had come home to relax, but my betrothed needed me to go to the store, so I went, and while I was there, the coffee just smelled so good that I decided to have a cup." Here the clerk hesitated, chewing on his lip subconsciously as he thought of the reason to give for drinking his coffee before bringing it home. He could have told the truth—that his betrothed would have protested to him having a cup of coffee in the evening before bed, but he was too embarrassed to give that as the reason, so he said, "And since I didn't want it to get cold before I got home, I decided to have the coffee right then and there."

His interrogators looked at him with suspicion as they interrupted him. "You didn't stop and drink the coffee tonight! You were walking with it!"

"Yes," the clerk said, feeling like he had a smooth

answer. "Yes, that's true, but tonight I am in a massive hurry and you are delaying me to the detriment of my career. Of course I would drink my coffee on the run when I need to get to work."

"Why would a government clerk need to be working at this hour?"

"Because I was unable to finish all of my work today, there's so much of it. I wasn't even supposed to stop back at my flat, but I did for a bite to eat, and I accidentally fell asleep. My manager even came to get me because I was so late!"

"Manager, huh? See if his story's legit."

Suddenly a flurry of images were rapidly changing on the screen. It stopped on the outside of his apartment building, and the image began to zoom in on a window. Now they were all staring at an image of the clerk's nude backside as he stood on his bed, the two women at the edge looking up at him.

"Well that's just great," the clerk muttered, his cheeks turning bright red. He wanted to bury his head in his hands, but they were bound behind him.

"That's his manager, alright. Looks like his story does check out."

"Bollocks! I thought we had her this time! Get him out of my sight!"

"Alright, come with me. You're free to go." The clerk was being pulled out the back of the van.

"Hey, c'mon! You never even told me who you guys are!"

He was dragged back onto the sidewalk where he had been, and the person who'd done the dragging was unbinding his wrists. "Aren't you obligated to tell me who you are? If you're a government worker, we both ultimately work for the same purpose!"

"Look, we're military contractors. Don't worry about it so much."

"Military contractors? I thought you weren't with the military."

"We're not."

"And what about my coffee! You spilled all my coffee!"

"Nothing to be done about that," the person said, disappearing into the shadows of the side street.

"Are you okay, little buddy?" the clerk asked, reaching into his jacket pocket. It returned with the little black mouse happily wiggling its whiskered nose. "Thank heavens they didn't harm you! I'll get you a treat when I get a chance, little guy." He returned the mouse to where it had been.

"Wonderful," the clerk said, taking a few deep breaths as he remembered that he was supposed to be at work already. He felt terrible. There was a general feeling of malaise overwhelming his body. He wanted to curl up on the sidewalk and fall asleep, but there was work to be done, so he began to shamble on toward his cubicle, dragging his heels a few inches at a time.

At last he stood before the government building. He tried the door and found that even at this time it was open. The security guard at the desk looked up at him with a bleary-eyed gaze. It was not a guard he recognized.

"Hi there," the clerk said. "I've just got some work to catch up on."

"Identification?" the guard asked.

"Right, right. I've got my government identification card here somewhere," the clerk said, searching through his pockets. "I'm sure I have it. Just give me a second." A rolled up piece of paper fell out of his pocket onto the floor. The guard was looking at him suspiciously, but he picked up the paper realizing that it was the mysterious note about the 195 that he would need to follow up on in the afternoon. *"Sadly, it's not that long until afternoon,"* he thought. His hand finally wrapped around what he thought was his ID. He pulled it out and said, "Here we go!"

"Go right ahead, sir," the security guard grumbled.

"Thank you."

As the clerk took the lift to his floor, he could hear loud dance music pumping through from another level. When he exited the lift to the hallway of his floor, he could still hear the dance music quite loudly. He suspected it was coming from the floor below. "Strange," he muttered. It was all dark on his floor, and he worried that a drill might have still been occurring, but he cautioned a few steps anyhow and the sensor kicked on and lit up the whole floor around him. He could see over the tops of cubicles to the other side of the building. The fluorescent lights in the darkness reminded him of a cloudy day as he shuffled down the hallway. He was passing by the kitchen and muttered, "I think I'll make a cup of coffee since some mean fellows calling themselves 'military contractors' decided it was their responsibility to dump mine out everywhere." The coffee supplies were left in the cabinet for everyone to use, so before long he had a pot grumbling as the water brewed through it. He left it to its business and decided to drop in on his manager's office. "I know she said she was going home, but for some reason I feel as though she may have stopped by here. Maybe even just to check up on me!"

He found her office door open and stepped inside, but her desk was empty and he didn't see her hiding behind the plant. "Well then," he muttered, and let out an unexpected sneeze. "Ugh." He grabbed a tissue out of the box on her desk, and as he blew his nose, he realized he'd taken the last tissue from the box. "Oh no! I need to replace that! I don't want her to find out that I was in here using her stuff." He didn't have any tissues at his desk—he usually went to the lavatory and used toilet paper if he needed a tissue—so he was going to have to hunt one down. He stalked down the nearest aisle of cubicles looking for a box of tissues, but not finding one, he grumbled, "These cheap people probably lock their tissues up when they leave because they don't want anyone to take one! What is that bloody music?!" He hadn't realized it was irritating him so much, but even over here near his manager's office, the music was quite loud. "How's a guy supposed to concentrate on his late night work over that racket?" He weaved in and out of the rows of cubicles, searching for a tissue, but as he got through the last of them, he was still empty-handed. "Oh, I know," the clerk said, "I'm sure there's a tissue in the break room! I should have checked there first." In the break room, he found his pot of coffee was finished brewing, so he poured a cup and fixed it. "Hmm. Not as good as the cup they spilled, but it will do." He proceeded to rifle through the cabinets in search of a tissue, but the closest he found was a roll of paper towels. "I guess this is my only choice," he muttered as he peeled off a sheet of paper towel. He ripped it a little bit to make it about the size of a tissue, and then he folded in the two ends the way the tissue had been. He walked this creation back to his manager's office and tucked it into the tissue box with care so that it was sticking out the top the way the actual tissue had been. "Man, when she blows her nose on that rough thing she's going to know something happened. My only hope is that she's not the first one here and there are other people around for her to suspect."

The clerk dragged his feet along the gray carpet and plopped himself down into the chair in his cubicle. "Now I'll have a chance to get some work done, at last," he muttered, but his eyes were closed while he said this, and he found himself feeling very comfortable sitting in his chair. *"Good thing that music's playing, or I'd fall asleep for sure."* He thought he said this, but at the same time, the words seemed to be floating before him in neon lights that flashed and danced.

"Wake up! What are you doing?!"

The clerk was being shaken by the shoulders quite violently and his eyes blurred into focus as he realized that his betrothed was the one who was doing the shaking. "I'm up! I'm up! Honey? What are you doing here?"

"I came to bring you brekkie. I felt bad you were stuck working all night, and seeing as it's almost dawn, I figured you were exhausted."

"Oh, I'm quite exhausted."

"Why don't you just use a sick day and come home with me?"

"I could never do that! You can't just take sick days willy-nilly around here!"

"Why do you have sick days if you can't just take them?"

"They're just there for show, so no one can whinge that we have inhumane working conditions or something. But don't suggest that you can actually use them! There are projects to be finished, deadlines that must be met! If I were to shirk all my responsibilities and just stay home in bed all day, how do you think that would look on my performance review?! There's a promotion at stake here! We'll never improve our living situation if I don't put all of my effort into it!"

"But look at you! You can barely keep your eyes open. How are you going to get any work done?"

"Don't worry. I'll make sure it gets done."

"But sometimes your health is more important than work!"

"How could you even think to separate the two? I'll have no health without my work! At least now if I'm taken to the hospital, I'll have a tiny bit of insurance to cover me. It might be just enough to save me. If I were to lose my job, I'd surely be left for dead should sickness befall me. Besides, I've worked too long and hard at my career to just let it slip through my fingers now. If I mess up this job and my references, I may never get another job in our province!"

"Well, maybe I'll get a job for us. I've had some promising interviews!"

"Maybe, but I have this job now. I can succeed at it. I know I can!"

"Well, if you say so," his betrothed muttered, looking at him suspiciously while she leaned on his desk. "Here you go. Have this. It will be good for you." She unzipped an insulated lunch bag and began to extract tubs of food and liquid.

"Wow, thanks! You're the best." As he sat munching in silence for a moment, he said, "Hey, how'd you get in here anyway? You don't have a government ID."

"Oh, apparently they started renting out the government offices for dance parties overnight. The guard assumed I was attending one of those and let me right through. He was very nice."

"He didn't seem so nice to me," the clerk grumbled. "How can they be having dance parties in here? There's all sorts of sensitive government documents! Do they really need a little bit of extra income that badly?"

His betrothed shrugged and stole a bite of his bagel. Before long the food was finished and she was excusing herself to a day of job interviews, urging the clerk to take it easy.

"Okay. To work, to work," the clerk muttered. His in-box was flooded with work he had to take care of. His eyes widened and he swallowed heavily, his throat still feeling sore. "C'mere little buddy. I need a pep squeak!" He took the mouse out of his pocket and placed him on his desk. The mouse started running around on his desk, gobbling up miniscule crumbs that the clerk hadn't even realized were there. As the mouse ran from crumb to crumb, the clerk watched him attentively, giggling with delight. However, after a moment, his giggles turned into a coughing fit.

When it subsided, the clerk opened a bottle of water and poured some into the cap for the mouse to drink before he looked back to his inbox. The backlog in the inbox seemed like a monumental task. Looking at that pile of work made the clerk feel the equivalent exasperation of being on the ground floor of the government building in the bigger city, and, realizing that the elevators were out of order, he'd need to climb the stairs to some ridiculous-numbered floor like 67 or worse. He sighed, and the simile made him realize that he should focus on the work the director needed him to do, as that far outranked the piddling work that the manager wanted him to take care of.

"Alright, let's see here. The director told me to record the number in a spreadsheet. What's this note here say?" He fished the note out of his pocket and unfurled it. He stopped to smile briefly as the mouse smelled the phone on his desk. "Okay, well, this note isn't very helpful right now as I must decipher it to figure out what to do tomorrow." He frowned as he realized that it was already tomorrow. "I have to remember what the director said. What did he say? What did he say? I know he said to record the bowling numbers in a spreadsheet. He said to label them something. What was that? Oh I remember, 'Fat!' the opposite of skinny, which I found strange, because I thought he was rather hefty. Anyway, that was the way to remember it, and remember it I did! What else did he say? He emphasized specifically that it was very important I write down the exact number of the opponent's bowling score. What was that?" He reached around for the notebook from his satchel and flipped through the pages until he found where he'd written the bowling scores. "Alright then. I've written here the number 'minus one.' Should I actually subtract the one or not? This must be a test. A test of my judgment. My bowling opponent was desperate that I subtract one from the score. Perhaps the director provided a set number to bowl and that supposed professional bowler bodged it up. Wouldn't it be impossible to bowl one exact number? Bowling didn't seem very easy to me. Then again, it's possible the director's instructions were to beg me to change the number so that when I actually change it, the director can say that I didn't follow his orders and therefore have failed at his task! Oh, I can't let that happen. No matter how much the person begged and pleaded with me to change that number by one, that person has no ranking over me. I mean, maybe—I have no idea, but as far as I know, the director is the one in charge of this task, and how could the director fault me with following his very own orders? Ah ha! I've got it! I'm sure that's right! I'm sure I passed the test and now I'm one step closer to that promotion!" The clerk made a column entitled "FAT" in the spreadsheet and wrote down the number of the bowling score without subtracting one. He felt pleased with himself, but he also felt like falling asleep. However, sleep he must not. There was a week's worth of work and he was pretty sure that his manager expected it done by the time the office opened in the morning.

His manager arrived shortly before opening. The clerk had let the mouse return to his pocket for a nap some time earlier, and he had made an honest effort on attempting the overwhelming pile of work. However, despite his best intentions, feeling sleep deprived and annoyed, only moments before the arrival of his manager, he'd begun to take out his frustrations on the document that was currently before him, filling it with curses and repeatedly calling the whole thing stupid. Thus, it was to his horror that his manager appeared behind him, immediately snatching up the document. All he could do was to look up with helpless eyes as he watched her scanning the document with a stern expression on her face. Her nose looked raw, scratched and red. He wondered if that was his fault, and if it was his fault, if she would discover that fact.

"Glad to see you're still here working," she said, focused on the document. "I don't want to have to keep checking up on you all the time."

The clerk bit the inside of his lip as she continued reading. He wondered if it would be better to just snatch it out of her hands and run away to the men's room where he could flush it down the toilet before she was likely to run in after him.

Before he did anything so rash, she said, "This is good. This is good. Keep up the good work. Sometimes we have to take a firm hand when these other departments try to boss us around. I'll let you continue. It's vital that you remain diligent," she leaned over as she slapped the document down on the desk and whispered into his ear, "You know important people are watching you. Your performance will determine your future face."

As suddenly and silently as she'd appeared, she was gone, and the clerk sat there with his face twisted up in a perplexed expression.

Out of his peripheral vision, he saw a greasy forehead

retreating down on the other side of the cubicle wall.

By now, the office was buzzing with people, so the clerk thought it would be perfectly appropriate to slip away for another cup of coffee. He thought it was just his luck that when he returned to his desk, his phone was indicating that he had a missed call from his manager. "She's onto me now," he whispered. "She's discovered I took the last tissue." His heart was racing as he called her back.

She answered the phone with no greeting and spoke as though she were mid-sentence. "What's this about you agreeing to recreate an encrypted report for someone in the Federal Notary Department?"

"Oh, that, uh, I don't know, I kind of knocked some of her files on the floor during the drill."

"You what?! Take care of this immediately! Make it your first priority! If this gets out, I'm going to be held responsible for your blunder!"

He heard the sound of the phone slamming in his ear. He sighed and opened the drawer where he'd left the stack of papers, but as he plopped them onto his desk, he saw that it was already 12:02pm. "Lunch time already? But it was just morning!" he whispered. He flicked from his tongue to his brain so his rival wouldn't spy on him. *"Looks like I've got another important decision to make. My manager says to make this top priority, but the director put me on a special project, and he outranks my manager by far. However, what if it gets held against me that I ignored a command from my direct supervisor?"* He glanced at the clock: 12:03. *"Oh dear, this is not good. I can't ignore the director though. I just can't!"* He grabbed the stack of papers and shoved them inelegantly into his satchel as he rushed out of his cubicle. He thought he could hear the sound of his rival snickering on the other side of the cube walls, but he had no time to worry about him. For all he knew, the rival thought he was slacking off and actually going to eat lunch. There was too much stressful bile churning in his stomach for him to be hungry at the moment.

He attempted to jog once he was out on the sidewalk, but the pain in his inner thighs was too great. "Ugh, I must be more knackered than I thought, Ellem," he muttered. He stopped for a second and attempted to massage his thighs, but the skin hurt, so he winced in pain and continued on his journey in a hobbling fashion. He collapsed his weight onto the bench at the bus stop and decided he would wait until one rolled up. He realized that a giant tortoise was the first vehicle to appear offering a ride. He wondered how much the bloke sitting on his head holding the reins would charge, and, more importantly, whether it would be faster than waiting for the next bus.

A bus appeared before him and he realized he'd fallen asleep. "Right, then," he mumbled to himself as he climbed onto the bus. "Bigger city?" he asked. He accepted the affirmative nod and shambled to a seat in the back of the bus.

He tried his best not to fall asleep since he didn't want to miss his stop. He opened his satchel and pulled out the bunched mess of papers. He thumbed through them a bit, but muttered, "I can't do anything with these from here. I'm going to have to figure out some way to deal with it." He shoved them back into his satchel. "What about you?" he asked the slip of paper he was unfurling in his hands. *Today the alley. Tomorrow 195. Continue the rotation.* "Well, the alley has to refer to the bowling alley. That seems obvious enough. 195? What could that be? There's no highways or streets around with that high of a number. It's got to be a floor in the building. That thing reaches up into the sky forever." Feeling proud of himself that he knew where he'd be going, he slipped the rolled up paper back into his pocket and slumped back in his seat. "You keep me awake, Ellem." He placed the mouse on his lap with a smile.

Back in the government building, the clerk had the same problems he'd had since the first day he arrived. He had no idea what happened to his clearance card, a security guard tackled him, and a woman in maroon appeared to save him, although she was very annoyed about it and threatened retribution.

"I hope she's not related to any department that could affect my performance review," the clerk thought to himself as he waited for the elevator to arrive. The doors slid open and he punched in the numbers for floor 195. The elevator whizzed up quickly, and when the doors reopened, he stepped into the sky.

"Huh?" He was staring up at the crystal-clear blue sky. A smell of cooking meat filled his nose. He looked down to realize he was in a city. It was tough to place the architecture. He couldn't decide between an ancient desert city or a futuristic city the likes of which he'd never seen. It must have been a synthesis of the two. He was strolling through some sort of market. People were bustling all about, talking and shouting. There were carts of food, shops and restaurants that people hurried in and out of.

"Excuse me," he said to a shopkeeper with a walk-up window. "Where am I?"

The shopkeeper looked at him with a confused expression and spoke in a language the clerk couldn't understand. He didn't think he'd ever heard it before. He was so upset and thrown-off by the whole thing that he turned and fled back toward the elevator, running at full speed, weaving through people, kicking up sand and gasping for breath in the dry air. He ran until he could scarcely breathe, his thighs burning. He was hunched over with his hands on his knees, practically choking as he inhaled air. *"I don't get it,"* he thought. *"I didn't walk very far from the elevator. It couldn't have been this far away, but it's gone and I seem to be deeper in the city."*

Once he regained a bit of strength, he started walking around, looking at things, listening to strange words, and attempting to get his bearings. "I must be in a foreign land," he muttered. "But that makes absolutely no sense."

The sun was beating down on him, and he was drenched in sweat. He continued to wander at random, attempting to read signs, but everything was in an indecipherable alphabet of hieroglyphics. He walked until his legs were trembling, and when he stopped for a rest, he realized he was standing directly in front of a massive cathedral. Its spires stretched into the sky like a thousand fingers reaching for meaning. The stone was old and ancient, cracked and crumbling in places like a clay pot left too long out of the kiln. He strained to see the top of it, to view the intricate carvings throughout—there may have even been statues worked into it—but craning his neck as far back as it would go, he couldn't see the top of the cathedral. He could see nothing but the bright glare of the sun that the cathedral partially eclipsed.

His left nipple suddenly felt ticklish. He looked down to see the little black mouse descending the buttons of his shirt as though they were a tiny ladder. "Wait, come back! Where are you going, little guy?" the clerk asked as the mouse ran down his trousers and hopped off his shoe.

"Wait! Come back, my friend! Wait for me!"

The mouse was sprinting forward in the direction of the cathedral. The clerk was following closely behind, but before he could grab it, the mouse had managed to scale the first stair and climb up onto the ramp accompanying the stairs for the purpose of human handholds.

"Ellem! Don't leave me behind!" The clerk was on the narrow stone stairs, climbing up them as fast as his aching legs could manage.

The mouse had a smooth climb up the ramp and was now climbing down in the direction of the two great wooden doors.

"Ellem! Wait!" The clerk was close now, but just as the end of the stairs was in sight, he saw the mouse's tail disappearing underneath one of the massive wooden doors. "Ellem, no!" The clerk arrived at the doors. There was a huge circular knocker on each door. He grabbed the one that was attached to the door the mouse had slipped underneath and realized that an apple was carved into the metal. He pulled and at first thought the door was locked, but second-guessed his thought and considered that maybe he had moved it a little bit. He threw all his weight toward the ground on his next pull and saw that it was moving back just a little bit. "Wait up, Ellem. I'm almost in," he muttered between breaths. Another round of pulling opened a sliver of door that he thought was just wide enough to fit through. He sucked in his breath as much as he could and just barely managed to shimmy his way into the cathedral. It was so dark within that immediately he couldn't see anything. His heart was pumping quickly and he didn't dare take a step forward into the unknown. Once his eyes adjusted to the extreme dimness, he was surprised to realize that he was in a very small room, surrounded completely by stone resembling the walls of a cave. He'd been expecting to look up upon a limitless ceiling, in a massive room with some sort of altar at the front, but enclosed as he was, there was only one way to go: down. A mouth in the floor opened up to stairs that extended down into farther darkness.

"Ellem? Did you go down there, little buddy? Ellem?"

If the mouse was present, it gave no response.

"Well, I guess I've no choice," the clerk muttered, and stepped toward the stairs.

For the first hour, he would periodically call, "Ellem! Ellem!" but then he gave up and hoped he would find the mouse at the end of the stairs. At that thought, another, more terrible thought bubbled up into the bog of his mind: *What if there is no end?*

But never-ending stairs was a ludicrous idea, and he moved forward with determination that he would find the mouse.

The first set of stairs was as claustrophobic as the antechamber had been. He'd moved down them slowly, often sliding a hand on the stone wall as he went down, stabilizing himself. After what felt like thousands of stairs, the clerk found the stone surroundings had disappeared, and what stretched before him was a spiral of stairs that went down into the mists of shadow, with no walls or enclosures that his non-crepuscular eyes could make out. "Ellem? If you're close, buddy, I think we should go," the clerk muttered, swallowing heavily. He went down more slowly now, fearing that he'd fall to his doom at any moment, but the stairs were so eternal that at a certain point, he was moving on autopilot, his head lolling dangerously to this side or that.

His mind snapped back to consciousness when he heard a voice shouting. He hurried down the stairs more quickly, moving in the direction of the screams. At last he could see a stone ground, and a man in a long black robe was shouting in a language the clerk couldn't understand as he ran away from the direction of the stairs.

"Don't run away!" the clerk called out to him. "I won't hurt you!"

Hearing the clerk's words, the man turned, but still backing away said in the clerk's language, "Help! Get that foul creature away from me!"

The clerk noticed that the old man was pointing at the ground nearby.

The clerk stepped off the stairs, and could see a tiny shadow shifting across the gray ground—then he realized it was the mouse. "There you are Ellem! Why'd you run off? You wanted to find this bloke?" The clerk rushed over, knelt down, and scooped up the mouse into his hands. He held it so that its head stuck out from between his thumbs, but the mouse seemed content to remain in his grasp. "You don't have to be afraid of this cute little guy," the clerk said.

The old man had stopped running, but he still stood some distance from the clerk and had a mixture of revulsion and terror spelled out on his face. "I thought you'd save me by stomping on that vermin, or some other act forbidden from one such as myself, who is sworn to pacifism—not by cradling it! Are you mad?"

"Man, what kind of a priest are you? You should respect all life, especially innocent creatures."

"I am not a priest; I am a philosopher. And who are you to judge? You who keep the record of murder and carry death?"

"I do no such thing!"

"So say all who seek ignorance," the philosopher said in a sad tone, more to himself than to the clerk. He groaned and slowly lowered his body to the ground.

The clerk also collapsed to the ground, holding the mouse on his chest. "Man, I finally find someone who speaks my language and he speaks in riddles," thinking to himself that it was dangerous to be throwing around the word, "philosophy."

A long moment passed in silence. The clerk almost fell asleep, but managed not to. "Where am I?"

"Exactly where you entered," the old man responded.

"A strange cathedral?"

"You seek a less specific answer."

"A strange city?"

"You seek a less specific answer."

"The government building?"

"Of course."

"Oh. So I haven't left? Then maybe I'm not so far off my task! I got a note to go to 195. I assumed that was here, but, here is huge."

The philosopher let out a sigh. "The stronger half of my theories say I oughtn't help you on such a task. The other half say it doesn't matter anyway."

"I think you should help me," the clerk said.

The philosopher sighed again. "Follow the language of the universe."

"What's that mean?"

"I'm not saying any more."

"Not even an inkling to your clue?" the clerk asked, but the philosopher didn't answer. "I guess I'll just lie here and think about it." He promptly fell asleep.

When next the clerk opened his eyes, he was laying in sand gazing into the orange haze of late afternoon. He sat up and saw that he was at the foot of the stairs leading to the cathedral entrance. He checked his pocket and found the mouse snuggling in a circle, as usual. His brow was furled as he climbed to his feet. He felt annoyed more than anything else.

As he walked, he noticed an unattended fruit cart in the street. As casually as he could, he slipped an apple into his sleeve when he walked past, and continued walking as though he'd done nothing.

When a few more minutes of walking passed with no signs of retribution, he took out the apple and began to feast on it, saving the core for the mouse in his pocket.

He shuffled along narrow alleys. Sometime earlier, he had realized that rectangular, ceramic signs were attached on the corner walls of buildings at intersections, but since the language was unreadable, he'd considered them worthless. Now he realized that he was staring at one with very recognizable numbers on it. "This is a breakthrough!" He sprint-walked in one direction and checked the sign: Gibberish to him. He backtracked to the numeral sign and walked in a different direction up from it. "A number I recognize! A lower number. What if I—?" He jogged back to the original number he'd discovered, and kept going past it to the next sign. "Ah ha! A higher number! I'll just follow these!" And follow them he did, enjoying his progress at each intersection as he saw a higher number, until finally he was standing on a street marked, "195."

"Alright. It's got to be around here somewhere. I'm sure of it. It must be the 195th building of the 195th street of the 195th floor. Ellem, could you imagine if there was another city in that building and this whole thing started all over again? What would you do if that happened, Ellem? I don't know what I'd do."

He continued down the 195th Street, searching for addresses—or at the very least, numbers—on the buildings he passed by, but he had no such luck—until suddenly an out of place, boring, rectangular structure stood out before him. It had square glass windows and above the doorway in bold, black lettering were the numbers 195. "That's it! I'm here! I'm here!"

The clerk rushed up the stairs of the building and pushed

the glass and metal door open, bursting through into an office lobby. There was a circular desk right before him, restrooms to the left, a hallway to the right, and some scattered potted plants.

"Good afternoon, sir," the receptionist at the desk called to the clerk.

He hadn't yet moved from the doors. A look of horror had been frozen on his face as he examined the new surroundings and expected the worst.

"Do you have an appointment?" the receptionist asked as he approached.

"Uhm, yes," the clerk muttered. "I'm here for one nine five," he said more distinctly.

"One nine five? Yes, of course. I'd be happy to send you up to the chairman if you'd just provide me with your identification."

"Oh, right," the clerk muttered, shoving both hands into his sandy pockets and feeling around. "Here we go!" he exclaimed, holding the card up into the air before handing it to the lady.

"Thank you very much, sir," she said, picking up a phone with her other hand and dialing four numbers.

"I have a—" she was squinting at the identification card, "I have a clerk from the small city branch here to see the chairman." There was silence. "Okay, thank you very much." She held the phone to her chest and said softly, "The assistant's checking with the chairman."

"Thanks," the clerk muttered, but he continued to eye the place suspiciously.

"Okay, I'll send him right up," the receptionist said, hanging up the phone. To the clerk, she said, "Here you are," handing him his card. "Take the lift to the first floor. Go down the first hallway on your right, and you'll find Room

195 at the end of the hall."

"Great. Appreciate it," the clerk said, stalking past the desk and down the hallway where he could now see the elevators. The first floor looked rather similar to the lobby. There were gray walls and beige carpets with an occasional potted plant for decoration. Off to the left he could see a cubicle farm, but down the hallway on the right, he passed by offices where people in business clothes talked on phones or worked on documents.

Sure enough, he found Room 195 at the end of the hall. He did the standard office knock-on-the-doorframe-of-an-open-door. "Excuse me. I'm here to meet with the chairman."

"Ah yes. I'll inform the chairman you've arrived, sir. Please have a seat." The assistant indicated three chairs that were aligned on the wall next to the door.

As the assistant went into a back room, the clerk sat with his satchel on his lap. He rubbed his pocket and could feel the mouse's warmth. He thought it was asleep. "Why'd you run away before, little guy?" he whispered.

"He'll be with you shortly, sir," the assistant said, returning to the room and retaking the seat behind the desk.

"Thanks," the clerk responded.

He sat there for a few moments before a portly gentleman in a tight-fitting suit appeared, and in a booming voice said, "There you are, my boy. I've been expecting you!" The clerk thought the small goatee around his mouth looked as though it were falling off. He walked forward to the clerk, and as the clerk stood, they shook hands and the man put his other hand on the clerk's back in a half-hug thing that the clerk found uncomfortable. "C'mon, c'mon. Please come into my office. Did they offer you coffee? No? Bring the boy some coffee!"

"Yes, sir," the assistant said, rushing off.

"Have a seat, my boy," the chairman said. "Did you have any trouble finding the place?"

"Well, actually—" the clerk began, but before he could finish, the chairman had rummaged a torn scrap of paper out of one of his desk drawers and was sliding it across the table to the clerk.

"Here's what you came for, my boy."

The clerk picked up the scrap and looked at it. There was a number printed on it.

"What's this?" the clerk asked.

"What you came for, I said."

"Oh, right," the clerk said.

The chairman leaned over the desk, close to the clerk. This seemed a big strain for him, and his belly was being crushed against the corner of the large desk. He said in a soft voice to the clerk, "You'll want to add this in a column alongside your FAT values. Label these LONG." He dropped back into his seat with a loud thud.

"Right. Fat. Long," the clerk muttered, extracting a pen from his satchel and scribbling a note on the scrap of paper before stuffing it into his pocket.

"So then," the chairman said, before looking up at the doorway. "Ah, here we go."

The assistant placed two cups of coffee on the desk. "Will there be anything else?"

"No, this is great, thank you," the chairman said. "Well, go on then," he said to the clerk, motioning toward the coffee.

"Oh thanks," the clerk said, lifting the cup to his lips and taking a sip of sweetness. "This really hits the spot."

"Glad you like it, my boy," the chairman said, lifting his cup and seemingly drinking half of it in one gulp. "So. Can I expect you the day after tomorrow? Same place, same time?"

"Actually," the clerk muttered. "Could you give me directions?"

"Directions to what?" the chairman asked, twisting his eyebrows. The clerk thought his eyebrows looked like they were falling off too.

"Uh, well. I really have no idea how I even got here."

The chairman let out guffaws of laughter. "Well at least you made it one way or another, my boy!"

"So, uh. I guess I need directions back from here. And, well. Directions *to* here for next time."

"Of course, of course." He picked up his phone and dialed four numbers. "Can you write up some directions for our friend, here? Yes, yes. Get him back and get him here again." He hung up the phone, smiled at the clerk, and gulped down the rest of his coffee.

With horror the clerk realized he'd only taken a few sips of his coffee, barely making a dent in it. Steam was still rising from the cup into his eyes as he inspected it. He flicked his eyes back to the chairman: He was just sitting there smiling at the clerk. *"Oh no!"* the clerk thought. *"I've got to finish this thing! It will be too awkward and impolite to sit here poring over my coffee while he's long since finished with his!"* The clerk attempted a big gulp of coffee. He forced a smile as it burned his tongue and heated down his throat.

The chairman sat smiling at the clerk with his patchy goatee.

The clerk took a deep breath and then attempted a big finishing gulp of his coffee. It worked, but he could feel it searing through his insides. He was still attempting a smile, but it was clearly a pained smile.

"Good stuff, I know," the chairman said, his smile unmoving.

"Well, thanks very much," the clerk said, standing and

extending his hand toward the chairman.

"Oh, you're welcome, you're welcome, my boy," the chairman said as he hefted himself out of the chair, nimbly appeared on the clerk's side of the desk, and enveloped his hand over the clerk's as he smothered the clerk's whole body in a mixture of handshake and bear hug.

"Cheers," the clerk uttered once he was free. "Should I leave it open?" he asked regarding the door.

"You can close it, my boy. Thanks," the chairman said.

"I'll be done with these in just a minute, if you want to have a seat," the assistant said. He was scribbling notes on a clean sheet of paper.

"Okay, thanks."

With directions in hand, the clerk was navigating through the city streets like a fairly competent tourist. Before he knew it, he was facing elevator doors that were built into an massive sandstone wall that seemed to reach everywhere, from top to bottom, left to right. "Whatever," the clerk muttered of the strangeness as he used his palm to summon the elevator. The doors opened, and he stepped on.

The elevator was packed, but he squeezed in anyway. At the next stop, two more people got on, and the clerk was so smashed in there that his feet weren't even on the ground anymore.

The phone in the elevator began ringing. The clerk could hear somebody answer it and respond, "Oh, I don't know. I'll just pass it around."

"Not me."

"Who are you looking for? Oh, nope."

"I'm sorry."

This went on for some time until the phone made it to the clerk. It was hard to align the receiver properly with his head as the cord was wrapped around many people. "Hello?"

"Ah, there you are!" his manager's voice said on the other end. "I'd recognize your pep anywhere. I was just calling to see how you're doing with that project I mentioned to you this morning. Good progress?"

"Uh, yeah the project. I'm actually working on it now. It's become, uh, a bit more complicated than I expected, but don't worry."

"I know I can count on you to make sure it gets done ASAP!" She hung up without saying goodbye. The clerk let go of the phone and it bounced around the elevator as though it were on an overly stretched elastic band that the clerk had just let go of. People complained and said "ow" as the phone smashed into them on its way back to the corner.

"Sorry," the clerk muttered.

Back outside at the front entrance, standing in the chilly air of the bigger city, the clerk wasted no time in heading across the street in the direction of the 2nd Street Ave Building. Once inside, he slipped upstairs to the second floor and began to stake the place out. Many people here knew him, so they would offer greetings and say something along the lines of, "What brings you over to this side of the land?" and the clerk would give a vague answer like, "Oh, you know, meetings and such." He was keeping his eye on the youngest people wandering around though—people he didn't know, but who would be the most useful. He caught sight of a few. *"Definitely interns,"* he thought.

Realizing that he probably looked like he'd just traveled through a desert for a month and a half, he slipped into the lavatory and tried to clean himself up in front of the sink and mirror. He washed as much sand off of his clothes as he could. He redid his tie and attempted to smooth it out. He wet his hair and tucked it behind his ears as best as he could to hide its length. "Alright Ellem, you ready? I'm ready."

Back in the thick of the cubicle farm, the clerk caught sight of one of his marks. The intern appeared to be returning from the break room with a full cup of coffee, so the clerk assumed he would be the best one since he didn't seem too busy. The clerk appeared in front of the unsuspecting intern, blocking his path and shoving a stack of papers toward his chest. "You've just been moved to a top priority project. Data breach, data loss, this hard copy is all we have, as the digital was lost. You need to recreate the digital file as quickly as possible, there's just one caveat, use this cryptogram here on top—this paper, got it? Use this cryptogram to change the encryption when you retype it. It's fairly straightforward. You know how to do this, right?"

The intern looked bewildered, but after a moment he nodded and said, "Yes, no problem."

"Great! Drop everything. Do this. I'll be back in an hour to pick it up," and then, in hopes that it would ensure the project would really get done, since the intern was working long hours, getting the worst work, and wasn't getting paid any money for his troubles, he added, "If you do a good job on this, I'll make sure to personally put in a good word for you with your manager—help jumpstart the engine on your performance review." The intern, of course, knew that the performance review would be the only chance to land a job out of this, should his superiors decide to hire him on the team post-internship. What the intern probably didn't know was that it was most likely they wouldn't, and his internship would just be another line on his resume as he hit the cut-throat job market.

"Yes. I can do this right away!" the intern said.

"Great. Here you go," the clerk said, handing him the jumble of papers. "You'll have to put it in the right order."

The clerk slipped out of the office and down the street

to a fast food restaurant. He found the menu lacking, so he ordered an extra-large box of fries and a small soda. As he sat at a table to eat, he realized the fries were still too hot for his recently burned tongue. *"Ah well, just sitting and relaxing for a bit is nice,"* he thought. He leaned back in the seat, resting his head on the top and closing his eyes.

The clerk probably would have fallen asleep right there if a jovial voice hadn't suddenly interrupted: "Well, well, we meet again, my friend! Fate has brought us together once more so that you can keep your word true on your campaign promise."

The clerk opened his eyes in frustration as the street-person sat down across from him. He had a tray with a mountain of food piled on top of it, which he placed on the table across from the clerk.

"Now don't think I'm just going around looking for handouts, my friend. There are very serious issues that need to be addressed in our province and on our planet in these late days of civilization, and someone uncorrupted by money and power needs to be the one to fix them, and who better for that than me? For instance, how would you feel if I told you that you were being watched right now?" Before he gave the clerk the remotest possibility of answering, not that the clerk was particularly eager to answer, he continued, "And I don't mean being watched by me, or being watched by these other fine consumers in this here fine establishment, what I mean is watched by the government. Watched by the military. The very people you would expect to be protecting you, who you would expect to be watching out for real threats instead of harassing ordinary, hardworking citizens such as yourself. And what if I told you: What the government can watch, the government can kill. No trial, no due process. If they suspect you of something they don't like, they can press a button on their computer and a flying robot will have you dead before you're even aware that anything unusual is happening. And unfortunately, my friend, these things are becoming so common that it's not quite so unusual anymore, now is it? And I bet I know what you're going to say. I bet you're going to tell me, 'But that is unusual. I don't see robots blowing anybody up.' Of course you don't. Robots blow up people every day. Robots are blowing up people right now, as we're sitting here casually conversating and enjoying some delicious food." As if remembering, he unwrapped a hamburger and took three big bites out of it.

The clerk hadn't moved, his glassy-eyed expression staring through the hairy fellow.

"But we don't see the robots blowing people up," the man continued with a mouthful of half-chewed hamburger. "They're technically our robots, since the government technically belongs to its people, and we don't even see 'em."

As the man talked and talked, the clerk felt a hint of amusement pulling at the corners of his lips, because he wasn't paying any attention at all, and the man was so engrossed in his own words, that he wasn't really paying any attention to the clerk, just assuming that the clerk was listening.

"And they claim robot death-strikes are the only way to keep us safe—all their actions overseas are supposedly to keep us safe. Yet why do they arm a group with weapons and tanks one day, and then claim those are the primary dangerous people they need to blow up the next day? It's illogical. They need to create such saboteur cells because it's good for the robot-making business, I tell you!"

The clerk fell into a kind of trance as the man's many words reflected off of his ears, and an indeterminate amount of time later, the street-person managed to recapture his attention.

"I said, did you happen to remember that change today, by chance. The change you agreed to contribute as a campaign promise?"

"Oh right, that," the clerk muttered, drowsiness weighing down his syllables. "I don't have it."

"Quite alright, my friend. Quite alright. I know you'll keep your word."

"Well, I've got to head back to the office," the clerk muttered, squirming out of his seat and swimming his way through mountainous piles of crumpled hamburger wrappers.

* * * *

"How's that report coming along?" the clerk asked the intern, appearing behind him.

"I'm sorry, sir," the kid muttered, "But this thing's in shambles. It'd take days' worth of work to put it back together properly."

"Oh dear," the clerk mumbled to himself. "And here I was hoping you'd have it done already."

"No such luck, I'm afraid. I'm not so quick at all this bumf yet."

"Alright, just save what you've got and give it all to me. I'll keep working on it."

The stack of papers seemed worse than before, as if the kid had handed him a purposely crumpled up ball of scrap paper. The clerk jammed it into his satchel and skulked out of the office. It was quitting time, and he'd barely accomplished anything, and here he was in the bigger city so far from his bed and his betrothed. Truth be told, he didn't know where he was actually supposed to catch the bus back to the small city. All the stops around here only had busses that continued directly across the river to the big city. The place where he knew to catch busses back to the small city wasn't an official bus stop, and the busses wouldn't stop if there were any police around. To make matters worse, during the evening rush hour, almost no busses passed by the unofficial bus stop. When the clerk arrived at it, there were already ten or so migrant workers standing and waiting for a bus to arrive. They spoke to each other in the island language, and even though the clerk could only pick up spare words here or there, they sounded like they were having a nice time and joking with each other. He couldn't imagine how they had the energy to act that way when he was bone crushingly exhausted and he didn't have to do backbreaking manual labor all day like them. Only two of the people didn't seem like migrant workers to him—a man and a woman dressed in suits, who he took for lawyers. But they seemed to be joking and laughing in the island language too.

The clerk's thoughts kept running through his head, like a bus that drove past its destination of a small office parking lot and kept going forward, even though it was driving through a field made of pink marshmallows and weaving through giant turtles at the pace of a snail due to the stickiness gumming up the wheels. When the bus to the small city actually arrived at nightfall, one of the migrant workers picked up the sleeping clerk from the sidewalk and carried him onto the bus in his strong arms. Another migrant worker picked up the clerk's fare. The clerk continued to snooze in the seat he'd been deposited in, and when the migrant workers were getting off at their stop, one of them shook the clerk gently by the shoulder and told him in the island language to wake up so he wouldn't miss his stop. The clerk jolted up, disoriented and confused. "Thanks," he said, not really understanding. And as the man made his way off the bus, the clerk caught himself and shouted out the thanks once more, but in the island language.

A few stops later, the clerk shambled off the bus into the frigid air of the small city. He walked his blocks down from the main drag and made his way up toward his bed and his betrothed. The two large men had all the lights off while they watched a movie and ate a pungent-smelling meal. The clerk silently slipped by and into his room. He found his betrothed kneeling on the bed amongst a plethora of snail shells.

"Oh, you're home, sweetie!" she said, smiling sweetly. "I'm so happy to see you. How was your day? Oh, don't worry about all this, I'll clean it up. It's just that two of the hermit crabs started fighting over a shell, so I'm trying to get them to like another shell, but now they're just hiding in their shells and not coming out—or doing anything at all, really. Oh, it's hopeless. Don't worry, I'll clean all this up so you can sit down."

"Hermit crabs," the clerk muttered in a voice that showed he was quickly losing consciousness. He shimmied around the door to close it and crumpled into a pile in the sliver of floor in front of the door.

"Oh my poor dear! You're exhausted! Are you okay?"

"Mmm hmm."

Once his betrothed cleaned up the hermit crab project and returned them to their tank, she dragged the clerk up onto the bed, removing his shoes.

"Let me make you something for dinner," she said.

"Had fries," the clerk groaned with his eyes closed. "I'm fine."

"Are you sure that's all you need? How was work?"

"I'm not done. I just need a rest. Don't let me sleep for more than an hour. I have a big complicated project to fix in my bag. I'm going to do as much of it here, tonight as I can. I just need a rest."

"Okay, you rest," she said, holding her palm on his

forehead.

Daylight brightening the inside of his eyelids awoke the clerk, who sprang up in fear and agitation. "Morning?! But I didn't work on the report!" He saw that the little black mouse was crawling around on the blankets, weaving up and down his betrothed's legs and feet. The clerk shimmied down to the end of the bed and leaned down to the floor where he found his satchel. Inside, he discovered what had been a discombobulated pile of papers was now organized into a neat stack bound in purple twine, and attached to the front was a memory card along with a note from his betrothed that read, *I finished organizing this and typing it in the new encryption for you, my darling. We need to talk about you quitting this job. There's more to life.*

"More to life?" the clerk thought. *"Is she mad? We can barely afford to live now. How would we do it if I didn't have this job? How will we manage if I fail to get the promotion?"*

He carried the finished report and memory card gingerly, like a blessing from the gods emanating a glowing divinity, but the lady at the office didn't even seem grateful when he returned the report. When he told his manager that it was done, she didn't seem to care or even be relieved either, and the clerk could see his rival sneering in the reflection of his manager's glasses.

Shortly afterward, he caught his rival staring at him over the cubicle wall. "What's wrong with you?" the clerk asked.

"That's what I'm here to ask you," his rival responded. "Why are you incessantly scratching at your armpit like a flea-bitten dog? Don't you shower?"

"Of course I shower!" the clerk snapped. He hadn't realized he'd been scratching it so much. Once the rival disappeared back into his own cubicle, the clerk inspected his armpit. It seemed to be inflamed, and as he touched it, he realized that he'd scratched it so much that it started bleeding. The clerk sighed as he walked toward the lavatory. *"Just what I wanted, another problem."*

The rest of the day was chaos, as had become his custom. He was ensnared in his daily work, and found it quite difficult to escape the others who were working on the project with him, and who thought that it was better to delay taking lunch. His next problem was finding a bus, and it was so late by the time he arrived at the federal bowling alley, that he knew he must have missed his scheduled game. This nearly put the clerk in tears, as he couldn't bear to disappoint the director, so he sat with his head in his hands for some time, the girls in green occasionally asking him if there was anything they could do for him. Part of him was remembering all the work piling up back at his cubicle, and that part finally won him over. He began to trudge back toward the elevator. The doors split apart to reveal a person wearing a fedora, and holding the brim so that it covered most features. "Ah, my friend! Our game can begin anew." The person caressed the clerk across the cheek, slung an arm behind the clerk's back, and squeezed him close as they walked back toward the lanes. The clerk didn't care at all about bowling, and just wanted to chuck the ball as fast as possible so he could get back to work. *"This is work,"* a voice in his head told him.

However, his opponent couldn't have bowled slower, making a big show of every step, which made the clerk feel like the person was doing it as slow as possible just to annoy him. "The game is an art," the person said. "You have to make love to it in order to succeed. The ball is an extension of my soul. The pins are my hopes and dreams."

The clerk gritted his teeth and didn't say anything. *"Just toss the ball already,"* repeated through his head like a mantra. He petted the mouse through his pocket in an effort to contain his frustration.

The clerk knew that his opponent was really trying to rub it in his face now because whereas the clerk only had to toss the ball once at the end, his opponent somehow managed to extend this to three throws.

On his final throw, his opponent decided it was time for another soliloquy. "Now, my friend, I'll have the fortuitous opportunity to show you my true skill. Ten pins remain, and I hold this ball in the final moments. You would think that I'd aim for the strike, taking the lives of all these pins and securing myself the first perfect game in a long time. That's what you think, don't you?"

Before the clerk could even consider responding, the person continued.

"But I won't do that. I won't do that at all. For you and I, we're not here for the sheer beauty of a perfect game, are we? No, no, no. You and I are here for much grander purposes, aren't we? And so, with this final ball, I'll give you your number to record—I'll only take down half of the remaining pins. A perfect game? No. But a perfect throw? Definitely." The person kissed the ball, twirled around, and unleashed the ball like a fencer lunging forward with her sword. It careened down the lane, and smashed just left of the center pin, hurtling them about. They all fell save one, which rocked back and forth before deciding to remain standing.

"What?" the person uttered, sounding more like a sob than a word. "This can't be! No! This can't be!"

"Not again," the clerk thought, fearing deception. He took out his notebook, wrote down the real number and the proposed number, placed the notebook back in his satchel, and began to remove the grotesque purple shoes.

"Sir, sir. Kind sir, you must believe me that I've been

ill these last few days and it's throwing off my ordinarily extraordinary bowling skills."

The clerk glided across the smooth floor in his socks, the person pleading with him as he went to the counter and changed back to his shoes.

The clerk was boarding the elevator while the person continued, "It will be bad for both of us if we get these numbers wrong! There's so much at stake!" The doors closed, leaving the clerk to dread when he'd repeat the encounter the day after the next day.

* * * *

The little black mouse was standing on the clerk's desk, and the two were staring at each other with wide, unblinking eyes. The clerk had positioned himself so that his body would cover anyone's view from seeing the mouse if they were near the entrance of the cubicle, and he had an empty three-ring binder ready to shield the mouse from view in case anyone needed him.

His rival's nasal laugh continued to stream in from the other side of the cubicle wall. The clerk's eyes widened, stress written over his face, but he said nothing and continued to stare at the mouse, who stared back. It had been like this for more than an hour as his rival conducted his training session with five of the assistant clerks crammed into his cubicle. Why their manager had decided that guy was able to train anyone was beyond the clerk, but it was seriously hindering the clerk's productivity. His rival had gone on and on about the assistant clerks sitting at his feet and learning, and from the bits and pieces that the clerk was unable to block out of his consciousness, it didn't sound like his rival had even begun to cover anything related to the specified training topic of formatting memos into the revised department style and the protocol for sending, filing, and duplicating said memos.

"Your presence is requested in our manager's office," one of the part-time assistants said behind the clerk, startling him. He forgot all about his system for hiding the mouse in the three-ring binder and scooped it up into both hands, holding them on his lap as if he'd had his hands folded, which proved difficult because the mouse started burrowing through his hands with its ticklish little fingernails.

"Huh? What?" the clerk muttered as he spun around in his chair to face the assistant.

"You. Manager's office. Now," the assistant repeated and rushed off.

"Thank goodness," the clerk sighed, depositing the mouse into his jacket pocket and shuffling in the direction of the far wall.

"New assignment for you," she said, looking up from her cluttered desk before the clerk could even announce his arrival. "Honestly, I hate to do this to you, but I've gotta send someone and you're it."

"Really? What's—?"

"You're needed in the Shipping and Receiving Department in the bigger city. They're short staffed, behind on their work, and they're filching a bunch of employees from other departments because they need to get caught up and they can't hire more crew with the hiring freeze."

"Right."

"It's only temporary."

"What about all of the work I'm supposed to be doing currently?"

"Top priority projects, you need to keep on top of. Anything less, I'm distributing among the other clerks."

"Great."

"So go to the bigger city now and get started. Don't worry. It's only temporary."

"Right."

Back at his cubicle, he heard his rival proclaiming, "You're never going to learn if your hearts are not open to learning." The clerk rolled his eyes and sorted through his documents, determining the top priority projects he needed to bring with him.

The clerk held the little mouse in his hands and petted it while he strolled down the sidewalk, vaguely searching for a bus. He was thinking about his betrothed and how she would respond if he told her that they were making him help out in another department. "I don't think she'd like it too much, Ellem."

The mouse remained still in the clerk's palm, occasionally flicking its ear at the sound of a horn, or sniffing its whiskers at someone who walked by too closely.

"I think she'd say that I should have said it's outside of my job responsibilities and it's not right for me to do that extra work without at least getting additional compensation and all that sort of thing. But she doesn't know how these things work. They don't just go around handing out promotions to any clerk who shows up on time to his desk every day and sits there. They want to see someone who proves to be a team player—who can be versatile and adaptable— helpful in any situation."

Eventually, the clerk got on a bus, and he sighed as he looked out the window—some part of him dreading the forthcoming ordeals in the ominously named Shipping and Receiving Department.

He also didn't know where it was, and as he ascended the stone stairs to the government office, he dreaded asking the security guards out of fear he'd set them off. He checked his wristwatch and saw that it was after noon. "Maybe I should just stop by the bowling alley first and get that over with."

The whole thing felt routine by now—trading his shoes with the girls in green, chucking a heavy stone ball for no reason, listening to the inane entreaties of the person in the fedora.

"Hey, let me ask you something, Ms.," the clerk said to the girl in green as he was trading the ugly shoes back for his own. "Do you know where the Shipping and Receiving Department is?"

"Why? You need to send something? I can interoffice it for you. You don't have to go down there."

"Why do you say that?"

"Oh, it's dreadful down there. It's dark, cold, musty—I always get lost. Much better to interoffice your document, even if it takes a little longer."

The clerk sighed. "If only it were so easy."

"Why do you say that?"

"I have to go down there. My boss is sending me to help them with some sort of task or project."

The girl made a face and shuddered. "Well, good luck to you."

"Thanks." He remained leaning his elbow on the counter while he was waiting for her to direct him to the place, but she just looked back at him. The moment started to feel awkward, so the clerk said, "So uh, can you tell me how to get there?"

"Oh, right. It's simple, really. Just hop in the lift and hit the button for the lowest floor. It's B-something or other. Just, whatever the button all the way on the bottom is, hit that one."

"Great," the clerk muttered. "Thanks very much."

"Good luck to you, sir."

The clerk got in the elevator and followed the girl's directions. The elevator doors opened up to reveal a cavern with lighting rigged up via wires running through the rock ceiling.

"I'm creeped out already," the clerk whispered in the direction of his pocket.

Nearby, there was a guy in a jumpsuit pushing a trolley stacked with boxes, so the clerk walked up to him and asked, "Is this Shipping and Receiving?"

"Who wants to know?" the guy said with a sneer, continuing to push his boxes.

"Uh, me," the clerk replied, following along next to the guy. When he didn't respond, the clerk added, "I want to know. I need to know if I'm in the right spot."

"And who are you, Mr. high and mighty? So famous that everyone should just know who you are and how important you are?"

"I didn't say that," the clerk muttered.

"You did too say it!" the guy snapped. "You said it with your tone. With your lack of information and the expectations you placed upon me."

"Look, I don't want to be down here anymore than you do, but it's our job."

"Oh I see, this place is so awful that you don't want to be down here, and you dare to act as though we're colleagues?" The guy scoffed. "Forget you." As he resumed pushing his trolley away, a door burst open out of the clerk's peripheral vision and a massive guy stormed in their direction. He was so huge that he seemed to hunch over so he wouldn't drag his close-cropped hair on the low hanging stalactites of the cavernous ceiling, and his chest was so gargantuan that it was like a king-sized bed when compared to the clerk's puny folding chair of a chest.

"What's all this ruckus? What's going on here?" the guy demanded, spittle flecking out from between his pudgy lips.

The clerk's wide eyes shifted in the direction of the guy

with the trolley, but that guy was suddenly nowhere to be seen.

"Who do you think you are? Showing up late and having the nerve to interrupt our training session with all this meaningless commotion?"

"Uh, I—"

"Shut up! I know who you are. You're one of the pathetic troupe of clerks they've sent down here, supposedly to be of our assistance. Office clerks don't know the first thing about working in a mailroom. It'll take ten of you to do the work of one proper transaction processor, and they only sent ten of you to make up for *fifteen* missing transaction processors."

"Missing? What happened to—?"

"You're not at a high enough clearance to know the details of our personnel. All you need to worry about is that you're late for the training, you're holding everybody up, and if you're not in—"

"Hey! What's the meaning of all this?" a petite woman exclaimed, bursting through the swinging doors.

The massive guy's whole demeanor changed. He instinctively cowered, his deep breaths heaving his chest, and his eyes squinting in her direction. When she came closer, he gently spoke, "I—the person who happens to be this new recruit's shift supervisor—was just having a few words with him about his new position."

"Sounded more like shouting than words from where I was standing."

"Well it's echoey in here. A guy's gotta speak up."

The clerk remained frozen, only his eyes twitching to look at one, then the other.

"Why don't you just let the shift manager welcome the new recruits?"

"I really think that's more of a job for their shift supervisor."

"No, nope. This definitely seems like a shift manager responsibility to me."

"You say that about everything."

"Well, it seems to me that you claim you have jurisdiction over everything as shift supervisor, but we both know that's not true."

"Just you wait, little lady," the massive guy whispered, barely audible to the clerk over the sound of his heartbeat in his ears. "They're trimming the fat around here, and it's only so long before they realize that it's redundant to have a shift supervisor *and* a shift manager working every day in Shipping and Receiving. And oh when that day comes, and they review the performance evaluations and see how efficient the shift supervisor is, your reign of terror will come to an end."

"What was that?" the lady asked, cupping her hand over an ear. "Did you say you were going to get back in the conference room to continue the training?"

"After you, of course," the guy said, motioning in a slight bow.

"I need to have a few words with our quivering clerk here first. Something you wouldn't know anything about. People skills. Leadership skills. Human capital management. The leadership qualities necessary for a manager in the twenty-first century—the furthest progress humanity has yet made."

The big guy scoffed and shuffled back toward the conference room, muttering inaudible gripes.

She fixed her gaze on the clerk. "The Manager of Communication Security in the small branch sent you, didn't she?"

"Um, yes. That's right,"

"Well I'm sorry you received such a cold reception. I'm trying to run a tighter ship around here, but the ranks are somewhat divided. I can tell from your calm demeanor that you'll be siding with me. Don't worry about the shift supervisor anyway. I'm the shift manager. I outrank him."

"Oh. Okay."

Shouting could be heard from within the doors of the conference room. The clerk specifically thought he heard the word "maggots."

"We'd better get in there," the shift manager said. "I can't trust him alone with the new recruits. I can't have him scaring everyone away. We're short staffed as it is."

The clerk shuffled in behind her as she stormed into the conference room. She was a tiny woman dressed in a navy blue suit, and she carried herself in a way that demanded respect and attentiveness. Even though the shift supervisor continued his explanation of shipping protocols, it was clear to the clerk that his demeanor shifted and became more reserved the moment the shift manager stepped into the room. Many employees were sitting in folding chairs that faced the front of the room, where the shift supervisor was leading the training, but they all turned to watch the shift manager as she marched down the space between the chairs that created an aisle to the front.

The clerk found an empty chair in the back and slunk into it. The shift manager picked up a marker and began sketching out a diagram on a white board. Without announcement, she started talking over the shift supervisor. He glared at her and began to grind his teeth, but the clerk noted that he didn't attempt to continue his presentation. He remained quiet, essentially ceding the victory to her.

"Now then, recruits," she said. "This is what the org

chart looks like down here. You'll note it's different than what you're used to up there, but I've started up tall to trace down the connections. You see this area here, where it splinters into five major departments? You're all coming from one of these departments, and in Shipping and Receiving, we're primarily shipping documents and packages up to them." She began drawing arrows up and down all over her diagram. "Now, what you'll see happen most often, is that one of these departments sends some documents down here to us, and we sort it out and bring it back up here to one of these other departments." She started drawing more arrows off to the side. "Nevertheless, we also have to ship a fair amount of material to non-governmental sites." She waved her hand over arrows that pointed off the board.

The shift supervisor had been wringing his meaty hands and he finally threw them up into the air. "Okay! They get it! This is all obvious. They would have figured this out immediately just by the name of this department alone. Let me go back to what I was talking about. I'm explaining the important stuff to them—the protocols they'll actually need to know when they're working down here—what type of documents are received where—what type of documents are stored where—what type of documents are shipped where—how to mark them—how to know what phase of the shipping and receiving process a particular document or package is on. How are they going to get any work done if they don't know this stuff?"

"Look sir," she started. The fluctuating expressions on his lips indicated that he beamed at her use of this title, but poorly masked the fact that it pleased him. "I'm not denying the validity of the material you are covering with them, but that's all very micro-level information, and I'm trying to paint the big picture for them here. They won't understand the small aspects if they don't know what part it plays in the overall picture of the operation. We'll get to that later. If they understand the big picture, it will help them to remember your portion of the training. So why don't we do this, I'll finish going over this with them for the next few minutes, we'll all take a coffee break, and then I'll let you continue where you left off."

"Coffee break!? Are you serious? Are you for real? These people barely started their training. They don't know anything yet. They haven't accomplished anything yet, and I can sure as heck tell you that not a one of them has proved themself to me—and you want to give them a coffee break?"

"Coffee breaks are good for morale," she replied, absently brushing fuzz off of her jacket.

"And not only that, but this will spoil the momentum of everything I've started already. I'm going to have to go back to the beginning."

"That's fine, that's fine. You should have let me start at the real beginning anyway. Now, as I was saying," she turned to the board and began to draw more lines and boxes on her diagram.

The shift supervisor crossed his arms and clenched his jaw.

"You may need to personally deliver items to nearby recipients, or take them to the appropriate inter-province, inter-country, or inter-nation post. Some of you will be delivering, some of you will be sorting, some of you will be processing. We'll figure out the details of who's going to do what once you're all up to speed. We believe in a tightly structured bureaucracy down here. Each person needs to play an integral role, and with each person performing their specialized duty to the maximum optimization, the entire department will run smoothly, operating at maximum efficiency, and if every department runs at maximum efficiency, government operations as a whole will offer unparalleled functionality. That is the true essence of bureaucracy. It's kind of like a sports team—if each individual player does his part well and in unison with the closest teammates, the whole team will function as one."

Someone in the second-to-front row had raised her hand, and at this point, the shift manager nodded in her direction. "Yes?"

"I understand your point completely," the woman started. "However, my optimal role in this organization is as a clerk in the International Affairs Division. How can I perform that integral role optimally, and allow that division to perform optimally, thereby allowing the entire organization to perform optimally, if I'm also expected to perform this integral role in Shipping and Receiving? It seems impossible that I should have the time to perform both roles optimally, and therefore, either way, some sector of the organization is being dragged down."

The clerk couldn't see her face from here, but he thought she sounded smug, and he could tell that she was looking in the direction of the shift supervisor, but when he spoke, it was clear to the clerk that she had not gained any favors with him.

"You think that's funny? Well it's not funny," he burst out. "How dare you seek to destroy a perfectly valid explanation with your syllogistic reasoning? Do you think we don't know it would be optimal for us to have a crew one hundred percent dedicated to Shipping and Receiving? The fact is that we don't, and even though the HR reps give us all kinds of BS about electronic communications and the need for us to cut back and join the divisions that have gone green, the fact of the matter is that mountains of paper correspondence need to flow through this organization every day and it's on our backs to get it to where it needs to go. So don't come in here and act like there's some flaw in the shift manager's logic. Because the problem isn't with her; the problem is with the fact that every action and every person in this organization has a true essence that can be reduced to numbers. Every one of you is being paid right now for your butts to be in those chairs, and if there's not enough money to go around, then cuts have to happen somewhere, and we just have to do the best with what we've got."

"Well said," the shift manager responded, her thin lips upturned.

"And don't think you can just come in here and divide and conquer," the shift supervisor continued. "Because even though the shift manager and I may have our differences, and we may approach things from different managerial styles, the fact of the matter is that we both want the same thing: For the Shipping and Receiving Department at this organization to be the best it can be. So when it comes down to it, we work together to achieve that as equals."

"Very true, very true," the shift manager started, "Except that I outrank you."

The shift supervisor became red-faced and shouted, "Hold it right there!" before he composed himself a bit. "Maybe it's time we review the staffing table down here because I've got mine right here and it clearly shows that I'm the one in charge." He extracted a crumpled up piece of paper from his pocket.

The shift supervisor was erasing the board while he said this. "Sure, let's go over the organizational chart." She wrote "Shipping and Receiving" up at the top, and drew a box under it, in which she wrote "Director."

"So far we're in agreement," the shift supervisor

grumbled.

Under this, she drew two vertical lines with boxes, and under those, another two vertical lines with boxes.

"Hold up! Hold it right there!" he called out, holding up his crinkly piece of paper. "You've got way too many lines going on there. On my chart—which is quite official, as you can see; it was given to me with my job description—there is a direct line pointing from the director to the shift supervisor—me—as well as a second direct line pointing from the director to the night shift supervisor."

As he said that, the shift manager drew in boxes with those titles on the board. "Yes," she said. "But you've worked here longer than me, and your chart is outdated. We need to add in the day shift manager and the night shift manager." She wrote those titles in the boxes above the shift supervisors.

"But my job description specifically states that I'm responsible for supervising the daily operations of the Shipping and Receiving Department!" the shift supervisor objected.

"Yes, but the word supervise implies you need people to be supervising, which you are. But I'm managing the whole operation, which involves not just supervising you and the other employees, but also keeping on top of our long term strategies, coordinating our efforts to meet the needs of the other departments and maintain focus on our long term goals and objectives. Management is about a lot more than just supervising some employees."

"Wait, wait, wait," the shift supervisor said, holding up a massive hand. "Night shift manager? I never heard of a night shift manager. I never even met him."

"Her," the shift manager interjected. "I'm sure the director sent you a memo about it. They hired her right after they hired me."

"You just leave correspondence with the director up to me."

"In that case, I wouldn't get anything done. A large part of my responsibilities involve directly working with the director."

"I bet," the shift supervisor grumbled.

"Okay everyone," the shift manager said in a peppy tone, turning toward the seated employees. "I can smell that the administrative assistant just brewed a fresh pot, so let's take a fifteen-minute coffee break. Grab a cup of joe, use the bathroom if you need to, stretch your legs, and we'll meet back here in fifteen."

Everyone immediately got up and began to shuffle toward the door. The shift supervisor was still fuming.

* * * *

The clerk was sitting at the table in the break room where a handful of other clerks were milling about. He sat there silently sipping his coffee, occasionally reaching into his jacket pocket and petting the mouse. The other clerks were all complaining about having to help out in the Shipping and Receiving Department. They were saying things like, "Why should I have to work in this mismanaged department?" and "This is putting me behind on all my projects. I better not get any negative feedback on my performance review because of this." The clerk could tell that they all thought working in the Shipping and Receiving Department was beneath them.

Everyone stopped talking as the shift manager strode into the break room. "Here's my loyal crew," she said, smiling at them all. "We're so happy that you were able to come down here and help us out. We can't thank you enough. Shipping and Receiving wouldn't be able to function without you, and the whole organization will benefit from your hard work."

The clerks muttered indistinguishable things.

"I apologize that you have to be a part of the conflict of ideas between the shift supervisor and myself, but that's an important part of the age we live in. Once these conflicts are ironed out, our department will function in perfect harmony."

The clerks nodded and muttered.

"Well, I'm going to head back in, but you've got a few more minutes," she said, turning to leave.

Back in the conference room, the shift manager mostly turned things over to the shift supervisor. He was describing the workflow, and the systematic way that documents and parcels would be collected and distributed. The process was so complicated and confusing that the clerk started jotting down notes on a napkin in case he was actually going to need to know any of these things to do this job. The more the shift supervisor explained things, and the more the clerk tried to figure things out, the more the clerk thought that this whole operation involved a lot of meaningless transportation of a document to different spots in the massive Shipping and Receiving facility before it actually was sent to be delivered to its intended recipient. *Maybe I'm wrong. Maybe I just don't quite understand the whole thing yet. Whatever. I'm just going to pass the time down here until they send me back to my regular post.* The clerk wondered if the shift supervisor was simply trying to obfuscate a rather simple process. He stopped taking notes because he was too confused. A couple of other people asked questions, but the shift supervisor shouted at them and started drawing elaborate diagrams on the board that were so twisted in on themselves that they were meaningless to the clerk.

The clerk was leaning his elbows on his knees with his hand running through his hair when he heard someone say, "Um, it's after five." He glanced up to see that it was the woman near the front who had questioned the shift manager earlier, and then he glanced at his silver wristwatch and saw that it was 5:01.

"I see the kind of lazy crew they sent us," the shift supervisor bellowed. "Clock-watchers who are ready to just run out of here at the first possible opportunity and not pay any mind to the task at hand."

The shift manager stepped in front of him and spoke in a soothing tone, "It's been a long day and you've all taken in a lot of new information. So let's end here for now and make sure you all get plenty of relaxation and rest tonight to let all that information sink in. We'll start fresh tomorrow and do some role-playing and hands-on training. Have a good night everyone."

The clerks jumped up and shuffled toward the door as quickly as possible. The clerk did his best to blend in with all of them and avoid any interaction with either of his new bosses. He counted himself fortunate that he made it into the first elevator heading toward the ground floor. All of the other clerks in the elevator were complaining about the new assignment and claiming that they were going to be up all night catching up on the work they didn't have a chance to do today. The clerk was already dreading how his betrothed would respond when he told her about his day.

Once he was out on the street, the clerks scattered in all different directions, and the clerk could see the street person who usually harassed him for change bothering one of the other clerks across the street. He walked down the block quickly in hopes of getting away from him.

* * * *

The clerk was relieved that his betrothed didn't seem to be too upset. He explained the situation to her, and she frowned and stared off into space for a long moment. A budgie kept chirping and interrupting the silence. Then she said, "Well it's not your real job, so don't let them work you too hard."

She faced her back to him on the bed as she crouched over a notebook all night. The clerk took advantage of her keeping busy by working on his documents that he was behind with. He suspected that she knew what he was doing, but she didn't say anything.

* * * *

The role-playing session of the training had been awkward, and it only got worse when it ended with the shift supervisor shouting obscenities and storming out.

Now it was the portion of the training when the clerks were supposed to shadow the transaction processors. The clerk was part of an expanded group of about seven clerks who were shadowing one grumpy transaction processor. He moved slowly and didn't provide much explanation about what he was doing. The clerks didn't ask questions either. Most of them seemed as disgruntled as him.

The clerk was anxious because lunchtime was drawing near and he hadn't heard anyone mention a lunchbreak. He was going to have to somehow slip upstairs and get his daily number.

The transaction processor apparently forgot something and turned around to go back to the station he had just come from. They were currently in the middle of a winding cavern. None of the walls were finished, and this place seemed as though it was carved out of rock by a mixture of ancient water and prehistoric humans. The clerk decided that he was going to have to slip away, which didn't seem like a problem because his two bosses were nowhere to be seen.

They were already heading back toward the elevators, so when they came to a fork, the clerk lingered toward the back of the crowd and slipped down the other corridor. He thought this would lead right to the elevators, but he came to another fork, and he wasn't sure if he should go left or right.

The left path looked darker and windier than the right path, so the clerk went right. It seemed to go on for longer than expected. "Shouldn't I be back to the lifts by now, little guy?" he whispered to the mouse, who was very still in his pocket.

Around another bend, the clerk froze in his tracks as he saw a pair of eyes gleaming in the shadows up ahead. They were low to the ground, and the clerk imagined a beast crouched on all fours, waiting to pounce as the clerk approached. He froze in place, uncertain of what to do. A long moment passed before the clerk began to creep backward. The creature didn't seem to be moving to follow him, so once the clerk was around the next bend, he broke into a full run. "I don't know what that thing was, and I don't want to find out," he whispered between breaths as he leaned on the wall.

Eventually, the clerk recognized the fork in the road, and he took the darker path. This corridor opened up into a wide area of stalagmites and stalactites, and he could hear water dripping in the distance. He could feel himself trembling in the cold as he pressed on, suppressing the fears on the edge of his consciousness that he would never find his way back to civilization. He found an opening in a wall where the lights seemed to be strung up more regularly, and he followed it down a narrow corridor.

He stopped abruptly as he heard sounds approaching. Before he decided to run or stand his ground, they were upon him—it was the transaction processor and the crew of clerks shadowing him. The clerk stood there, looking confused, and none of the other employees even acknowledged their colleague, they just kept walking, so the clerk fell in with them as they made their way back into the cavernous depths.

It was almost two hours later when they returned to the lobby of the underground complex and decided to take a lunch break. The clerk rushed to the elevator and hit the buttons for the 195th floor. This part of his daily quests had become fairly easy and routine—he just had the problem that there was always sand in his hair. He commended himself on the nice work he did navigating the desert city today, only getting lost twice.

"There you are, my boy!" the portly chairman exclaimed when the assistant walked the clerk into the office. "You're running late today—but perhaps just in time. We are sitting down to some brownies."

"Wow, really?" the clerk said. He hadn't even thought of actually eating anything during his lunch break.

* * * *

"So uh," the clerk muttered, glancing down at the parcels he was supposed to deliver and back up at the shift supervisor. "Can I get a map of the area down here or something? I got lost last time."

"What?" the shift supervisor said, looking up from the mess of documents and manila envelopes he was in up to his waist.

The clerk thought it was a rhetorical "what?" but the fact that the shift supervisor just stared at him expectantly caused him to repeat, "May I have a map?"

"A map of what?" the supervisor snapped, an edge to his words.

"This facility. I got lost the other day."

"You've gotta be kidding me," the supervisor moaned. "Where's your sense of direction? It's not *that* big. All of the tunnels intersect in one way or another."

"I don't know," the clerk mumbled, since he didn't know what to say.

"I tell you what, I'll put in a formal request for the director to send you a map, but I wouldn't hold your breath. It's going to be a while until she gets around to that. I put in a request to her for documentation about this so-called 'shift manager,' and she hasn't responded. I haven't caught her in her office in a long time either."

"Where is she?"

"Who knows? She's always got meetings and all kind of BS up in the sky."

"The sky?"

"Pie in the sky. The office complex smothering us. You know—where you came from. Where you usually work."

"Oh, I don't usually work up there," the clerk said. "I usually work in the branch in the small city."

"Whatever," he grumbled. "I'm asking for maps for all the new temporary clerks down here, but like I said, don't hold your breath."

"Okay, thanks," the clerk said.

"Just get those to where they need to go," he said, nodding at the documents in the clerk's wheelbarrow.

"Yep. You got it."

The clerk's wheelbarrow squeaked when he pushed it, and as he navigated the winding corridors of the underground caves, the squeaking echoed and freaked him out. He thought there was a creature around every corner, but he'd been wandering down here for hours and hadn't seen anything other than the occasional other clerk pushing their parcels along in whatever makeshift thing with wheels had been available.

A chill ran down the clerk's spine and he whirled around to see what was behind him. Glowing eyes were in the distance, low to the ground and moving closer to him. He instinctively began to back away, not turning from the creature. He was becoming distant from his wheelbarrow, but the creature was almost next to it. As the thing stepped into the light, the clerk could see that it was a ragged animal on four legs, brown fur clinging to it in mats, a limp, misshapen tail, pointy little ears, and a long, whiskered muzzle.

The thing was so pathetic that the clerk forgot to be afraid of it. He crouched down, crawling forward slightly and holding out his hand. "Are you friendly, little buddy?" the clerk whispered.

The animal let out a low growl and the clerk pulled his hand back. The animal stepped forward, put its front paws on the wheelbarrow and took a parcel with its teeth. When it hopped down, it knocked over the wheelbarrow and sent items flying all over the floor. As this happened, it scampered back the way it'd come, and the clerk could make out that it had rejoined others of its kind, hidden in the shadows.

"I wonder what that was all about, Ellem," the clerk whispered as he quickly gathered up most of the items, shoved them back in the wheelbarrow, and hurried back in the direction in which he'd been travelling.

The clerk couldn't understand why the work he was doing was necessary. He understood the people who were bringing the mail down from the upstairs offices, he understood the people who were sorting that mail once it got down here, he understood the people who were delivering that mail back up to the offices, and he understood the people who were taking things out into the city for delivery, but he couldn't understand all of the people—including him—who had to take mail to different areas of this underground facility for "processing," whatever that meant.

By this point in the evening, the clerk was longing to

be home eating dinner with his betrothed, but he was still trapped down in the underground caverns. He saw another clerk pushing a shopping cart full of mail and he rushed to catch up with her.

"Hey, do you know the way out?"

"I think it's this way," she said.

"Great. Let's get out of here."

"But we're not supposed to leave until we get all this post to the right place."

The clerk made a noise in his throat. "We'll figure that out along the way."

Another clerk was up ahead and called out to them, "Hey! I've got the solution right here." They walked up to the other clerk, who led them to an alcove in the cavern where there was a hole in the ground that seemed to lead into a pit of foul-smelling water.

"We all just dumped our leftovers in there and now we're heading home."

"But what if there are important documents?" the clerk asked. "I don't think it's fair to stay here forever, but I also don't want to destroy these permanently."

"Suit yourself." Both of the other clerks finished dumping the documents and continued their journey with empty trolleys. The clerk could see a group of other people ahead. Not wanting to get left behind, the clerk took out his documents and gingerly placed them on the cold ground, a couple of feet away from the hole. He rushed to catch up with the group.

* * * *

"What's the meaning of this!?" the shift supervisor shouted the next morning as he slammed a pile of envelopes down on the table in front of the clerk.

"Uh. I don't know," the clerk mumbled.

"Do you want to take a guess about where we found these?"

"Uh."

"Don't you have anything to say for yourself?"

"Well the thing is, there was a wild animal, see, and he uh, kind of chased me, so I, well you see, the thing is, I lost a lot of the parcels, and it was so dark and creepy down there, especially with the wild animals, that I didn't get a chance to find them again."

"Wild animal? That's preposterous," the shift supervisor snapped. "Don't go showering me with your outlandish excuses."

"I've seen wild animals in the caverns before." The shift manager had appeared in the doorway behind them.

The shift supervisor glared at her, but he held his tongue.

"They usually scamper off, but they're down there. I think they're dogs."

"They could be dogs," the clerk muttered. "I was a little busy fleeing to notice."

The shift supervisor started to open his mouth to speak, but he closed it again and stormed out, slamming the door behind him.

"You're the clerk from the small city branch, right?" the shift manager said in sweet cadences, sitting down next to the clerk.

"Yeah."

"Don't let him get you too riled up. That's just his management style," she said. "I think I have a calming effect on him."

The clerk didn't think that was the case, but he didn't want to say anything about it.

"Yeah, you know how it is managing a team of people. Everyone's got their own personalities and ideas—their philosophies of life that color their perception of the work they're accomplishing." She was smiling, looking longingly at the gray, stone wall just behind the clerk.

"Yeah," he muttered.

"Say, what's your philosophy of life?" she asked, leaning forward in the chair, her light eyes penetrating into his, even though he did his best to avoid her gaze.

"Uh." The clerk squirmed in his chair. He could feel sweat pouring down the groove of his spine. "I don't know."

"C'mon now," she said, giving a friendly laugh and patting him on the arm. "Everyone has a philosophy of life. Even if you don't think about it, it determines your motivations, your dreams, your goals."

She stared at the clerk, waiting for a response. "Uh huh," he tried, hoping she'd go away.

"I think this is one of the best ways to think about it. I think about this all the time, and it really helps me get a handle on the real meaning behind the work our department is performing as a part of this exceptional nation's government." Her wistful gaze moved away from the clerk to the gray wall before snapping back on him. "Imagine if you were in charge of this planet. You could remake a world society to be however you wanted. How would you make it? What would it look like?"

She had a slight smile on her lips, like someone who just told a joke and was waiting for him to understand the punchline and start laughing. She leaned forward, eager.

"Uh," the clerk uttered, swallowing. He could feel his clothes sticking to his body now, sweating all over and feeling wet as if he'd been caught out in a summer rainstorm. "Well, I guess." He was having difficulty comprehending her question, and rather than wanting to actually answer her, he just wanted to say whatever it was that would make her go away. "Right then," he muttered, smiling.

"What would your world look like?" she asked, her smile widening. "C'mon. Think of it like an ice-breaking exercise for you and me. The kind of things they teach you in Human Resources school. It doesn't have to be your final answer. I just want to get a feel for where you're coming from. Imagine you were queen of the world, righting wrongs and fixing injustices. What would the planet look like under your command?"

He could feel the mouse wiggling in his breast pocket, thinking that perhaps it wanted to relocate due to the sudden and excessive moisture. "I guess—it would have more animals," he muttered in one quick breath.

"Animals?" she said, nodding appreciatively and stroking her chin. "A most unexpected answer. Almost the opposite of the type of answer I would give. You see, when I think of animals, I think of the law of the jungle—the strong eat the weak, that sort of thing. I imagine that humans have moved beyond nature. We've developed so that we can find new routes that don't rely on mere instincts for survival."

The clerk was wide-eyed, fearing that he'd offended his temporary manager by saying the wrong thing. Would she be contributing to his performance evaluation to document the work he's doing here? He had to find out, somehow. He glanced up at her and saw that she was still smiling, her face contemplative.

"Think about your answer further. And I'll think about mine," she said, "and when we meet up again, we can continue our discussion. Actually, I wanted to tell you—I've got an office in the caverns, and since we've got so many newcomers here, I converted it into a little break room for everyone—well, everyone except the shift supervisor; I don't want to tell him about it. I know it's silly, but I'm thinking of it as the Café in the Caverns. He'd just be a downer if he found out about it. Never mind, I don't even know why I'm bringing him up. The point is, it's just past Station Seven, so when you're in the area, feel free to stop in, take a load off, and grab a cup of joe. And I hope that we can continue this conversation there." She smiled at him and stood up.

Her expression changed when she noticed the parcels on the table. She picked them up and gave them a meaningful look, turning them in her hands. "The packages you didn't get to deliver yesterday?"

The clerk felt his cheeks burn red, but before he could answer, she spoke again.

"Don't worry about them. I know it's a tough job and you're behind. I'll deliver them for you." She walked out of the room, clasping the parcels to her chest.

* * * *

Hours later, the clerk found himself amidst a group of other clerks in the shift manager's secret break room in the cavern.

"People around here keep talking about pie, but I've never seen anything other than coffee in these break rooms."

"Forget about pie. They can't keep pie down here. The dogs would get it."

"What dogs?"

"There's whole packs of wild dogs down here."

"They're not wild. They're friendly."

"No way! One growled and chased me the other day."

"You guys are putting me on. How would dogs even get down here?"

"Beats me, but they're definitely down here."

"There's probably a hidden tunnel that leads to the surface. They follow it down here for warmth or food, I bet."

The door swung open and the shift manager strolled

in, a smile spread across her thin cheeks. "Now isn't this nice? Such camaraderie! This is how you build a real team." Everyone stopped talking. The shift manager walked over to the pot of coffee and poured herself a cup. "A team can only function if the members know one another well. A team needs to interact so much that its motions become like one, and that's what we're building down here in the Shipping and Receiving Department. Each of you will know your own role flawlessly, but you'll be familiar enough with the roles of your fellows that you'll know how to rely on them, how to help them out of a tight spot. A true team is able to move as one, and seamlessly adjust to difficulties or contingencies. We are definitely moving in that direction." She was still smiling as she sat down in one of the empty chairs.

The clerk had been watching the person next to him discreetly write a note hidden from view of the shift manager, and he caught a glimpse of what it said: *"Don't know why she's thinking so big picture, pie-in-the-sky type stuff. As soon as we get the O.K., we're all out of here."*

Moments later, every employee stood up at once and muttered excuses about getting back to work, quickly disappearing out of the door. The clerk immediately regretted he hadn't rushed out with the rest of them—he still had a decent amount of coffee left to finish in his cup—and he found himself alone with the shift manager. She smiled at him. "Why don't you come sit a little closer?"

Seeing no way to make an excuse, the clerk stood up, grabbed his coffee, and took his seat next to her.

"So, do you agree that any random group of people thrown together isn't necessarily an effective team?"

The clerk saw no way to answer this question other than to nod his head and say, "Yes."

She liked that answer. "And do you agree that the

members of the team each need to understand their own role properly?"

"Yeah."

"But in knowing their own roles, it isn't necessary for them to know the roles of the others in order to function properly, is it?"

The clerk could tell this one was a trick question, so he thought for a second. "They need to have some idea of what their fellows are doing if they're a team."

"Yes! Definitely! This is one aspect of an effective bureaucracy that is often overlooked. People imagine that a bureaucracy has a few at the top who are overseeing everything, and it is only these select few who need to understand the big picture of the whole operation. But I say no. I say that an effective bureaucracy needs to consist of a series of teams. Does every member know exactly the big picture of the whole operation? Not one hundred percent. But—but," she was excited. Her expression was like fire, and her arms waved with each point, "each team, or department, in the common parlance, has to have a strong understanding of its overall goals, and each member's responsibility, and how they interact with their closest departments. That's something I'm trying to build here."

"I see," the clerk said.

"But if a bureaucratic solution could work for an operation as big as this one, couldn't it have other, even grander applications?"

Her eyes were glistening intensely in the clerk's direction, so he knew he had to answer. "Uh," he muttered, buying time. Sweat was beading down his back and forehead now. He could feel the little black mouse stirring, climbing out of his jacket pocket. Part of him wanted to adjust the mouse, but he had to focus on giving the shift manager an answer. "Yeah, I guess," he spat out finally.

He could feel the mouse climbing his shirt like a rope-ladder as the shift manager continued. "Yes. That's exactly what I'm thinking! Imagine if society itself was a grand bureaucracy—artificers at the top, each town and city its own team working together toward the greater whole."

"Isn't it kind of like that now?" the clerk muttered without thinking, being struck with fear as the mouse's advance continued.

"But 'kind of' is not good enough. It can be improved. We'd probably have to start small. Town by town, city by city. When each is a team, they can combine forces with their fellow teams, the country forming together into a harmonious whole—and once this is in place, it can be expanded to other countries—to become the world's society. And please don't think I'm making this sound easy—because it's not easy. It would be filled with struggle, but each struggle would result in unquestioned progress. And the long road would lead to the end of history, to the utopian society that has—hey, is that a mouse?"

The clerk's eyes went wide. He could now see that indeed it was a mouse, nestled on his shoulder, looking out at the break room and flickering its whiskers in the direction of the shift manager.

Before the clerk could react, the shift manager continued, "She's cute. Is she friendly?"

"Uh, yeah," he muttered.

The shift manager stood up and reached her hand toward the mouse. It flinched at first, but she moved slowly and scratched it on the back with one finger. The clerk thought the mouse seemed to like her.

"You let her stay in your pocket?" she asked.

"Uh, yeah."

"That's very cool. You did say you like animals. Well, we'll talk more later. We better get back to work." The shift manager put her mug in the sink and washed her hands.

* * * *

The clerk found himself alone in the front office as he dialed his manager's extension and stood in silence save for the ringing in the phone's earpiece. One of the other clerks had found him in the cavern to give him an urgent message to call his manager. The phone stopped ringing, but no voice came from the other end. He thought maybe the call had been disconnected.

"Hello?" he said.

"Hi. Who's this?" a voice on the other end said. It was male, so it couldn't have been his manager.

"Who's *this?*" the clerk retorted, upset at the man's poor phone etiquette. He knew that if he answered his boss' phone, he should say, "Communication Security Department, Small City Branch. How may I help you?" So what was wrong with this person?

"Hold on. I forgot the name of the department."

"What? Where's the manager?"

"She's in a meeting. Can I take a message?"

"She called for me."

"Oh!" the guy shouted, holding the word out for several beats. "You're the guy in the uh, mailroom type place?"

"Yeah."

"She needs to meet you. She said there's a big meeting in the main office and you're to go with her."

"Ack! What? When?"

"Now, I guess. I don't know. She like, left already."

"When?"

"Hmm—That's a good question. Let me think; let me think. It had to be, geez, I don't know, a good twenty minutes to an hour ago."

"But you're one of her assistants! Don't you have her itinerary? Her calendar?"

"Look man, I'm sorry, but I'm like, only part-time, you know? And I haven't been working here very long—only a few months. So I don't quite have everything down yet, you know?"

The clerk grunted in frustration and hung up the phone without saying goodbye.

He rushed upstairs in search of his manager. He didn't see her at the lobby, so he decided to ask the security guards about her.

"Now just why do you think we're here sir?" was the security guard's response.

"Uh."

"The lady asked you a question. You'd best answer her."

"Uh."

"Surely even amid all the important thoughts going on in your mind, you must have at least given some regard to us lowly security guards?"

"Well, she deserves an answer. Why do you think we're here?" The guard pointed at a patch on his uniform that read "Federal Security."

"Uh, for security, I guess."

"Yes! For security! And how secure do you think it would be if we just gave out itineraries of every important official who came in and out of the building?"

"I don't know."

"Let me give you a little idea. It would be the opposite of secure. A security guard is to ensure that the important information and people who work in this office are not compromised. We can't have these things falling into the wrong hands."

"So do your hands look like the right hands?"

"Well—she *is* my manager."

"Wrong answer, sir."

"There you are!" his manager's voice came from behind, saving him from the ominous approaches of the security guards. "What took you so long? My assistant called you an hour ago."

"Ma'am! I only just got the message," the clerk said, rushing in the direction of his manager and away from the sinister stares of the security guards.

"Well let's hurry. This is a very important meeting. And if you're going to become a very important person, you have to attend important meetings like these."

"Yes, without a doubt!" the clerk exclaimed, understanding the hints at the promotion that lay behind her words. He was already following his manager down the corridor in the direction of the elevators. She placed her palm in the spot between them and it glowed to life, opening the doors for them. As they rode in the elevator, his manager briefed him about the upcoming meeting.

"And of course the director will be there," she added.

"Of course." the clerk muttered, looking all around the elevator. He considered mentioning collecting numbers for the director, but decided that was too secretive to mention. "Do you know how long this meeting will take? I'm supposed to deliver a lot of parcels today."

"Who cares? That's stupid. Just dump them in a lake or something. I only sent you down there to appease the Director of Official Transport after her shift manager relayed all of the information to me. She's not going to pay close attention to the day to day stuff." His manager took a deep breath. "Now this is of the utmost ultra-importance—You have to pay careful attention to me and follow my directions exactly. We can't go in there together. The last thing we want to do is give them the impression that I'm babying you or something. You may be young, but you're a mature, responsible employee who can get things done and take on a leadership role when necessary. You can follow orders too, but you're able to seamlessly adapt yourself to challenges. Your greatest weakness is that you care too much. So when we go in there, you'll be walking into a room of your superiors, already seated and expecting you. You're going to have to control your gaze, because it would be wrong to look at one of them but not greet them, but it would also be wrong to greet them in the wrong order."

* * * *

As the clerk sat at a long board table, his manager seated several people away from him, he kept replaying his entrance in his head. He feared that he'd done the exact opposite of his manager's expectations. He felt like he had been a whirlwind of awkward looks and unintelligible utters of "Sir," and "Ma'am." Most of the people paid him little mind, but he distinctly thought that the director flashed him a disapproving look.

"You all know why we're here," the director said, calling the meeting to order. "We've had many disturbing reports from a variety of sources. I fear we may have an infestation on our hands, the likes of which we've not had to deal with in decades. However, they haven't yet made their move, so we may be able to cut off their head before they really get going. You see, from what we know of these people, they probably have one leader pushing the whole thing. If we stop the leader, it's likely the others will abandon their philosophy. These people like to look to the teachings of an old master. They believe in a 'Philosopher King.' We neutralize the king, we kill the movement."

The clerk watched the director continue to speak, the dull lights of the conference room producing an inordinately bright glare off of his bald head. His thick hands gesticulated in menacing movements as he spoke of thwarting secret saboteur cells. His muscles bulged beneath his suit, the bulky veins of his neck threatening to tear the fabric of his tie.

"We've been fortunate that our nation has only rarely suffered a severe saboteur attack," the director continued. "There are desert cities on the other side of the world where such attacks are a sad fact of daily life. People lead lives of fear, sadness, and death. Our military fights in such situations, suffering losses themselves, keeping back the tide of instability to safeguard our people. We must do our part to prevent this from turning into anything of consequence. It's a common misconception that these extremists are fringe, underground men. The fact of the matter is that philosophy has historically been a bourgeois undertaking. Another wrong point is that people assume philosophers are all thought and no action. The truth is that the most dangerous philosophers stop thinking once they develop their ideology, and they then become all action from that point, impossible to reason with. I suspect at this stage, their only thoughts are to do harm to this organization, to create instability in our government—in our great nation. We must develop our own systematic plan of action to thwart theirs."

* * * *

It was a couple of hours later when the clerk and his manager were walking down a desolate hallway on the 94th floor.

"I want to see if the Director of Human Resources is in while I'm down here," she had said. "You can come along."

Now as they walked, she broke the silence. "So, any thoughts about the meeting?"

The clerk pursed his lips. "Well, I don't know if I was able to follow the whole thing. It was about philosophers, right? But they took it so seriously. It's not like philosophers are going to blow up a building or something—are they?"

His manager gasped and grabbed him by the shoulders. "You know something!" she whisper-shouted, shoving him into the wall.

"Uh—"

"Not here!" She maintained her grasp and shove-walked him down the hall and into the women's bathroom, sitting him down on one of the toilets as she maintained an intense gaze into his eyes. She leaned over and flushed the toilet. "Now talk. What do you know?"

"Uh. I don't know."

"You've been in the main office much more than me. Have you heard any sort of philosophical talk?"

"Uh—"

"Dialogues?"

"Well—"

"Debates?"

"Um—"

"Arguments? Treatises? Provocations? Manifestos? Polemics?" She shook the clerk by the shoulders. "Talk!"

"Pie!"

The manager flushed the toilet again. "Pie?"

"People keep bringing up pie. Pie in the sky. Sometimes I think they mean this building, since it's above us when we're in the basement, but sometimes I think it means lofty ideas."

"Lofty ideas? I don't like the sound of that. That sounds like philosophy! These philosophers get in here with their crazy pies in the sky, getting the employees' heads filled with all these ridiculous ideas, and before you know it they're all forming unions and we have to lay off whole swaths of people—or worse. It's a mess. Good thing you brought this to our attention." The manager unhanded the clerk. "This conversation never happened!"

She stormed off, leaving the clerk sitting in the women's room.

* * * *

The clerk was sitting in the main office of the Shipping and Receiving Department. He'd been staking it out for a while, and he finally found a private moment to use the phone. This whole thing about the philosophical saboteurs infiltrating the government had his stomach sick with stress. He had no idea what to do, but he remembered a long time ago, he'd read something in the employee manual about a "Problem Department." It was some kind of service to assist employees that any employee could get in touch with if they had an issue that they needed help resolving. If he recalled correctly, the information listed about the Problem Department was so vague that it seemed they could assist with work or personal issues, and there was some sort of limited confidentiality clause. He tried to reach an operator for the number, but there were no operators, only automated menus. He used the numpad to search by name for "PROBLEM."

"Do you want to be connected with the Problem Department?" a robot voice said.

"Yes," the clerk said. The phone rang eight times. The clerk was tempted to hang up.

"Problem Department," a breathless voice came on the line. "How can we help you?"

"I need you to help me figure out something. You see, my—"

"Just come in later and we'll help you. All of the Problem Specialists are busy assisting other employees right now.

However, I think that later on tonight there should only be a few hours' wait—" the clerk could hear muffled shouting and discordant noises on the other end of the call. "Actually, just come in tomorrow."

"Where are—?" the clerk stopped speaking because he heard the click of the call disconnecting. "So much for that," he sighed, no closer to figuring out if he should mention this whole philosopher thing to his manager.

"What are you doing just sitting around?" the shift supervisor yawped, bursting into the office.

The clerk scrambled to his feet and tried to rush out the door.

"Not so fast," the hulking brute of a man shouted, holding his hand to the clerk's chest to prevent his leaving. "There's no slacking off in this department. Just for that, you're going to personally be delivering this new stack of parcels that came in." He shoved a bunch of envelopes and small packages into the clerk's arms. "And I've got my eye on you, so don't think I won't notice if these don't end up where they're supposed to end up."

The clerk shuffled back out toward the caverns, pushing his parcels along in the wheelbarrow. He stopped and looked back at the elevator doors. It wasn't long until he'd need to sneak upstairs to the bowling alley, but every time he wandered into these labyrinthine caverns, he had great difficulty finding his way back. "I'm going to settle this once and for all, Ellem," the clerk said, extracting a big bundle of twine from his satchel that he'd acquired during one of these elaborate deliveries specifically for this purpose. He crept over to a nearby shelf and tied one end of the twine around its lower leg. He kept the roll of twine up on his wheelbarrow and let it unspool as he pushed the wheelbarrow along farther into the caverns, delivering parcels to the designated delivery stations. He wound around deep into the caverns, through areas dark and light, wet and dry. At one point, he could see animals creeping in the distance, so he wound around through an out of the way tunnel.

"Alright, I'd better get back," he said, having delivered the majority of his pile. He turned around, feeling confident as he followed his twine back through the myriad of pathways and tunnels. He focused solely on the thin rope, rather than his actual surroundings, retracing each step with care as he leaned over the wheelbarrow, regathering the small rope.

"How far did we wander, Ellem? We're still winding back around this twine." As the clerk looked around, the tunnels seemed dark and unfamiliar. They seemed to be shrinking—getting smaller so that it was to the point where it was difficult to negotiate his wheelbarrow, which just barely fit. In fact, he got to a point where the path turned up steeply, and there was no way he could push his wheelbarrow up any farther. "This seems much steeper than I remember it," he muttered. He thought he could hear growling in the distance, so he grabbed the handful of remaining parcels and stuffed them into his satchel, abandoning the wheelbarrow and using both hands to scurry up the rocky path.

After a time, the tunnels were so narrow that the clerk began to fear he wouldn't even be able to fit his body through this area of the caverns, and still his twine stretched ahead, designating the way he had come. Just when he was beginning to be overcome with claustrophobia, he saw the end of his twine—wrapped around a stalagmite and tied in a knot as the tunnel descended into a path of a size only mice could fit through. "What?!" the clerk exclaimed. "This can't be!" He tugged on the twine and shouted in rage. But what was to be done? He wanted to be out of these blasted tunnels, so he began to shimmy backward, descending bit by bit.

The clerk was dirty, damp, and exhausted by the time he shuffled back to the entrance of the cavern. He shambled to the elevators without bothering to be sneaky, and made his way to the bowling alley.

* * * *

"So, I've got a big problem," the clerk said. "And you're the only one I can trust."

His betrothed smiled. "Of course you can trust me."

"It's about a dinner party."

Her smile got bigger. "A dinner party you say?"

"Yeah, see. There's all this stuff about philosophers going on at work."

Her smile got smaller.

"Do you know anything about philosophers?" he asked.

"Not much. Just what they say in school. I didn't really pay attention."

"Well, the management is trying to weed out secret philosophers that they think mean us harm or something."

"Okay? Why did we get derailed from the dinner party?"

"Well, my shift manager for my temporary assignment invited me to a dinner party at her house."

"That sounds lovely." Her smile got big again.

"Yeah, but see, I'm worried she might be—or at least, is suspected of being—one of those secret philosophers they say are so dangerous."

"So you think she means us harm? That the dinner party is a trap to ensnare us?"

"Well, no, not really. She's usually quite nice."

"So then what's the problem? Let's go to the dinner party."

"Yeah, but, you see, since I'm worried that my manager and the director are suspicious of the shift manager, it may reflect poorly on me if it gets back to them that I attended her dinner party."

"Nah," she said, turning her big smile to the bird cage. All the birds flocked close to her face and started chirping at her. "It won't. And if anyone says anything, just explain that since she was your temporary supervisor, you thought it might be held against you if you didn't attend." She opened the cage and let one of the brightly colored birds perch on her finger. "Oh, this will be fun. When I'm out tomorrow, I'm going to buy something for us both to wear."

"Okay," the clerk said, frowning and petting the little mouse, who remained in his pocket.

* * * *

When the clerk had been at his cubicle the next morning, he had remembered to check his employee handbook to discover the location of the Problem Department, which turned out to be located on the 157th floor of the branch in the bigger city.

As he exited the elevator, he walked into a hazy hallway that was filled with guys in suits smoking e-cigarettes. The clerk sniffled as the water vapor entered his nose in various fruity flavors, which mixed together in his nostrils like a fruit salad. The men were muttering things related to accounts and audits, sprinkling in a lot of profanity about the various tasks they needed to do.

As the clerk approached, they all stopped talking and stared at him, still taking drags of their e-cigarettes, which caused the tips to light up in different neon colors. Feeling uncomfortable, the clerk tried to rush past them, but then a very short man blocked his path and addressed him. "Hey buddy, where do you think you're going? You're not authorized to be in here."

The clerk darted his eyes around, not sure if he should stand his ground. All he saw were the intense stares of the other men. His eyes were starting to water from the puffs of vapor bouncing into his irises. "I—I'm looking for the Problem Department," he managed, his voice coming out tiny and being overwhelmed by the mist.

"Well you're in the wrong spot, pal," the short man responded. The clerk could smell mangos on his breath. "You can't just go waltzing through our area, looking at all of our confidential files. Don't you know we've specifically been told to keep an eye out for suspicious characters?"

"And he looks mighty suspicious!" another man behind him exclaimed, the blue glow of the light on the end of the e-cigarette reflecting off of his glasses.

"You're scaring the poor wanker half to death," another man in a long brown coat said, putting his arm around the clerk and pressuring him to walk back down the hallway. The clerk could smell watermelons. "You know the kind of confused schlubs who visit our neighbors," he continued, still not addressing the clerk.

He walked the clerk back the way he'd come and spun him by the shoulders so that he was facing a different direction. "Godspeed, you poor bastard," the man said as he walked away. This time, the clerk thought that he was the one being addressed.

He realized that he was facing a door, and next to the door a paper sign was taped on the wall that said, "Problem Department."

The clerk pushed down on the handle and pulled the door open, a multitude of voices and cacophony entering his ears. He took a step into a room that was no larger than two busses placed side by side. There were people milling about all over at various workstations and tables. The clerk couldn't help but notice piles of unorganized papers shoved in nooks or on surfaces here and there, and he saw office supplies scattered about the various desks and tables. Everyone was so engrossed in animated conversations, many people hunched over others as they wrote or typed, that the clerk's entrance had seemed to go unnoticed. The clerk strode forward into the room. There were desks blocking his path, but he shifted toward the center of the room and walked to where there were several windows. He was thinking that there would be a nice view from all the way up here, so he leaned in close to the cold glass. A gray haze was all he could make out of the world beyond the office building. He could have been two feet up or two hundred feet up from all he could see. "Oh well, Ellem, it was worth having a look, don't you suppose?" He sighed.

As he turned around, he took one glance at all of the busy people and started back toward the door.

A young guy with shaggy hair was walking past the clerk with his head down, and he bumped into the clerk. "Oh," he said, looking up, a confused glaze over his eyes. "You're the guy who needs a Problem Specialist to go with you to haggle down the price of a used car, right?"

"Uh. No," the clerk muttered.

"Oh. Really?" the guy said, scratching his head. "Are you sure? I could've sworn it was you."

The clerk didn't respond.

"Wait, wait—I got it! You called before, right?"

The clerk gave an apprehensive nod.

The guy continued, perhaps not even noticing that the clerk had nodded. "You were the one who needed a Problem Specialist to *jump-start* your car because the battery died! See, the thing is, only one of the Problem Specialists has a car, and we haven't been able to get a hold of her since she went off with a client to stake out a suspected pen thief."

"Look, don't worry about me," the clerk muttered. "I'm

just going to go."

The guy nodded.

"Wait!" a woman's voice shouted, cutting through the discordant voices in the room and directly into the clerk's ears.

The clerk turned his head to see a woman hopping down a rope ladder from the far corner of the room. She nimbly landed on the ground and took several long strides, slightly shifting her body to maneuver around a portly woman, and stood before the clerk with her shoulders held high. She had long dark hair and skin like coffee. In fact, the clerk thought she smelled like coffee, which he considered a good thing. She held out her hand. "I'm the problem specialty officer here," she said as they shook.

"Oh," the clerk muttered.

An annoyed look flashed across her eyes. "It means I'm in charge of this area. I run the Problem Department. I supervise the problem specialists. And of course, I'm an expert problem solver, if I can say that ever so humbly."

"Oh," the clerk managed once more. He was filled with a serious regret that he had come to this place and his stomach had started to churn and feel nauseous. The chaos of everyone shouting and running around was filling him with anxiety, and he figured it'd be peaceful enough to just zip down to the basement and push his stupid wheelbarrow around in the caverns—assuming he didn't get eaten by a wild animal, that is.

The woman's shoulders seemed to drop at the clerk's reaction, but she retook her proud posture and tried another route. "I'm sorry that we weren't more attentive to your problem upon your first arrival in the Problem Department." She shot a sidelong glance at the shaggy-haired guy, who had already wandered to the other side of the room. "We only have interns instead of proper receptionists, and you know how interns can be."

The clerk remembered the intern handing him a jumbled ball of what was supposed to be a document in the 2nd Street Ave Building—the document that his betrothed had ended up completing for him. "Actually, yes. I do. It can be quite frustrating when they don't perform a proper job."

"Did my intern at least help you to complete the necessary paperwork?"

"Uh, nope," the clerk said, not knowing about any paperwork.

The woman sighed, visibly frustrated. "If you'll just come right this way and have a seat," she said in a peppy tone that contrasted with her arched eyebrows, "This should only take you a moment." She sat him at a table with a pen and a sheet of paper. "It's best if you can complete the whole thing, but the starred lines are absolutely required."

The clerk glanced at the form. It was printed in tiny font and there were a lot of questions crammed into it. "My answers can't be used in anything related to my performance review, can they?" the clerk asked.

"No, this is just for our records," she said. The clerk glanced at a nearby leaning tower of papers, wondering how accurate those records could be. "Please take your time and fill out the form. I'll be right over here, so just let me know when you've completed everything."

"Okay," the clerk muttered, reaching into his satchel for a pen. He bent over the form, just barely making out the tiny text for "Name" and "Employee Identification Number." He tried to write in tiny, boxy print letters so that the form would be neat, but there was such little space in which to fit any words that all of the ink seemed to be running together into an indecipherable blur. When he was down on the next line and had to write in his title and department, he went back to put a clear cross on a letter, and that seemed to blot the whole word into sludge.

"Hey," a voice came from behind him. He shot up, his spine cracking as he straightened back into a normal sitting position. It was the intern, but the clerk didn't say anything; he just looked at him. "My boss says I have to make a photocopy of your ID card. We have to make sure everyone we assist actually works here."

The clerk didn't see why they should have to do that since the security was so tight to get into this building in the first place, but he was feeling so exhausted that using any energy to speak more than was absolutely necessary didn't seem like the best idea. He fished the card out of his wallet, handed it to the intern, and hunched back over the document. He had difficulty concentrating on answering the questions that came on the next lines. His fingers were hurt and cramping from attempting to write such tiny letters, and he could feel an ache pulsating through his entire body, particularly in his head and joints. As he sat up for a moment, he realized that the conversation that was closest to his ear—the one that was actually disturbing him the most—was coming from the so-called problem specialty officer, who was having an animated conversation in the island language with a hefty fellow. The clerk hunched back over the paper, but before long, he gave it up, shuffled out of the seat, and shoved the paper in the direction of the woman.

"Oh, all finished?" she said.

"Yeah," the clerk said.

"Let's get started then. What seems—"

"Can I have my ID back? Before I forget?"

"Your ID?"

"My government issued identification card," the clerk

uttered through gritted teeth.

"Yes—right, right—of course. Uh, where is it?"

The clerk's face was incredulous. He looked around the room and found the shaggy-haired guy sitting at a desk creating a pyramid with post-it notes and paperclips. The clerk pointed at him, and followed the woman as she walked over to him.

"This gentleman needs his identification card back," she said.

"I gave it back to him," the intern said.

"No," the clerk said.

"I could have sworn I gave it back to you, man," the intern said, a defiant look on his face.

"Where is your copy machine?" the clerk asked.

"It's over there," the woman said, pointing to a desk in the corner of the room. The clerk walked over to the desk and looked all over the top of it, but he didn't see anything related to his identification card or a copy machine. He glanced under the desk and noticed there were all kinds of junk and compartments down there. He knelt down onto hands and knees and crawled underneath the desk. Someone had carved out an insane amount of elaborate shelves into the desk. There was a water cooler, bottles of hand sanitizer, a paper shredder, some sort of plastic melting machine, a dollhouse—which required the clerk to take a moment to extract the little black mouse from his pocket and allow it to run around in the tiny house as he took much amusement at the fact that the furniture and kitchen appliances seemed like the perfect size for the mouse to use—assorted other personal affects that didn't seem like they belonged in an office—which the clerk did his best to avoid touching—and finally, squeezed into the far corner, a copy machine. He crawled over to it. He could barely get the lid open the way it was jammed into the close-fitting space, but he found his card inside. He also found the paper copy of his ID in the tray. He started to back up and immediately hit his head on a corner, causing him to cry out in pain.

"Are you okay down there?" the problem specialty officer asked.

"Yeah. Fine," the clerk mumbled a few moments later, after he'd managed to crawl backward and extract himself from the escritoire. He looked down and saw that his nice work clothes were completely covered in dust and grime. He patted at them a bit, but it didn't help anything. "Here," he said, shoving the copy of his identification card at the woman.

He couldn't help but realize that since he'd been here, not only had his headache become worse, and not only had his problem not yet even been discussed—let alone solved, or at least progressed toward solving—but a *new* problem had been created—the loss of his identification card—which he'd had to solve himself, and in the process he had solved a problem for these alleged problem specialists by giving them the photocopy of his identification card and thus ensuring that the documentation about his visit was properly completed.

"So what problem can we help you with today?" the woman asked.

The clerk thought for a moment, wincing and rubbing his forehead. "Is there someplace quieter we could speak?"

"Of course. Right this way." She strode to the exit, holding the door for the clerk. She paused in the hallway, but before she spoke, a fruity cloud of water vapor wafted between them, so she continued walking, holding the door for the clerk as they entered the stairwell.

"So what can I assist you with today?" Her voice echoed

in a place that was concrete and unfinished, as if they'd travelled behind the scenes of a play.

"It's about my—"

Before the clerk could continue, the door burst open, bringing two men and a cloud of tropical water vapor. "—And then that son of a bitch has the nerve to say that no one told him to keep records back ten years! No one told you? Are you kidding me!"

"Did he really think that was going to save him?" the other man shouted, bursting into laughter and clapping his abettor on the shoulder.

With another wince from the clerk, the problem specialty officer said, "Let's just continue this down a couple of flights." The clerk was shambling behind her as she went down several flights of stairs—many more than the clerk thought was necessary. Just as he was about to voice a complaint, his toe got stuck on the edge of a stair and he went tumbling down. With precipitate reflexes, the woman whirled around and grabbed the clerk mid-fall, hoisting him up by the underarms with her muscular grip—he started to cry out in pain as her powerful fingers dug into the sore under his armpit—and depositing him safely to the ground. His legs immediately buckled and he became like a puddle in the cement, wheezing with his eyes wide. "What happened? Are you okay?"

The clerk nodded. "Fine. Fine," he rasped. "I wanted—" he continued at a whisper. She leaned in close to hear him. "I wanted to discuss my shift manager."

"She's your supervisor?"

"No, I don't think so," he continued to murmur. "I've been assigned to temporarily help out in the area where she is."

"So she's your temporary supervisor?"

The clerk made a dissenting noise in his throat. "Occasionally she tells me something to do, but there's a shift supervisor there, and he tells me what to do a lot."

"Okay. So what's the problem with this shift manager?"

"She keeps asking me a lot of—" the clerk took a deep breath and then said in an even softer voice, "—philosophical questions."

"And how does it make you feel when she asks you these questions?" the woman said with a serious expression on her face, leaning in closer still to the clerk so that he could feel her breath on his cheek.

"It doesn't matter how I feel when she talks to me," the clerk responded, thinking that he felt pretty uncomfortable at those times as well as right now. "What matters is that I think she's a—well—I think she's a—philosopher."

"In what way?" the problem specialty officer asked.

The clerk's eyes were wide. "I've said too much!" he shouted, pushing on the woman as he attempted to get up. His push didn't move her, but once she saw that he was agitated, she rose and stepped back. He scrambled to his feet and started to hobble down the stairs, grasping at the handrail.

"Sir!" she shouted after him. "Please give me more time to discern the issue you're working with!"

The clerk kept moving.

"Don't you want to at least—" She stopped shouting at this moment, and, glancing over her shoulder to make sure that no one was around, switched to a quiet voice, "—complete a brief evaluation report about our services?" She looked down the stairs the way the clerk had run. "No?" she whispered with a smile, shrugging to herself. "Well, I *did* ask him."

The clerk could see her heading back up in the direction of the Problem Department as he took the stairs one by one.

At the landing, he shoved the door open and found himself in a long hallway that had several beds arrayed in a circle in the middle of it. There was a man in a cerulean bathrobe friendly waving his arms in the air as three billy goats hopped from bed to bed, occasionally letting out a bleat.

The clerk's eyes went wide and he quickly turned away, finding the spot to summon the elevator on the wall. The elevator arrived shortly, but as he stepped in and turned back toward the hallway, he realized that one of the billy goats was running full speed down the hallway straight at him. "Oh no!" he shouted, wondering if billy goats ate mice. He slammed on the zero button several times, four zeroes lighting up on the LCD display. The doors closed as the goat's triangular horns were disturbingly close to the clerk's vision. He knelt and sat back onto the ground, awaiting his arrival in the Shipping and Receiving Department.

* * * *

The night of the dinner party arrived, and the clerk found himself standing with his betrothed at the stone staircase of a massive old apartment building, the flourishes and ornate details of a past era's architecture adorned the building, and as the clerk squinted up at it, he thought he could make out gargoyles peering down at him from the upper echelons.

His betrothed led the way ascending the stairs. He remained behind, staring down the street where cars and busses were stopped at a five-way intersection.

"Aren't you coming, dear?"

"Yeah," he grunted, sprinting up the steps behind her, feeling the ache in his shins.

She hit the button for a buzzer, and they waited for a moment, but nothing happened. She tried the huge glass door and it opened, so they slipped in. The foyer was lavish with red carpets, golden trim, little tables with vases and plants, and a pair of elevators. Before they reached them, a stern voice from behind said, "Can I help you?"

They whirled to see a tall woman dressed in a stiff black and white tuxedo, complete with bowtie.

"We're here for the dinner party," the clerk's betrothed responded.

"Oh my," the woman said. "You're quite late."

"Really?" She turned to the clerk. "You said it started at nine."

The clerk shrugged.

"No matter. Right this way," the woman said, summoning the lift and inviting them to enter.

"A lot of people must live here. This is quite a building. I didn't realize such buildings still existed downtown. I thought it was all new construction."

"Well there aren't many like this ma'am. But don't you know? This is the nomarch's mansion. Only she and her family live here."

"Oh, I'm sorry. This is our first time here. It's great to see behind the scenes of a public servant's life." She shot the clerk a quizzical look. He shrugged.

They exited on the 25th floor and followed the butler (the clerk supposed) down the hall. She pushed open oaken double-doors, and held them for their entrance into a grand ballroom. The first thing that caught the clerk's eye was a crystal chandelier—larger in size than a whole bus—that took up the expansive ceiling and glittered like a field of stars. There were balconies filled with orchestras and choirs. Many people were dancing in the center of the room, but there were also tables with food and people milling about all over the place. The clerk shrunk back toward the hallway, but his betrothed looped her arm through his and pulled him forward. "I'm sure the nomarch is still making her rounds.

She'll greet you in due time," the butler said. "In the meantime, please feel free to help yourself to something to eat. The tables are all arrayed over there."

"Thank you very much," his betrothed said, walking them in the way the butler had indicated. She whispered to the clerk, "You didn't tell me this was a party at the nomarch's house!"

"I didn't know."

"Your shift manager is the city's nomarch?"

"I don't think so," the clerk muttered. "Maybe we should just get out of here."

"Are you kidding? I want to dance. C'mon. Let's dance."

The clerk didn't want to, but he didn't protest. He fumbled through a few songs. His betrothed pulled him this way and that, and he did his best to imitate her, only stepping on her a couple of times, and bumping into another group of dancers only once.

"Mind if I cut in?" asked a woman with vibrant green eyes that matched her dress.

"Uh," the clerk uttered. He thought that his betrothed shared a meaningful look with the woman. "Sure," he muttered. The other woman wrapped her arms around his betrothed and whisked her away in a fast-paced dance.

The clerk shuffled away from the dance floor to find some food since he hadn't yet had any dinner. He passed by a few tables that were piled high with meats and found a table with cheese, crackers, raw vegetables, and various spreads. He immediately took two pieces of cheese and put one on his dish and the other in his jacket pocket.

"*Psst!* Pass some cheese down here."

"Huh?" the clerk muttered, looking around.

"Under the tablecloth. Be discrete."

The clerk finished piling some cheese on the small dish.

"Cheese is one of those moral gray areas," the woman's voice under the table whispered. "I decided it would be okay to serve it at my party though. See, I don't know the specific details about how this cheese was procured, and it's unfortunate the animals were probably mistreated. However, it is not outside the realm of possibility for cheese to be made in an environment that is entirely pleasant for the animals involved, and you don't have to kill them to make cheese, of course. So in an ideal scenario, while meat would never be permissive for pleasurable eating—a utilitarian perspective, you know?—the suffering and deaths of all those animals— dairy products would be okay in an ideal scenario."

The clerk slipped the dish, now piled high with white and yellow squares of cheese, underneath the tablecloth. He caught a glimpse of the woman crouching down there. It was his shift manager.

"Why are you under the table?" he whispered.

"A more pressing question would be why are you—who are clearly an uninvited guest—out in the open?"

"You invited me," he whispered down in the direction of the table while he piled vegetables onto a new plate.

"Yeah, invited you to *my* party."

"Isn't this your party?"

"Would I be hiding under the table at my own party?"

"Uh."

"That's really what you think of me, isn't it? You think I'm so weird that I would just be hiding underneath the table and greeting my guests like this as a mere eccentricity."

"No. Well, I—"

"I'll take that too," she said, reaching an arm up from beneath the table and taking the veggies away from the clerk before he could even eat one. His stomach grumbled as he grabbed a third dish, and he used tongs to pile up random food. He put down the tongs and grabbed a piece of cheese to eat. His shift manager slipped the dish out of his hand, and before he could get the cheese to his mouth, he realized the little black mouse had scampered down his jacket sleeve, climbed onto his hand to snatch the cheese, and retreated back down the sleeve. The clerk grunted in frustration.

"Don't worry," his shift manager said. "You'll have plenty to eat at my party, which, if you'll recall, my good sir, starts at ten p.m. sharp."

"Ugh," the clerk muttered.

"Now do me a solid and pass down the whole platter of vegetables," she whispered.

"How am I supposed to do that?"

"There's no one right next to you. Just do it right quick."

"Ugh," the clerk groaned as he complied.

She passed back the large platter, which was now empty.

"Excuse me, sir," a voice said behind him. "I'll take that. I see we need more vegetables." The waiter took the platter and added it to the cart he was pushing, which had other empty plates and glasses.

"Is that enough?" the clerk whispered to the table once the waiter had left. There was no response for a while as the clerk piled cheese and crackers into his mouth. Crumbs fell out of the corners of his mouth as he chewed. He lifted the tablecloth and glanced under the table. His shift manager was gone.

"What are you doing?"

As the clerk turned around, he said, "What?" in response, but it was poorly enunciated due to the large amount of cracker crumbs and partially masticated cheese occupying his mouth.

"Chew with your mouth closed!" his betrothed scolded. "You're not a little kid. And why are you poking around under tables and such?"

"We have to get out of here," the clerk said, coughing a bit. He took the fluted glass out of his betrothed's hand and drank the rest of it. He coughed more at the foul-tasting alcohol.

"We just got here! I haven't even had anything to eat. We're not going anywhere."

"Yeah, but see," he whispered. "We're at the wrong party."

"Wrong party? You said this was the address."

"Hmm—I did, didn't I?"

"So why do you say it's the wrong party?"

"Because I just talked to my shift manager and she said as much."

"Why would she be at the wrong party instead of at her own party?"

"She said her party starts at ten."

"Ten? You said nine. And where is this supposed other party?"

"I don't know."

"Well ask her."

"I don't know where she went. She was under the table a minute ago."

His betrothed narrowed her eyebrows. "Look. Just forget about the whole thing. We're at a nice party now. Let's get some real food."

The clerk didn't like the scenario he found himself in as he shuffled behind his betrothed. He sent furtive glances around the room, wondering who all of these people were, when he recognized a hulking man engaged in serious conversation near a fireplace at the end of the dance floor.

"Hey!" he whispered, grabbing his betrothed's bare shoulder. "That's the director."

"Huh? Where?"

"Don't look! Over by the fireplace. Let's get out of here."

"Don't be ridiculous. If he's here, you should be here too. C'mon, let's go say hi to him. You can introduce me."

"Oh, I don't think that's a good idea."

"Well, how do you think he'll take it if you just ignore him."

"Let's get out of here."

"We're staying, and you're not going to pull a social *faux pas* and ignore him."

Her hand was pressing into the small of his back, pushing him in the direction of the director. The clerk could see him, shaking his head as he responded to another guy in a three-piece suit. The director took a sip of clear liquid from a wine glass. The clerk tried to back up, but his betrothed put both hands behind him and shoved him forward. The director glanced in their direction and an expression passed across his face. The clerk thought that the director recognized him. The clerk raised his hand to wave and suddenly the director was gone.

"He left!" the clerk exclaimed. He tried to stop walking, but his betrothed was hunched over, shoving him forward.

"I'm not falling for that."

"Look!"

She stopped shoving and saw that now there were only a few confused people and a broken glass of spilled liquid on the marble floor.

"Where could he have gone?" his betrothed asked, looking all over the room.

The clerk looked toward the door to leave.

"There!" his betrothed shouted, pointing. The director was crouching behind a waiter who was pushing a cart of drinks.

"I think he's trying to get away from me."

"Don't be ridiculous!" his betrothed said, grabbing him by the arm and rushing toward the director. A group of people danced in front of them, and when they whirled away, the director and the waiter were out of sight. "Now where did he go?" his betrothed asked, rushing them forward and scanning the room. "There!" she said, pointing at a spot further along the dance floor where the director was army-crawling between groups of dancers. "We've got him now," she said, trying to weave between people waltzing back and forth. "Ugh! Now where is he?"

"Uh. I think that's him," the clerk said, despite himself. There was a woman with a big fluffy dress walking toward the food, and the clerk was pretty sure that the black dress shoes sticking out from beneath her dress gave away the fact that the director was crawling along beneath her.

"He won't get away this time!" the clerk's betrothed shouted, dragging him off the dance floor. As they rushed along, the clerk suddenly shouted and fell down, the world going dark.

"Hush," his shift manager said. The clerk realized that she had pulled him beneath the cloth of a waiter's cart. "Now we've just got to collect your wife."

The clerk didn't bother to correct her. His betrothed was pretty much his wife anyway.

His shift manager was peeking out from beneath the cloth. The clerk could tell that they were wheeling along near where the food was set up.

"There she is. Closer. Closer. Almost got her. Yeah!" She scooped up his betrothed and deposited her next to the clerk, holding a hand over her mouth to keep her from screaming. "It's okay. I'm his boss. I invited you to my party."

"Huh? Where are we? What's going on?"

The clerk shrugged.

"We're on a first-class trip to a world-class kitchen, where we'll pick up some drinks and make our way to the real party. Pleased to meet you, my dear." His shift manager held up his betrothed's hand and kissed it.

His betrothed frowned. "Why was that guy running away from us?" she asked the clerk.

"I haven't the foggiest," he muttered.

"We're almost there," his shift manager whispered. "Stay low and follow me." She hopped out of the cart while it was still in motion, and they followed her, rolling out into the heat of a bustling kitchen. The clerk looked up at chefs and waitstaff rushing all around. Peering up at them from the ground, the clerk thought they looked like giants. He was in the back of this line, and he crawled behind the women, weaving between people's feet and sometimes cutting between counters and stacks of food supplies. People were shouting and there was the sound of pots and pans slamming about. They negotiated their way into a back room. It was quite cold, and the clerk realized it was some type of walk-in refrigerator. The shift manager was on her feet, throwing all sorts of bottles into a big sack that she then slung over her shoulder. "We're going to make a run for it," she announced. "Follow me to the back corner."

So they were running through the kitchen, and the clerk saw his shift manager shove someone out of the way, and a guy shouted, "Hey! Get out of my kitchen!" The shift manager hopped up into a little cubbyhole in the wall, and the clerk saw no choice but to force his way in with her. The three of them didn't quite fit—his leg was bent in an uncomfortable way—but suddenly they were sliding down through the wall.

They fell out in a pile with the clerk crumpled beneath the women. "Ah, almost there," the shift manager said as she stood up, surveying a hallway with deep green wallpaper.

"Where are we going?" his betrothed asked.

"To my humble abode, madam. To my dinner party."

They went down several flights of stairs, but in the middle of one section of stairs, the shift manager said, "It's through here," and she forced her sack of drinks through an opening between two stairs before shimmying in after them. The clerk helped his betrothed in, and then clambered in himself, sliding down some chute and landing in a cavern.

"My place is beneath the house proper," the shift manager said as she led the way, her voice echoing through the dark cave. "There's a series of caverns leading out of—or into—the basement. I think it was used for smuggling in olden times."

"And the nomarch lets you stay down here?" his betrothed asked.

"In a manner of speaking," his shift manager said, laughing.

The clerk figured it was dark enough to hold the mouse in his hands and pet it as he followed behind the two women, not paying much attention to their small talk. "Everything fine with you, Ellem?" he asked as he scratched the mouse under its tiny chin.

Lights were strung up at the end of this passageway, and it opened into a larger area where people were milling about. "Drinks are served!" the shift manager said, holding up the big sack. The clerk recognized some of the other clerks he worked with, but there were a lot of people he didn't know.

The clerk was sitting on the cold ground, wanting to go home to bed. His betrothed walked over and handed him a plate of food, taking a seat on the ground next to him.

"Thanks!" the clerk said. "I'm so hungry."

"Me too," his betrothed said between mouthfuls of *hors devours*. "I would have been back sooner, but I got to talking with your manager. She's really interesting! She was telling me all these cool ideas she has."

"She's not my real manager," the clerk muttered.

His betrothed went on as if he hadn't said that. "She has all these ideas about how we could create a worldwide bureaucracy as the ultimate society with a perfect balance. She said that all the chaos we suffer now is due to change, but once we resolve that, the unchanging society would be the end of history as we know it, and the start of a utopian society that doesn't change. You know, because it's achieved balance. Perfection."

"Wouldn't an unchanging society be inherently bad? I don't think that could be a utopia."

"Perhaps I just explained it wrong. It was a really interesting conversation. She was asking me all these questions about my thoughts and beliefs. I really had to think."

The clerk just chewed his food. At some point, his betrothed got up to get them colas and came back.

"Hey guys," the shift manager said, taking a seat. "Whatcha talking about?"

"Nothing," the clerk grumbled.

"I was really interested in your ideas about creating a utopia," his betrothed said.

"Oh really?" the shift manager said, flashing a shy smile. "I'm glad. Thanks for saying so. I think it's really important that we try to better our world. And I mean, here, we have a pretty good life, even if there are a lot of the less fortunate who have a much harder life, and we give up all of our privacy. But to support the wealth of our country, a lot of terrible things are done to the less fortunate of other countries—and I'm not just talking about children making our stuff—that kind of thing. What's really terrible are the wars waged in our names. We're led to believe that these faceless aggressors hate us and want us dead, but if they hate us, it's only because we've occupied their country for years and killed their loved ones. We have an incredibly advanced military, and we're fighting guys who are lucky if they can even get their hands on real weapons, but we're supposed to believe that they are a constant, credible threat to us here at home. We bomb them with robot planes that they can't shoot down, and for all that robotic targeting, it's not as accurate at the government would lead you to believe. They kill a lot of civilians, but they downplay that. Downplay is an understatement."

The clerk took a sip of his cola.

"You sure know a lot about foreign policy," his betrothed said.

"Nah, I know more about philosophy. But it's philosophy that could repair the damage done to our world. We just have to act on it."

"How did you learn all this?"

"Oh, learn?" The shift manager laughed. She fluttered her sparse eyelashes in a way that made her seem shy, yet the twitching corners of her mouth showed that she was excited to talk about herself. "I suppose learning's been a whole big lifelong process. I mean, I don't wanna give you my whole life story, but see, when I was a kid, my biological parents died during a trip overseas. Yeah, it's sad, but I don't really remember them. My paternal aunt stepped in to take care of me and my brother, but my brother was older and he ran away from home and none of us ever saw him again. So then they deemed my aunt unfit to raise children and sent me to an orphanage, and I got adopted by this philosopher. But see, she didn't tell them she was a philosopher or anything. She presented herself as a dealer of rare books—which she was, that's how she'd amassed most of her money. She knew what to buy, what to sell—the whole bit. So, you see, I was suspicious of her at first, but very impressionable, and I eventually came to look up to her. I can't tell you for sure why she adopted me, but I can present to you my two leading theories. Both are for philosophical reasons, of course, but that goes without saying, if you knew her. The first is that she chose to adopt a child for utilitarian reasons. Here she was, alone with more than enough food, shelter, and money for herself, so it would be part of the greater good for her to adopt and raise an orphan who would be in otherwise unfortunate circumstances. The second is that she believed she could acquire a child at just the right age to mold her mind into the perfect philosopher. A better philosopher than even herself because of starting so young and being shaped in just the right way. You see, my mum was on the bleeding edge of the underground philosophical movements at the time, and before long, she took me overseas—the whole adoption process was very much more laissez faire back in those days—and back then, philosophers were running with some pretty seedy crowds. By no means was it the first time philosophers engaged in subversive political action, but it was the most violent—and of course, I mean violent in the philosophical sense of 'extremely disruptive'—not blood and guts. Most people would tell you it was no place for a kid, but I wouldn't be the woman I am today if it wasn't for my mum bringing me along—militia meetings, army meetings—I can't tell you how many times my mum and her team of philosophers were granted audiences with kings, queens, emperors, sultans—and of course, their enemies—princes in exile, ex-military factions plotting revenge— To bring new thoughts into the world is—well—"

The clerk leaned his head back and looked up at the craggy ceiling. His betrothed leaned forward, eyes wide. "Well?"

"Well, the trouble came when my mum's team hooked up with some known saboteurs. These were some dangerous guys, and they had been involved in some real violent acts— violent in the sense of blood and guts—attempted coups— You know how it is. There are many countries where the ancient struggle over who is entitled to what land still goes on to this very day, and it's generations upon generations of revenge acts that still fuel it—Son A today has to kill Father Y because Father Y killed Father A and Father A's ghost said to Son A, you must avenge me and lead our people to victory—but this is ignoring the fact that Grandfather A killed Grandfather Y and Son Y, but they'd only done it because of earlier familial killings at the hands of the A family, etc. etc.—expanded to warring clans, warring countries, land that was promised by gods who never show up, the only godlike presence ever showing up being the unbelievable firepower of the world's largest militaries that have arrived to claim what resources they can steal amid the chaos, or even just to use the chaos as an excuse to intervene, which means they can charge money for building the expensive war machines, and they line their pockets—!"

The shift manager had jumped up, shaking her fists in the air, her hair whirling around behind her like a fallen manila folder of loose-leaf paper. Her face shifted to apologetic. "I uh, don't mean to rant." She plopped herself back down on the ground. "Suffice it to say, a deal was hashed out with the saboteurs, but no one was to be hurt—my mum's team just needed their connections and knowhow, but there was a mole, and well." Now a battle was struggling across the shift manager's lips and eyebrows, one side for stern stoicism and the other for tearful remembrance. "I don't know exactly what happened, but I was left with a friend at the scriptorium, and I never saw my mum or her team again, and, well, I followed the path of texts to my current position."

The clerk glanced at his betrothed's rapt expression. "What an incredible story," she started. "I'd love to find out more about that path of texts—"

The clerk jumped to his feet. "Well, thanks so much for inviting us. We had a great time, but it's best we get going."

"So soon?" his shift manager asked, shaking her head in an effort to return her face to its normal features.

"Yes, yes. It's getting late," the clerk said, helping his betrothed to her feet.

"Let me walk you out," his shift manager said. She walked them down a series of winding tunnels that became increasingly dark. "Okay, you just follow this stairway up to the surface and then you'll be out on the street. Thanks again for coming. It was great to talk to you. If you'd like to discuss more philosophy and foreign policy, we meet here every third Saturday night. You're always welcome."

"Yeah, yeah," the clerk muttered, already ascending the stairs.

"I can't thank you enough for having us," his betrothed said. "And thank you for the future invitations. I would love to engage in further discussions." The women hugged and pecked each other on the cheek.

"Why'd you rush us out of there?" she asked the clerk as she joined him on the sidewalk, heading in the direction of the five-way intersection. "I was having a good time."

"Did you hear that propaganda she was spouting?" the clerk asked. "My worst suspicions are confirmed. She's a *philosopher.*"

"So what? That's not against the law."

"It is when they start blowing up buildings!"

"Huh?"

"Look, I just don't think we should get involved with her. It's too dangerous."

"Sometimes the life worth living involves taking a few risks."

"Hey, I take risks every day. It's not easy to make a living."

"Sure. Okay."

"Look, she's a *philosopher* anyway. She probably made all of that stuff up to try to alter our thinking and make us do something in some scheme."

His betrothed's reply was interrupted by a shadowed form emerging from the pile of detritus lining an alley.

"Why good evening sir and madam," the street person in ragged clothes called out in an amiable tone. "Sir, you are so finely dressed tonight, and clearly out on the town with your lady friend that I won't take up much of your time except for to inquire as to if you'll be making your campaign promise this very night."

"Uh."

"What promise?" his betrothed asked, her eyes darting from the clerk to the homeless man.

"I, uh. Well, I guess I told him I'd give him some spare change."

"Well then give him some."

The clerk made a show of reaching into his pockets and thrusting his hands about to demonstrate that no jangling of change was to be heard. "Sorry, I don't have any."

"Oh sir, I'm sorry," his betrothed said to the man. "Unfortunately, I don't have any pockets in this dress, so I didn't bring anything with me."

"Fear not, madam. I won't take up any more of your evening. I am sure that your lovely husband will keep you informed about the campaign he has agreed to sponsor, which is of course a campaign of the utmost importance for the future of our nation."

"We're not married," she blurted.

"My apologies, ma'am. And my apologies once again if I was at all discourteous in interrupting your intimate night out on the town. Please do enjoy yourselves and get home safely," the hobo said as he shifted back into the shadows.

"Do you know about this campaign he's going on about?" she asked as they approached an intersection.

The clerk shrugged.

Their walk home became silent save the hum of traffic in the distance.

* * * *

"Look, I don't see what could possibly be so confusing about the caverns," the grumpy transaction processor said to the clerk. "The layout is very simple. In fact, I think I have an old diagram in the office. Hold up for a minute; I'll be right back." The clerk's eyes shot around as he sat near the messy pile of papers on the desk. At every movement in the hall, he thought he saw the shift supervisor, but it was always just another clerk going by.

"Here we go, guv," the transaction processor said, throwing down a big tattered paper on top of the other papers on the desk. It was filled with creases where it had been folded and refolded again, and the thing was tattered, with a few rectangles that had fallen out. "You see. This is where we are now," he pointed. "This here's the lifts."

The clerk rubbed his chin, puzzling over the diagram as he hunched over it. It was basically a figure eight with two different tunnels crisscrossing the shape. "There's no way it's that straightforward in there," the clerk argued. "I've been lost in there, and there's all sorts of dead-end tunnels."

The processor was already crumpling up the diagram, re-forcing it to fold into rectangles before the clerk could scrutinize it further.

"If you'll excuse me, some of us have packages to process."

Feeling exhausted, but knowing he still had to finish delivering those packages and catch up on a couple of the top priority projects from his real job, the clerk decided that he would help himself to a sweetened cup of coffee in the shift manager's break room.

"They're abandoned show dogs," one of the clerks was saying as the clerk took a sip of the hot coffee and decided to stir in some more fixings. "I have a friend who works in the industry. You know, they do the whole beauty contest thing for dogs? When the dogs lose or they're not up to standard, the people abandon them down here in these tunnels. I mean, I don't think they specifically mean them to be in this mailroom area, but these tunnels branch all throughout the city. They're from back before the era of the great fire, when they rebuilt the city on top of the ruins. The dogs eventually wander over to our area."

"I've gotten a good look at those beasts a couple of times. They're no fancy show dogs," one of the other clerks interjected.

The clerk glanced up at the shift manager's workstation, wondering if she was listening to any of this. He could only see the back of her head.

"No, they are though! Don't you get it? They may start out pretty, but when they're forced to fend for themselves, they form packs, become feral—their fur gets all messy because there's no one to comb and shampoo them anymore."

"Yeah, I think he's right," another clerk interjected. "I caught a good look at one the other day, and I could've sworn I'd seen that beast before. I think it was on the telly—in that advertisement where the guy refills his bottle of water in the loo. Remember that one? A few years back it was on nonstop, and that dog looked like that dog, just older, you know?"

The conversation was cut short as everyone looked toward the doorway, where they could hear a lot of people stomping through the cavern.

The clerk could see a whole group of soldiers rushing through the tunnels in their direction. They were wearing big, sturdy helmets, green military fatigues bulging with pouches for extra equipment, thick combat boots, and each held some sort of long machine gun in both hands as they ran.

"Freeze! Nobody move!" the first soldier to burst into the break room shouted. The clerks all looked terrified.

All of the soldiers rushed through the center of the room and two of them burst into the shift manager's workstation. "Hands up where we can see them!" a soldier yelled. All of the soldiers had their guns pointed at the shift manager.

The clerk was peering through the soldiers, trying to see what was happening. Two soldiers holding onto a woman were walking back toward the entrance. Her hands were clearly strapped behind her back, and they had a firm grip on her as they led her back toward the entrance. The clerk got a clear look at the woman as they passed him, and he was positive that it was not the shift manager. This woman's hair wasn't even the right color—it was a sandy blonde—and he could have sworn it was one of the girls who worked at the bowling alley.

The clerk realized that the director, his manager, and the shift supervisor, among other high-ranking officials, were awaiting the soldiers in the caverns. When the soldiers were near, the shift supervisor shouted, "That's not her! That sure as hell is not her!"

"What do you mean it's not her?" the director demanded.

"It's not her! It's not the supposed shift manager!" the shift supervisor replied.

One of the soldiers took out a communication device and started shouting into it, "TE to FD—we are on Code X—repeat we are on Code X. Lock down everything!"

The soldiers all started running back toward the exit to the caverns, save one who stayed behind at the entrance to the break room, and the officials followed not far behind. The clerk noticed that they'd taken the woman with the sandy blonde hair along as well.

The clerks were all wide-eyed, making faces at one another but not sure if they should speak.

* * * *

The staff were all corralled in the area near the front Shipping and Receiving office. The soldier had eventually led them over there, and everyone was waiting for some news. The clerk didn't engage in any of the wild speculation that was going on, being content to sit on the cold, stone ground and pet the mouse through his jacket.

It was a long time of anxious waiting that was finally broken when everyone realized that the elevator was coming down. The doors opened and the clerk was surprised to see that his manager was the only person to walk through the doors. He jumped to his feet to meet her.

"Everyone," she said, raising one hand to quiet the crowd. "I'm the manager of communication security. You are all to return to your official posts. Transaction processors should remain here and await instruction from your shift supervisor. Clerks, return to your departments and report to your supervisors. Your time in the Shipping and Receiving Department is over."

Since she was his supervisor, the clerk followed her, and as they walked toward the front entrance on the first floor, she said, "I've arranged a car to take us back to the small city."

The clerk thought it was fancy—an all-black sedan with tinted windows. He sat in the back with his manager, who sighed and looked exhausted. "I'm sure you're curious about what happened," she said.

"Uh huh," the clerk responded.

"Well, you know the shift manager in the Shipping and Receiving Department?" she said.

"Yes, of course."

"She wasn't a real employee. She didn't even actually work here!"

"What?!"

"She was a spy—a saboteur—a philosopher! She in-filtrated this organization. Got her hands on fake security clearance—acted like she belonged. Took over that whole downstairs operation."

"Wow," the clerk said.

"And you know what the worst part is?" his manager asked.

The clerk started to answer, but it had been a rhetorical question.

"We didn't catch her. She got away. Somehow, she must have known her secret was blown. The soldiers grabbed an innocent administrative assistant. We tried to lock down the building, but we could see on the security camera that she had already made her escape."

"Wow," the clerk said.

"The director thinks we're in the clear now, but I don't

know. If she managed to infiltrate us for that long, I'm worried there could be others."

"The director doesn't think so?"

"No. She was a known radical. He says she pulled this operation off on her own, hoping to build followers over time. He said she was a philosopher queen. He thinks it's like taking out a beehive—with no queen, the whole thing falls apart. But I don't know—I'm not so sure—I'm nervous. I'm going to suggest a full review of all our security protocols."

His manager leaned her chin on her hand and looked out the window. She sighed and became silent for the rest of the trip.

* * * *

The clerk would have preferred to spend the day in his cubicle, just catching up on his work and performing his usual tasks, but he hadn't heard any word from the director. He didn't have to go back to the Shipping and Receiving Department, but he still had to go back to the main office for the director's secret mission.

The clerk lost track of time as he went through the routine of work and collecting numbers to add to the spreadsheet. Between moments of pandemonium, the clerk had the occasional silent bus ride to contemplate whatever stray thoughts entered his mind. Most of them were about work, but increasingly, memories of the time before he'd come to live in this part of the province slipped in. As a boy, he'd grown up on a farm with his parents. They were still there, living out their lives in the quiet monotony of farm chores. Thinking upon it now, he felt a mixture of nostalgia to go back, and relief not to be there anymore. He suspected that his father always wanted him to take over the family farm, but he wasn't made to be a farmer. He was always screwing up his chores or cutting corners, and his father was always stern, yet forgiving, but the clerk could see into his eyes and sense the sorrow and disappointment that his father's farm, which he'd inherited from his own father, who'd inherited it from his father's father before him—all the way back to the time of the first settlers—would be passed down to this sorry excuse for a farmer, who would let it fall into a state of disrepair. On the other hand, the clerk sensed that his mother didn't want him to become a farmer, but wanted him to grow up and become "successful," which was why she seemed so disappointed that he received such poor marks in school. Yet how did she expect the clerk to do well in school, that place of endless torments? The girls laughed at him, the boys bullied him every chance they got, especially in sports, which they all loved, and the clerk loathed. Every game was an excuse to trip him and shove him. When, by chance, he began correspondence with a young girl from a distant city, he finally thought he found someone else whose mind was similar to his, and he thought that perhaps the city would be a place of like-minded individuals, unlike this land of farmhands and tradesmen.

The clerk leaned his head back on the seat of the bus and sighed. The vibration of the wheels jostled his brain and rattled his teeth. He opened his satchel of envelopes and important documents to remove a thermos of coffee that had been prepared for him by his betrothed. The refreshing warmth of the liquid swirling in his mouth reminded him of her tongue in a moment of passion.

The smile faded from his mouth when he remembered his final days back on the farm. He took the little black mouse from his pocket and gazed into its tiny sparkles of eyes. His father had commanded him to slaughter a pig—a pig the clerk had secretly named Stephenson. The clerk had secret names for all the animals on the farm, and he talked to them when no one was around. The clerk knew this was a test of sorts, arranged by his father. If it was a chicken, maybe the clerk could have forced himself to do it, just to appease his father. But not Stephenson—he was so friendly and intelligent—the clerk thought all the pigs were as smart as human children, and to kill a pig or child was an awful thing to do. He often imagined a world that treated pigs with the respect afforded humans, and the pigs would grow to be just as smart, to develop their own pig society with accomplishments to rival that of humanity. No, the clerk couldn't go through with it. He'd taken Stephenson out into the woods and set him free, knowing that he'd have at least a chance for survival, rather than let his trust lead to an axe in his throat.

He didn't tell his father what he'd done, but his father knew. "For goodness sake, he's a man grown! What are we going to do with him?" he heard his father say to his mother downstairs, more sorrow in his voice than anger.

When he announced that he was moving to a coastal city on the other side of the mountains, he thought at least his mother would be happy—that it was the kind of success she'd always wanted for him. But she wasn't happy. Apparently, her idea of success was only something like running a business in the village, something close to home. He thought of his younger sister, who had always been more suited to farming than he was. If he wasn't in the way, maybe his father would realize it was time to pass down the farm to a woman.

The clerk wrote his parents sometimes, but—He replaced the mouse to his pocket and wiped his face with his sleeve.

He glanced at the important documents and remembered what he was doing. He looked out the window and didn't recognize any of the surroundings. "Oh no! I've missed my stop!" He shouted "Next stop!" and then shook his head and corrected himself by shouting, "Next stop!" in the island language.

He got down on the sidewalk and started walking back the way he'd come. At the intersection, he looked at the street signs. "Wait a second—28th Street? Oh dear." He turned around and walked back in the direction the bus had been traveling. He hadn't missed his stop, he'd just failed to recognize his surroundings, so he was going to have to walk the rest of the way to the bigger city.

* * * *

The clerk shielded his eyes with his arm as he stepped out into the 195th floor, sand whipping into the pockets of his dress jacket. All around him, people were shouting in an unfamiliar language. He knew it wasn't the island language because the cadences were all wrong, and he could at least pick out some words from the island language, whereas he couldn't even discern where one word ended and another began in the vernacular these people were speaking. He chanced a glance from underneath his sleeve and saw that the people nearby were agitated and gathering up their sundries in preparation to take shelter from the sandstorm. Even though he couldn't understand them, he could tell that they were upset about the wind and the weather.

As the clerk moved away from the elevator and into the city streets, he found that on some blocks the buildings shielded him from most of the wind, although it was impossible to avoid entirely. Navigating the streets was difficult, but between the fact that the streets were numbered and he carried directions in his pocket, he couldn't get too lost.

After some time, tired, sweaty, and sandy, the clerk collapsed into the corner of an alley.

"Welcome, my brother," a deep voice said.

"Huh?" the clerk uttered. He saw that there was a woman sitting cross-legged next to him. She wore some kind of tattered headgear and a thick gray coat, despite the heat.

"Don't mind me," she said. "The fringes of society belong to us all. Make yourself at home."

"What are you doing here?" the clerk asked, wiping sweat from his brow.

"Oh, you know—nothing much. Loafing. Idling. Drifting." She made a noise in her throat. "You probably think it's best to have a job and work as much as possible, right?"

The clerk shrugged. "Yeah. You're supposed to work."

"That's what I used to think too. I mean, I was skeptical of it, but you know, how else are we going to keep society running? Yet as I've been sitting here, able to get some real thinking done with no expectations weighing down my spirit, I've realized just how good idleness is—I've been building up a sort of defense of loafing in my head—"

The clerk coughed a few times and gagged. "Do you have any water?" he asked the hobo woman. "I think I've got sand in my throat."

"Sure. No problem." She rifled through a plastic bag that was jam packed with miscellany. "Here you are," she said, handing the clerk a brown canteen.

He tipped his head back and took several long draughts. It was warm but refreshing. He wiped off his mouth with his sleeve, the sand scraping on his lips. Then he poured some water into the cap and offered it to the mouse.

The woman made a horrified expression when she saw the mouse lean out of his pocket, but she said, "Cute." She rubbed her hands together, eager to continue. "As I was saying, society's got us all convinced that everyone needs to get up every day and spend eight hours a day—and really isn't it more like ten or twelve these days?—toiling away at some inane job. Do you know how many people there are in society? They've really all got to do this? Leaving behind their whole life to waste it on another life that supposedly supports the original lost life? Do you follow my train of thought here?"

The clerk looked at her. He considered getting up and running away, but she had been nice enough to share her water with him, so he gave a vague nod.

"Don't you see that in this late age of civilization, we shouldn't be clinging to the outmoded mentality of the virtuousness of work? We're not all farming to sustain our very existence."

"Farmers," the clerk whispered.

"We're performing all sorts of uselessness. It should be our prerogative as a community to split up the necessary tasks smally and fairly, so that we share our leisure hours and distribute them amongst all. Leisure is in fact crucial for a civilization, but those tiny few and powerful at the top don't want us to know that. We have such a high level of productivity that, in fact, it would actually take a small number of people at work to keep all of society in relative comfort. Due to that fact, we could, say, reduce everyone's working hours to three per day, or maybe only a few longer days per week—but our present society with its outlandish worship of work would never allow this. Instead of cutting working hours in half for all, they would rather have anyone with a job be overworked, and those employees deemed redundant by the high productivity will be kicked out to the streets, where rather than finding any joy in leisure and idleness, they are made to feel failures who lost their means to survive. Now instead of being idle they must toil unpaid as they constantly beg for a new soul-destroying job. No one really likes to work, right? People always say they hate their jobs, if they're with friends, seemingly away from the prying eyes of their bosses—who can ever be sure in this age of unprecedented mass civilian spying?—so we can safely assume that work is unpleasant. And if work is necessary for the basics of existence, then everyone should work their own fair share—are you with me?"

"Huh?" the clerk muttered, taken by surprise that she'd addressed him in the middle of her monologue. He'd been pondering the existence of a cloud overhead. "Oh—yeah, right."

"Very good," she said with a beaming smile. "So it is only right to work enough for one's own necessities—it seems unfair not to—but by the same token, isn't it unjust to have to work more hours than is necessary, since we determined that no one really likes work?"

"Unjust?" the clerk thought with suspicion. *"That sounds like the kind of word a philosopher would use."* He squinted at the woman, trying to discern something in her face.

"Now, it is in fact not right at all that people should have such small amount of leisure time given the fact that so many of the best things in life happen in what we would determine leisure time," she continued, oblivious to the clerk's scrutinization. "But the present cult of work that controls our society would not like to admit this. Endless work is not what people will recall fondly, and in fact, people would do better 'work' if they had the free time to commit themselves to their passions instead of our endless struggle for survival. And I can just imagine the reactions of the pundits now, claiming that if people only had to work a few hours per day, they wouldn't know how to spend the rest of their time—a sad fact indeed if that turned out to be true. What happened to fun and joy? Why does everything have to be done for the

purpose of something else? Why this obsession with productivity at every second? I'd guess that many of the best
advances in society were thought up by those who had the
leisure time to have an idle mind to think them up—like I
said, just hanging out here recently has given me much more
time to think."

The clerk, fearing this all sounded far too much like philosophy, bluntly changed the subject: "Why don't you speak
a foreign tongue like the rest of them?"

"Huh? Oh, I'm not supposed to be here. I'm just hiding
out here. When I found out they were canning me before I
was supposed to know, I took off, hid out. Now I'm still in
hiding. I don't know if I've been officially fired yet— maybe not. Maybe I'll have a bunch of checks to collect if I'm
lucky—heh. But either way, I figure I can stay here on these
fake streets that are actually a government office, and maybe
after I've built up enough experience, I'll try my hand living
out on the actual streets. I can blend in with the actors here
well enough that I haven't been caught yet."

"Actors?"

"Yeah, they've recreated one of the cities on the other
side of the sea here. They want it to be authentic for the soldiers. See? Like them." She pointed.

The clerk squinted his eyes and he could see a group
of people in military fatigues carrying long machine guns.
They moved quickly through the street as people filtered
around them. "Oh. I hadn't noticed."

"Yeah, I noticed a lot just loafing here. And to be doing
nothing in this place of business—of great commerce. Because don't let them fool you, running a government is just
running a business on a larger scale—"

"Well, uh," the clerk shouted, jumping to his feet. He
knew he needed to interrupt her and get out of here before

she tried to corrupt him with more philosophy. "I need to get going. You know, there's work to be done—time is money and all that."

"Everything is money," the woman grumbled. "But perhaps soon we'll have a society where sacred things cannot be reduced to a monetary value."

"Right—yeah—of course," the clerk muttered as he backed away from her. He rushed down the street and rounded the corner.

He checked his directions and made sure he got to the right thoroughfare. Now he could just follow the ceramic plates on the buildings until he saw number 195 and he'd be there.

Pushing the glass and metal door open, he arrived in the office lobby. Sand was falling from his clothes as he walked up to the receptionist's desk.

"Here to see the chairman?"

"That's right."

"Let me just make sure he's available."

Before long, the clerk was escorted into the chairman's office. "Ah, there you are, my boy," the hefty man said, clasping the clerk on the back. "I've been waiting for you. I've got a big project for you to work on today."

"Big project?" The clerk muttered. "But I'm just supposed to collect my number."

"Yes, yes. There will be time for that later, but for now, there's something you need to take care of," the chairman said, idly rubbing his fat fingers over his mustache. The clerk worried that the whole thing would fall off, leaving the chairman in an embarrassing situation as he poked around under the desk trying to find the fallen mustache. "The crew in this building have been giving me trouble as of late. We're kind of isolated out here, outside the buzz and lifeblood of the office work happening on the other floors. And I really need them to get their acts together for this big presentation late this afternoon. If I try to go rally them, I know I'll just be met with the same dead-eyed fish stares and shrugs I see every morning during our forenoon meeting—but you! You're young. You're cool. You're fresh blood to wake them from their slumbers and get them cracking! I've known you long enough to know that is true beyond the shadow of a doubt. So what do you say, my boy? It's a simple project, really. There are seven techs, each trained in some arcane art," he laughed his hearty laugh and slapped the clerk on the arm. "You know what I mean. I'm from before your time. We did things differently back when I was cutting my teeth, but now I'm in charge of overseeing this operation, yet it relies on each of their individual technical know-hows. You've just got to convince them to set up their equipment in the multi-purpose room ASAP, report back to me once it's taken care of, and we'll all be happy little larks."

The clerk didn't respond. He needed his number, so he didn't want to upset the chairman, but he was trying to figure out how to escape this elaborate task that was being forced onto his shoulders.

"Ah, but where are my manners? You're still weary from the sun and the sand!" the chairman said. "Please, have a seat." The clerk obeyed, and as he took a seat, the chairman returned to his seat behind the desk, collapsing into it. He rang a bell on the desk.

"Yes sir?" the chairman's assistant said, poking his head in the doorway.

"Brew up a pot of espresso for me and this good man, will you? And use the good stuff!"

"Right away, sir!" his assistant said.

"Thank you, my boy," the chairman said, smiling. He

looked at the clerk and said, "He's a good kid. And so are you!" He laughed, shaking his head back and forth with memory. "When you get to be my age, everyone's a kid."

The clerk didn't respond. The chairman's twinkling brown eyes were still staring at him, expectantly, so he said, "Yeah."

The chairman smiled, still looking into the clerk's sandy face. The clerk looked down at his scuffed shoes. Some time passed in this fashion before the assistant returned with a tray containing a tall, hexagonal metal pot with two tiny mugs. The assistant plopped the tray down on top of all of the papers on the chairman's desk.

"Thank you! Thank you!" the chairman was saying as the assistant poured the brown liquid into each tiny cup from a great distance of height, which concerned the clerk—and rightly so, as he could see that tiny brown circles had splashed all over the chairman's paperwork.

"Would you like any sweetener?" the assistant asked.

"Yes, please."

"I told you," the chairman said with a big goofy grin under his tattered mustache. "He's good!" The chairman took a big swig of espresso. To the clerk's horror, the chairman had emptied his tiny cup all at once.

The clerk looked down at his tiny mug. He could feel how scalding hot it was just from where his two fingers gripped the miniscule handle. Steam was rising up from the cup, heating the clerk's eyeballs.

The chairman put his little mug down not on the tray, as the clerk had expected, but on a hill of papers covering the desk, which wasn't even a flat surface and left the mug looking as if it would tip over and crash to the floor, which would surely break its delicate handle. As the clerk looked up from that mess, he saw the chairman's eyes were on him.

They were friendly eyes, to be sure, but there was also something expectant in them. The clerk felt like he should say something—make small talk—but he was dreadful at that, and the whole situation left him feeling awful. He looked back at his mug, steam still rising. He had still been waiting for that assistant to return with the sweetener, but it seemed like quite a bit of time had passed. The clerk considered just downing the strong coffee all at once, like the chairman had, but he remembered the last time he burned his tongue and his insides to get away from this uncomfortable scenario and he didn't think the pain was worth it. His body was already feeling so sore and achy all over that he couldn't imagine having to function with added aches.

The assistant returned and wordlessly left a small bowl of cubes with a spoon in front of the clerk. "Thanks," the clerk muttered. He caught the chairman's face, which was still beaming, and the chairman raised his eyebrows at the clerk. The clerk imagined the eyebrows getting stuck there, just a little bit higher on his forehead than they were supposed to be.

The clerk used the spoon to splash a couple of the white cubes into the espresso, which seemed to be as much volume as the drink itself. Then he used the spoon to furiously stir the espresso. After double the amount of time that would have constituted a polite and acceptable stir, the clerk was still stirring. He imagined that he could whisk all the heat out of the beverage. He was still going at it—he didn't dare glance up to make eye contact with the chairman—he just kept stirring and stirring with his eyes penetrating into the brown liquid.

"There you go, my boy! Stir it! Stir it!" the chairman said with excitement, laughing and clapping. "Why you are a hoot. I just love having you here."

Something about the word "hoot" was more than the clerk could take. He abruptly stopped stirring, dropped the spoon on the tray, and wide-eyed, he picked up the little cup and drank it down in a continuous series of small sips.

"Marvelous! Smashing!" the chairman cheered, still laughing. "What do you say we do this all again after you rally my troops?"

The clerk smiled, but it was a look of terror.

* * * *

The assistant had deposited the clerk on one of the few floors of this inner-building—the clerk assumed inner, since wasn't this little office building inside the government sky-scraper? What he was standing in was a square. There was a hole in the middle of the square, and if he looked down it, he could see the lobby where the receptionist was sta-tioned. Behind him was the hallway he had walked down to get here, and around the rest of the square were seven doors. He had a list of the seven technicians in his hands, but he really didn't want to go cavorting with these people. He con-sidered taking a nap in the corner, and then going back to the chairman and telling him he'd tried, but they wouldn't listen to him, so could he please have his number now? He needed that number. That was the only reason he'd go through with this—because he was compiling an important report for the director and he needed all of the numbers. He couldn't have any word of his slacking getting back to the director.

So, with the excitement and fear that had built up in his chest with the thought of the director and the associated report, he marched up to the first door and knocked loudly.

"What is it?" a voice came from the other side.

The clerk considered asking if he could come in, but he didn't have time for being polite. He needed to be assertive and just get this job done. He shoved the door open and was met by a horrified shriek from the technician inside.

"What have you done? What's wrong with you?"

The clerk could see that there was all kinds of computer equipment crowded into this office, and he must have knocked something over when he opened the door. The clerk remembered all the trouble that had occurred when he'd knocked down that stack of papers in the small city, so he quickly muttered, "The chairman said you have to set up for the presentation in the multipurpose room posthaste," and closed the door. He could hear muffled responses coming through the door, but he shuffled away to the next office.

He was about to knock when he realized that the door was cracked. "Excuse me," he tried, sticking his lips through the spot where the door was ajar.

"Can I help you with something?" the technician said.

The clerk used his forehead to push the door open enough to stick his face through. He could see the technician sitting at a desk. Not only was there a mess of papers on top of the desk, but there were towering, wobbly stacks of paper all over the rest of the office. "The chairman said you have to set up for the presentation in the multipurpose room posthaste," the clerk said.

"Oh, I would just totally love to do that," the technician replied, "But as you can see, I'm quite overtaken by assignments at the moment, and the project you're talking about is really low priority."

The clerk considered mentioning that since it was supposed to happen today it's now or never, but he shrugged to himself. "Okay," he muttered, sliding his face back out and shuffling over to the next office.

He knocked on the door.

"Come in."

He entered and saw that the technician in this office was

arranging a lot of tiny human figurines and buildings on the desk. "The chairman said you have to set up for the presentation in the multipurpose room posthaste," the clerk muttered.

"That's all well and swell," the technician said. "But I'm on an important assignment from my real supervisor. Quite frankly, I don't know how that bloke got this sinecure in the first place. He has no technical knowledge whatsoever."

The clerk tried the same line in the remaining four offices and recorded the responses as follows:

"If it's so important, why doesn't the chairman get off his keester and come tell me himself?"

"Who are you? I don't take orders from strangers. How do I know you're not a saboteur?"

"Yeah, yeah. I told him I'd do it tomorrow."

"I did the same setup for him last year! Why's he need me to do it again?"

Confirming that he'd hit all seven offices, the clerk trudged back down to the chairman's office.

"What can I help you with?" the chairman's assistant asked as the clerk appeared in the doorway.

"Can you tell the chairman that I'm ready for my number now?" the clerk asked.

"Sure thing," the assistant said, disappearing into the chairman's office.

"Ah, brilliant!" he heard the chairman say.

The assistant returned and escorted the clerk into the chairman's office.

"So they've all setup the multipurpose room then?" he asked the clerk.

"Well—not exactly, no."

"What?!" the chairman shouted, a look of shock passing over his face.

"I told them to—they all said they were busy," the clerk

muttered.

"No, no, no, no, no—this won't do! Did you tell them that this is a top priority order?—that the director will be here at any moment?"

"The director? Coming here?"

"Yes, of course! Didn't you read the note I wrote for you?"

The clerk looked down at the paper. The list of the seven technicians had been neatly written out by the assistant, but he realized that there was an indecipherable scrawl in the bottom corner of the paper. He squinted at it, but he couldn't make out one letter except for maybe a capital "T." The clerk darted his eyes back up at the chairman, who seemed quite upset. "Uh—" the clerk uttered.

"Well go back and tell them, will you lad! This is no time for dilly-dallying."

The clerk tripped over his feet and had to grab onto the wall for support to keep from falling as he rushed out of the office.

As the clerk walked back into the square of technician's offices, he was going to just knock on the first door again, but then he stopped himself, remembering that out of all seven offices, the technician at the second office seemed to be the most pleasant. He sidled up to that door, which was still partially open, and he gently pressed his face into the office. The technician looked harried as she rifled through a stack of papers. "Excuse me," the clerk whispered.

"Ack!" The technician jumped back, knocking over the stack of papers, which began to flutter throughout the room.

"Sorry," the clerk said in a soft voice. "I didn't mean to startle you. It's just that the director is on his way for that presentation in the multipurpose room, and it's a top priority project."

"The director is coming? Here? Now? Why didn't you say so before?" The technician hopped up, landing on a stack of papers, which the technician then leapt from, pushing the door open in an impressive spin jump. "The director's coming!" the technician shouted out in the square. "The director is coming! This is a top priority project! Grab your equipment and establish an assembly in the multipurpose room!"

The clerk was astonished as he saw the technicians running out of their offices sidled with backpacks and attache cases and carrying all manner of technical equipment and machines in their hands. With great agility, they dove through the open square in the center, landing gently in the lobby with their equipment unharmed. The clerk was now alone up in the square, looking down at them as they ran down one of the corridors branching off from the lobby. The clerk shuffled back down the hallway in search of the stairs.

Not much time later, the clerk was standing next to the chairman in the entrance of the multipurpose room as they watched the technicians buzz about in the final stages of assembling the necessary equipment. "I knew I could count on you, my boy," the chairman said in proud tones as he put an arm around the clerk's back. His arm was sweaty and uncomfortable, and the clerk was trying to figure out how to politely get away from it.

"There you are, Mr. Chairman," a baritone voice came from behind them. They whirled to see a whole entourage of people wearing masks with breathing apparatuses and gear that looked like it was made to survive the rough conditions of a desert. The man who had spoken removed his mask and the clerk recognized that it was the director—although through the gleam of sweat, the clerk could see stubble prickling out all over his head, which was unusual and suggested he had been on some expedition for the last few days. He shed his gear to reveal that he was wearing a suit underneath, and he walked up to the chairman and shook his hand. "It feels exhilarating to cross through enemy territory," the director continued, "knowing exactly how men and women in uniform feel to face these challenging times."

Once that greeting was complete, he turned toward the clerk and began to stretch out his hand, but as his arm was extending, the expression on his face changed to one of concern in recognition of who the clerk was, and he put both hands onto the chairman's shoulders, shoving the large chairman between himself and the clerk before rushing to the other side of the room.

"Whoa there, careful," the chairman said.

Before long, the lights were out, save for all the flashing lights on the buzzing equipment that now surrounded the room, and everyone was seated around a long conference table. The clerk realized that his manager was sitting on the other side of the table, and she shot him a quizzical look, mouthing, "What are you doing here?"

The clerk shrugged. He actually needed to get out of here, as it was now late, and there was no way he would get back to his cubicle in the small city before his shift was supposed to be over.

Yet the clerk still couldn't leave because he needed that number from the chairman. He could see the chairman, but he was sitting several seats away from the clerk. People were talking and seemed generally attentive to the meeting, so the clerk slouched down in his chair and let himself slide underneath the table. He was shocked to see that there were three women sitting cross-legged under the table. They were all in a row, writing notes in notebooks. Two of them were able to lean their notebooks on the back of another, but the girl in the front needed to lean her notebook against the thigh of someone who was sitting up at the table.

"What are you guys doing down here?" the clerk whispered.

They looked up at him with surprised expressions, all three of them putting their index fingers over their lips in unison. The woman at the head motioned for the clerk to come closer. For a moment, he took her for the so-called ex-shift manager from the Shipping and Receiving Department—but no, as he looked at her face, her eyes seemed to shrink and her cheeks began to expand. He felt dizzy and looked away. She motioned for him to come closer once more. The clerk crawled across the industrial carpet so that he was nearer. She motioned for him to come closer. He shifted forward a bit. She motioned for him to come closer still. He couldn't get much closer without sitting in her lap, so he gave her a puzzled face. She shifted forward a bit and cupped her hand around his ear, and when she spoke, she was so close that he could feel the disturbing, warm wetness of her lips and tongue. "We need to be as silent as possible because this is an extremely secure meeting," she whispered.

"What are—?" the clerk started to whisper, but one of the other girls hopped forward and slammed her hand over the clerk's mouth to keep him silent.

"Don't worry about us," the girl in his ear whispered. "We're supposed to be here. We need to take the notes for this meeting." His ear was all wet from her slobber. "And it's extremely secure, and they've got all this top secret security technology in here, so we need to take the notes by hand—so we need to listen carefully. We can't be making noise. Why don't you just lay your head down in my lap and take a nap? I can always give you a copy of the notes after. You're so weary, and you've had a long day. Doesn't that sound nice?"

She removed her hand from his ear, a line of spit going

with it, and the three ladies resumed their writing formation. The one in the front patted her lap and made eyes at the clerk. He started to back away, but she grabbed him and savagely twisted him around. He was taken aback by her great strength and use of force. She had her strong hands on his shoulders now. He was fighting her, but she was slowly pulling him toward her lap. Sweat broke out on his brow as he struggled to keep himself up, but he was losing the battle, and she was pulling him closer and closer to her lap. Out of the bottom of his peripheral vision, the clerk saw the little black mouse climbing up out of his pocket. The mouse climbed up his neck, over his mouth—tickling the clerk's nose—and hopped off of the clerk's head and onto the woman's lap. She started to scream, but the lady behind her clapped her hand over her mouth to silence her. In the commotion, the clerk broke free of her grip.

"Let's go, Ellem!" the clerk whispered as he scooped up the mouse out of the green skirt of her lap. The clerk crawled away on all fours. He needed to find the chairman, but he was totally disoriented as to what part of the table he was under. Before he could even start to examine the legs and feet that were all around him, he realized that the women were coming after him. One of them lunged at him, and he had to roll away to avoid her, slamming into people's legs. Someone kicked him in the shin. He kept moving, but the other two girls were now blocking his path. He grabbed onto one of the table legs to swing around in another direction and rolled past the girl who had lunged at him.

He was looking at the legs of the people now. *"The chairman! The chairman!"* the clerk thought. *"Which one is the chairman?"* All of the legs looked the same to him. He knew there were men and women seated at the table, but from down here in the darkness, all of the legs looked identical. He crawled forward, the women gaining ground behind him. He couldn't even tell the difference between left legs and right legs anymore. He was just passing through an endless stream of legs. The women had taken up a new formation to ensnare him. He knew in a moment they would be upon him again. He stopped crawling, gasping for breath as he inspected the legs. One pair stood out to him. They seemed like they could have belonged to a man of the chairman's girth. Suddenly he felt hands claw onto his own legs. He threw his arms forward at the legs he'd been inspecting. He tugged furiously on the pants. The women were pulling him away, so he grabbed onto the pants and tried to pull himself in the opposite direction.

"What in the—?" he heard a voice say above him. A face with a misshapen mustache appeared in the darkness— it was the chairman! He reached down, grasping the clerk under the armpits, and yanked him up above the table.

The clerk howled in pain, the sore under his armpit screaming as the chairman's fat fingers dug into it.

The chairman tried to hush him. "It's alright, my boy," he said, plopping the clerk onto his feet. "Just a moment." He put his arm around the clerk's back as he escorted him toward the entrance. Tears were welling in the clerk's eyes, so he couldn't discern the level of irritation that might have been showing in the director's face. One of the technicians prevented them from exiting, motioning to another technician who did something to a machine before they were permitted to leave.

"What was all that?" the chairman said once they were back in the lobby. "You shouldn't be crawling around under the table like a toddler during such an important presentation!"

"But there were these women down there!" the clerk

protested. "They were—"

"I don't want to hear it!" the chairman interrupted. "I don't want anything going wrong in my office when the director's here!"

"Fine!" the clerk replied. "I'm leaving. Just give me my number for today."

"Well, I'm afraid I don't have it on me," the chairman retorted.

"But I've been waiting patiently all this time, and I need to get back to my post."

"Well you're going to have to wait—I don't remember what the number is. I'll get it for you after the presentation."

"But I need it now," the clerk whinged.

"Fine, fine. I think it was this." He took out a scrap of paper from his pocket and jotted a number down.

"You think?" the clerk said with hesitation as the chairman handed him the number.

"It's close enough."

"Close enough? I need it to be accurate. I'm compiling a report for the director! I'm the one who's going to be in trouble if it's wrong."

"It's not wrong. It's right," the chairman said, patting the clerk on the shoulder. "I'm sure of it, my boy." He turned away, heading back into the multipurpose room.

* * * *

The next day, the clerk found himself heading to the bigger city on a particularly important task, but he didn't have to meet anyone at a specific time, so he was taking his time and walked part of the way. He was delivering an updated copy of the spreadsheet for the director. Whenever the director asked for the updated copy, it was always to be left in secret, odd places: rolled up inside a specific bowling shoe, tucked behind a bathroom hand-dryer, or folded into the inside of a phone that he'd needed to dismantle and re-assemble with a screwdriver—that kind of thing. It was all very secretive and could never have any identifying information written on it. The clerk had been working on it for quite a while now, and it was filled with rows and columns of numbers that were meaningless to him.

When the clerk returned home late that night, his betrothed was all eyes and no mouth. Her eyes seemed to have grown to take up her whole face and the room beyond, while her mouth shrunk to be itty-bitty. The clerk asked her questions, such as how her day had been, but her tiny mouth seemed able to supply only one-word answers.

The clerk had just finished mashing up a can of black beans with his teeth when her mouth decided to grow.

"I have a confession to make," his betrothed said. "I, well, how can I put this? You see, the thing is—I haven't been going to job interviews. For the beginning of the whole process I was—I swear! I always dressed my best and kept myself ultra-groomed. I ironed my suit-jackets; I had plenty of crisp copies of my resume. I was so focused that even while I was waiting in the offices, I was researching the companies, preparing the best possible answers to a wide range of questions. But going to dozens and dozens of interviews a day becomes quite tedious, quite quickly. One day as I was trudging along the main avenue in the business district, searching for a building that didn't seem to be where it should have been—my eyes lingered long on the large glass window of a café. The window was bigger than the average storefront window. It seemed as though it was a shimmering portal into a world much nicer than the one I was inhabiting. I stood staring at the window for a long time like a puppy watching a person prepare dinner as everyone on the sidewalk shoved past me. Red-painted wood framed the otherworldly image of people talking and relaxing, drinking and laughing, eating and creating. Yes, creating. I stood there for so long just trying to comprehend the idea that people could be creating things not of this world in there. I understood it so little that I didn't think I'd even be able to step through the doors, as if something would prevent it from happening—a force-field or something. Yet I knew this was preposterous—the entire time I was planted there, people were going in and coming back out with steaming cups of coffee and tea, and it had been so unusually frosty that I was shivering in my business clothes and strongly desired to grasp a warm tea or hot chocolate. However, there was still the fact that something was holding me back—perhaps it was the job interview that I was currently late for. But I'd made an earnest effort to find the place, I swear! I couldn't find it, and I didn't see why if I looked again I'd be able to find it, and besides, to show up late to a job interview was an assurance that I'd never get the job, and I probably wasn't going to get this job in the first place. It probably was impossible for me to go in that café though. It was another dimension. Some place I was never meant to enter—but the chaos of the world ensured that I'd arrive where I shouldn't. You see, at that very moment, a group of movers were clomping down the sidewalk carrying a massive armoire. They were clogging up the entire sidewalk and people seemed grumpy about moving out of their way. Because of the increased person-traffic around me, I shifted closer toward the entrance, pressing my chest against the cold glass of the window. People were exiting the café just as the movers were approaching, and others were shoving to try to get around the movers, and I found myself being jostled and bumped, and I was literally pushed into the open door of the café. I even tripped on the slight step of the door and went sprawling into the place, landing on my arse. The aroma of spices, herbs, coffees, teas, chocolates, pastries and other gluttonous delights overwhelmed me so much that I didn't even care, or really notice that I was sitting there on the stone ground. A wiry lady in a sleeveless tank-top—which revealed colorful tattoos on her arms—appeared before me. Her hair was mussed into an odd assortment of braids. She reached down and lifted me by the armpits, plopping me back onto my feet. She said she didn't want someone to trip on me and hurt both of us. I felt as though I were looking at a creature described only in mythology. Subconsciously, I followed her back to her table. She was in a nook of the café that had a shaggy brown rug spread over the gray stone floor. There were soft couches and chairs all over the perimeter of this section, with only tiny tables next to them for people to store their drinks. Her small end-table was covered with empty coffee and teacups, but one of the cups was filled with water and dirty paintbrushes, and she had a few upside-down lids filled with brightly colored paints. Next to her chair, she had an entire easel set up and she was painting indescribable geometric shapes in a variety of colors. I was mesmerized as I watched her pick up a paintbrush, dip it in her palette, and begin to create things not of this world.

"I have no idea how long I stood there just gawking at her before she finally glanced up at me with her bright green eyes for a moment and said, 'You know this is a capitalist establishment and non-utopian, right? They prefer if you pay a few bucks for a fancy coffee and take a seat. You can have a seat on the couch here and still watch me if you'd like, you pretty little thing.'"

"I must have blushed the same shade of pink she'd recently mixed, and I only managed to get out, 'Okay,' and shuffle back toward the front of the store where the counter of buzzing baristas were penned. I had no idea what kind of drink to order as I stood in the long line, and before I was ready, I found myself at the front of the line and needing to give the barista an order. 'Well what do you recommend?' I'd asked.

"'That depends. What do you usually like to drink?'

"I made a noise with my mouth but gave no real answer.

"'Coffee? Tea? Hot Chocolate?'

"'Uh, coffee, I guess,' I'd responded, as if my brain had no conception of a drink in a café beyond a cup of coffee.

"'Strong, sweet, or salty?' he asked.

"I managed to respond 'Sweet,'

"'Hot or cold?'

"'Hot,' I'd decided. I'd been expecting hot.

"With that answer, he dashed away to prepare an unknown drink. Another barista appeared to take my money, and then I had to wait a bit over near another counter while the drink was prepared. I was eventually handed a bowl-sized mug overflowing with whipped cream. I took it back over near the artist and sat on the edge of the couch where she had indicated earlier. I was still obsessed with what she was painting, but I realized she wasn't the only artist in this place. There were other men and women with easels over in this nook, and I had the distinct impression that people sitting with notebooks or paper in other sections were some sort of other creative types. Mostly though, I sat and watched the lady paint. Her paintings are so hard for me to describe to you. I can picture them perfectly in my mind right now, but to turn those images into words seems impossible, and I suppose the images have to remain permanently locked in my mind because my own hands are too imperfect to recreate the powerful images the way they're supposed to be. I'm still so entranced by them that I could imagine dedicating my life to attempting to show them to you. Just imagine it!

Every day I'd attempt to sketch and paint from my memory, slowly and painstakingly getting closer to what I'd seen. Maybe after years I could really do it. And then, I'd have to figure out how to create something new with my unexpectedly enhanced skills. But maybe that'd be impossible."

If the clerk was being honest, he'd tell you that he was fighting sleep while he listened to her detailed account, but he'd listened diligently nevertheless, and he took the opportunity of her wistfully looking out into nothing to say, "Is that what you want to do?"

"Huh?"

"Is that what you want to do? Teach yourself to paint? To be an artist? Is that what you want to do?"

She took a long time to respond. "Well, maybe I already started. You see, I got up early and pretended to go out for job interviews the next day, but in secret, I slinked away to the café—but the atmosphere was completely different. There was no one chilling or hanging out. The place was rather busy, but it was all people rushing in to get a cup of coffee, asking for it to go, and rushing back out. They were probably on their way to work, or maybe even job interviews—who knows? And so they weren't sitting there in the café. So I sat in the little nook by myself, feeling sad at the loss of creators and creation. I sat there for a long time with my briefcase on my lap, a different unknown hot tea drink on the little table next to me, and I realized that I myself could create if I so desired. I opened my briefcase and took out a resume and a pen. I decided to move from the couch to one of the regular tables, and once there, I placed the resume upside down on the table next to my cup of coffee. The blank paper needed me to create something on it, so I began to sketch. I hadn't drawn a picture since I was a child, so of course my little cartoon drawings of animals were simplistic. And I thought it was interesting. Why were animals the artwork I so desired?" She leaned over the bed and returned with her briefcase. She opened it and spilled out a stack of drawings on the backs of resumes, some in pen, some in pencil. "Look at them. These were some of my early ones. These ones are newer. I started sitting in here and sketching the animals while I can look at them, you know, sometimes when you're not here. They don't like to stay still though, which makes things hard. I think I've gotten better. Do you think I've gotten better?"

"Yeah, these are really nice. I think you've gotten a lot better," the clerk said, holding up a drawing of a particularly hairy hermit crab.

"So the artist types don't show up until later. I think some of them stay there all night, or at least until the café closes at midnight or something. I tried to tell the painter whose indescribable geometric worlds I so love how empty I'd felt without acts of creation surrounding me.

"'You know what the ultimate act of creation is, don't you, you pretty little thing?' she'd said, tossing me a sultry look with her green eyes, resting a hand on my shoulder, and giving me a wink. But immediately after, she laughed it off and said, 'I'm just kidding. I'm quite happily married, you know. My wife's off doing her own work right now. You are cute though.'" His betrothed laughed.

"Oh," the clerk muttered. He forced a smile because that seemed to be expected.

"So yeah. I've got all these sketches here instead of job interviews under my belt, but you know, getting a job is like winning the lottery anyway, so, maybe it's not too much lost. I'll get back out there eventually, unless you're—"

"You can get back out there when you're ready," the clerk said. "If you need to do this for now, you do this. I don't know, maybe you'll never get back out there. That's okay too. I'll be out there. I'm already out there. Sure I may just be a lowly clerk right now—one of the lowest of the low. Overworked, underpaid—expectations that are impossible to meet—but yet, I must meet them because that is the only way to get a promotion. And you'll see, after my promotion, I'm sure I can take us out of this place. I bet I can even get us a place so nice we'll have a private toilet, and a real kitchen area in our bedroom! That'll be luxurious! I'm willing to bear the brunt of the finances, if you'll put up with it. Maybe soon I'll be a senior clerk! And maybe some years after that, I could become an assistant head clerk, and if I work hard enough after that, maybe I'll become a head clerk! You'll see! You'll see!" At this point the clerk became dizzy and fell on his back.

"But—that's so meaningless," his betrothed whispered.

* * * *

The following afternoon, the clerk was just making his way out of his cubicle after a harried morning of bouncing between his co-workers on the three top blue priority projects he was currently assigned.

When he stepped outside onto the sidewalk, a confused-looking girl said something to him.

The traffic was so deafening that he didn't notice she was talking to him at first, and when he glanced over in her direction, she repeated herself. He scrunched up his face to indicate that he hadn't heard her. He shouted, "What?" and held his hand up to his ear like an old codger. She repeated herself. He heard nothing. He held up one finger. When the traffic stopped for a moment, he repeated, "What?" and she began to speak, but the traffic instantly picked up again. "I'm sorry. I can't hear you!" he shouted. The traffic slowed for a moment.

"You don't speak the island language?" the girl said,

clearly perplexed.

"Only a little bit," the clerk muttered.

"Really? Wow." She shrugged, muttered something in her own tongue, and walked inside the government building.

The clerk stuffed his hands in his pockets and pouted as he walked toward the street in search of a bus. "At least you—" he started to say, but his sentence was interrupted by one cough, then another, and followed by another. It was a downright coughing fit. After a few minutes of coughing, he was doubled-over in pain, and the coughing fit had brought him to his knees. He was holding his mouth with one hand and his throat with the other. He gasped for breath in the nanoseconds between coughs, and hot tears streamed out of his bloodshot eyes and down his cheeks. When it finally stopped, he fell forward onto his hands and gasped for air for a few more minutes. He took a deep breath as he started to recover, and when he opened his eyes, he saw a pool of blood between his knees. "Uck," he grunted, seeing that he'd coughed a mixture of red, sticky blood and phlegm onto his hands. He didn't have a napkin or water on him, so he wasn't sure what to do. He tried to remember if there was a water fountain that he could use to drink from and wash up, but he wasn't one hundred percent certain. He decided his best bet was to go back inside the government building and to use the lavatory.

The security guard at the door made a disgusted face when he saw the clerk holding his soiled hands in front of him like he didn't know where they belonged. "Are you okay, man?"

"Yeah, I just, uh, made a mess," the clerk muttered. "I need to wash up in the bathroom."

"I'll need to see your ID," the guard responded.

"C'mon, please. I don't want to get my clothes all dirty

retrieving it from my pocket."

"Alright. Go in real quick. Just this once, since I know you."

"Thank you so much!" the clerk said, walking back through the full body scanner. He washed his hands and face, and then cupped his hands to drink some water from the sink.

Back out on the street, passing quickly by the bloody wound in the sidewalk, he was once more in search of a bus. "What was I thinking of before the interruption?" he asked himself, and remembered the little black mouse. He stopped on the sidewalk, a few grumpy people muttering as they walked around him, and took the mouse out of his pocket, holding it up to his nose with both hands and giggling as the whiskers tickled him. "You, my friend, are the only one who seems to understand me anymore," the clerk said, smiling.

Hours later, the clerk was crawling through a tiny, dusty air vent deep in the heart of the bigger city's government building. "It should be about here, Ellem," he muttered, tugging on a grate. He dropped down onto a mountain of papers that began to buckle under his weight. As they toppled, he slid down them as if he were falling down an icy hill. He landed amidst more papers, while the other papers fluttered about like oversized snowflakes. "How's he ever going to find it in this turmoil?" the clerk whispered, surveying the room stuffed with papers in various stages of crumple, memory sticks and older forms of digital memory, as well as the odd artifacts like bicycles, beekeeping suits, braided wigs, and office chairs.

"Find what?" a perky voice said. A face popped out from beneath the junk in front of the clerk.

The clerk had been holding the updated spreadsheet for the director, and when she startled him, he squealed and dropped the paper. He went to pick it up, but he was holding what appeared to be a detailed list of endangered animal species. "Where did it go?"

"Where did what go?" the girl said, putting her face right in the clerk's and startling him afresh.

"Oh, it's you," he said, as he glanced at her.

"It's me?" she asked. "Well of course it's me. I know it's me, but you don't know it's me because you don't know me."

"Sure, I do. We met at that—" the clerk didn't finish his sentence as he peered into her eyes. Her sandy blonde hair and green tank top, those were obvious, but the more he attempted to recognize her face, the more it seemed to shift and change, making him queasy. "—that, somewhere," he muttered, shaking his head and giving up.

"Right," she said in a voice chilled by sarcasm.

The clerk had already gone back to searching for his paper.

"Watchya looking for?" she asked, putting her face in his face again.

"Nothing. I'm just looking for the way back out of here. There's no doors or anything? Maybe a trapdoor in the floor?" The clerk figured he'd left the document where he was instructed, so he might as well not worry about it.

"Oh, I'm afraid not," she responded. The only way out's the way you came in."

"Oh dear. How am I supposed to climb back up there? I knocked over the paper ladder when I came in."

"It's no problem. I gotchya!" She grabbed the clerk around the chest and hoisted him up by the armpits.

The clerk cried out in pain. "Let me down!" he shrieked. The sore under his armpit was raw and hurting, and she was making it worse.

"Don't be a baby," she said, and started spinning around

in a circle. She bounced onto a pile of paper and bicycles, which she used to propel herself onto the wall.

"Ow! Let me down! Let me down!" the clerk cried out as she ran alongside the wall perpendicular to the ground. She spiraled around and around the wall, building momentum until she tossed the clerk up the little air duct square he'd fallen from. He lay on his back in the air duct for a few minutes, groaning in pain.

"A thank you would be nice!" the girl called up from the room.

The clerk felt so weak that moving his body seemed like the worst thing in the world. He lost track of how long he'd stayed in that air duct. He didn't think he fell asleep, but he felt very odd, and wondered if he'd been fading in and out of consciousness.

When he finally dragged himself back out to the street, it was already nightfall. He made it to the unofficial bus stop where he discovered that there was no one else waiting there for a bus. His standing was wobbly, so he laid down on the sidewalk, feeling his headache vibrate from his head into the concrete. "I'm in pain, hungry, and I have to go to the bathroom, Ellem," the clerk muttered in slurred speech, regretting that he'd spoken because talking hurt too.

The loud noise of an engine awoke him. "Oh! Bus!" he muttered, scrambling shakily to his feet. He clambered up the stairs and into the bus, collapsing in the first open seat he found. He let his forehead lean against the vibrating window, where he could see the reflection of his half-closed, bloodshot eyes. "We'll be home soon, Ellem," he whispered. "We'll be home soon to my darling. She'll take care of us."

Through his blurry vision, he suddenly saw water. It was a deep, black-blue against the azure sky, stretching out beyond the horizon.

"Water. Water? Water!" he grunted, his eyes bolting open as he shot up erect in his seat.

He put his hands on two seats and used his arms to pull himself to his feet. He took one step into the aisle and cartwheeled backward, slamming into the back of the bus. People looked at him and whispered. He struggled back to his feet, and holding a seat in either hand, he pulled himself toward the front of the bus, bit by bit, as though he were travelling through a hurricane. He was drenched in sweat when he finally reached the front. "Driver!" the clerk exclaimed. "I think I got on the wrong bus! What bridge is this?"

"Why, it's the bridge to the big city, of course," the bus driver said, not moving his eyes from the road.

"Oh dear. You see, I need to be in the small city."

"Well you're going to have to take a bus back once you reach the terminal," the bus driver responded.

"You can't take me back?"

"Oh no, I'm afraid not. Once we stop, my shift's over and I'm heading home."

"I see. Thanks anyway," the clerk murmured. He turned to return to his seat, but the bus hit a bump in the bridge and he tripped, rolling end over end until he slammed into the back of the bus. His head was swimming in headache, so he decided to just wait there on the sticky bus floor until the bus stopped.

Eventually he found himself in a circuitous underground transit station. Everywhere he turned, he found trains and busses going to places he didn't want to go. He tried to ask a couple of people where he could get a bus to the small city, but they rushed past him. There didn't seem to be anyone who worked in the station that he could ask for help. Down one hallway, he found a flight of stairs. He ascended them and found himself out on the street.

The city was so densely packed with impossibly high buildings that the clerk felt like—rather than being outside, which he supposed he was—he was actually surrounded by walls trapping him inside of some labyrinthine megastructure. He craned his neck and gawked upward, searching for the tops of buildings or the light of the moon. He found neither, only a hazy, gray-black sky.

The clerk had to go to the bathroom so bad that he couldn't even think straight. Here in the heart of the big city—the capital of the world—business people rushed along the sidewalk with indefatigable speeds and amazing precision. The clerk needed to catch his bearings, which was difficult enough when he had to pee so bad, but it was especially worse because everyone on the sidewalk kept shoving into him, spinning him like a top and bouncing him around the sidewalk like a pinball. For these people, time was money, and they couldn't lose some money because of a confused tourist in their way, so they shoved him and let him be someone else's problem. "I've got to pee, I've got to pee!" he muttered through gritted teeth, holding his crotch as he took hard shoves from shoulders, elbows, and briefcases. One shove put him in the direction of a door, which he hurriedly scrambled inside. He found himself in a small deli—a counter of meat and cheese in the front, chairs and tables in the back.

"Please, I need to use your bathroom!" he said to the lady behind the counter. He was practically doubled over in pain from holding his bladder.

"Bathrooms are for paying customers only," she replied.

"But it's an emergency!" the clerk pleaded.

"Doesn't matter. Store policy."

"Oh, okay, fine!" the clerk grunted, squinting up at the menu. Everything was so expensive, and he needed enough money to get back across the river. He ordered the cheapest sandwich he saw. She took forever making it, peeling each slice of cheese apart as painstakingly as building a tiny ship in a tiny bottle. When she told him the price, he handed her his only bill, and she handed him back some change. He stuffed it into his pocket, and said, "Keep the sandwich there for a second!" while he turned to flee into the bathroom.

"Wait!" she called out.

But he had to pee, so he kept going.

"Ah, my friend!" one of the customers said, but the clerk had no time to pay attention.

He reached the men's room and tugged on the door handle, but it didn't budge.

"You need the key!" the lady said, holding up the key from behind the counter.

"Ack!" the clerk gurgled in his throat, rushing back to get it.

When he finished, even though relief washed over him, there was still a lingering pain in his pelvis. As he exited the bathroom, a smiling face met his. "Ah, my friend," the man said in a jovial voice. He immediately recognized the voice, even though the street-person had trimmed his beard and hair and was wearing a spiffy double-breasted suit with a starched white collar-shirt and a clean, paisley tie. "I knew fate would deliver us together so that you could contribute your campaign promise. And fate's on our side because every bit counts, and since we've managed to break through the walls of propaganda, and I've been elected senator, my campaign needs help now more than ever."

The clerk's heart dropped—he needed that money for the bus fare back across the bridge.

"C'mon now, grab your sandwich, and I'll tell you all about our progress." The heavyset man retook his seat at a table piled high with submarine sandwiches and pickles. He slid a chair out from under the table as an invitation to the clerk.

"I guess I have no choice," the clerk thought to himself as he retook his sandwich and sat down across from the new senator.

"You see, my friend," he said with a mouthful of sandwich, "I told you I'd come here to do what you'd do, if only you had the chance, and here we are. It's my job to expose corruption and right wrongs, so I'm starting with the most evil practice I could think of: Manufactured death from the skies." He took several huge bites of sandwich and chewed quickly. He resumed speaking before he'd finished swallowing. "I know it goes against every law we have on the books. Even the worst person has the right to a fair trial, but dead people don't get trials."

As the man droned on, eating copious amounts of sandwich in the process, the clerk fingered the change in his pocket. He was wondering if there was some way he could escape and keep his change for the bus fare. Sure, in theory he could just get up and run away right now, but something invisible was keeping him still, causing him to nod politely at words he wasn't paying any mind to.

"You know what? It's probably easier if I just show you. I'm a senator now—I have unrestricted access. You won't believe this thing. It's only a few blocks from here. Let me just finish my sandwich." He lifted a massive chunk of bread, meat, and cheese from his tray and crammed it into his mouth. The clerk figured he'd have had to unhinge his jaw to fit that in there, but he seemed to have no problem. The next words out of his mouth were indecipherable, but he gathered up his trays and crumpled napkins before heading toward the door. The clerk followed, carrying his uneaten sandwich outside with him.

The clerk took big strides in the shadow of the man's girth to navigate the bustling sidewalks, and before long, they were in a large marble hallway. "He's with me," the senator said at the security desk, flashing an identification card.

"We're going to need to see some ID for him too," the security guard said.

"Um, I should have it right here," the clerk muttered, fishing around in his pocket. "I know it's around here some- where." In his struggle, he dropped the remains of his sand- wich all over the shiny marble, splattering mayonnaise and tomatoes onto the bottom of the security desk.

"Don't worry about that, my friend. We'll get someone in here to clean it up," the senator said.

The clerk found his card, and as he went to hand it to the guard, the guard gave it a stray glance and said, "That's fine. You gentlemen can head inside."

"You ever been in this building before, my friend?" the senator said after they walked through the full body scanner and approached the lift.

"I don't think so. Where are we?"

"Why, we're where all the magic happens," he respond- ed. "C'mon, we'll take the lift and I'll show you the floor— where the senators debate, vote on laws—all that. It's be- cause of the support of people like you."

They stepped out of the hallway into a big, round room that the clerk recognized from videos. It looked much big- ger in person. It reminded the clerk of an ancient coliseum, where the spectators cheered up in the seats as gladiators battled to the death down in the center.

"Down there is the debate floor. You've got to be a mas- ter in rhetoric—the art of persuasion—in order to get all the senators up here to vote with you." There weren't any debates happening right now, but the whole place was filled with people in suits milling about. "Well, I thought you'd find it inspiring to see this place up here, but we're going to have to take the service elevator to the basement for me to show you what I really brought you here for. Just play it cool, okay, my friend? Not everyone's like-minded as you and I."

The clerk followed him down a series of serpentine hallways, which took several narrow, mazelike turns before they reached a dead end stacked with crates and boxes.

"Do me a favor and help me shove these out of the way." So shoving commenced, along with pushing and pulling, and it took a while until a little square hole in the floor was uncovered. The clerk considered expressing his disbelief that they—particularly the large senator—could enter this square without becoming hopelessly wedged within, but his body was trembling and speaking seemed like it would waste energy unnecessarily. "Follow after me, my friend," the man said, gracefully sliding into the square as though it were bigger than it looked. The clerk did as he was told, feeling cramped, claustrophobic, and too close to the man's rear-end. He bumped into that end just as the man announced, "We've made it to the service elevator."

Sure enough, the clerk could stand almost to his full height in the small service lift.

"Where would you like to go?" a butler holding a mechanism of ropes and chains asked.

"Basement. All the way down," the senator responded.

The butler began tugging ropes and cranking the mechanism. The whole box they were in shook and swayed as they descended deep beneath the earth. Just when the clerk was on the verge of working up the energy to ask, "Will this take much longer?" the butler lifted the latch on the doors as the elevator box slammed into the ground, sending the clerk tumbling out. He spun in a circle as he tried to catch his balance and landed flat on his bottom.

"Up, up, my boy," the senator said, giving him a strong hand. The clerk looked around to realize that he was in some sort of aeroplane hangar.

"Ah, senator, good to see you," a military-looking man said as he approached. He shook the senator's hand and then shook the clerk's. His grip was too strong, and the clerk imagined his hand cracking and crumbling into pieces. He wasn't sure if he let out a yelp, but he was definitely wincing. "I see your admiration has brought you back, and with a colleague, no doubt."

"Yes, yes, of course," the senator said. "That's her right over here, isn't it? The newest model." He continued walking away from the elevator and the others followed.

"What am I looking at?" the clerk muttered as he saw a shiny, black triangle the size of a house.

"You are looking at the future," the military man said. "The future is now. The future's been happening for the past decade. The future is safety. This is the soldier of the future."

"What do you mean? This thing's a soldier? You mean—a robot?"

"Yes, it's a robot plane. Autonomous. We can win the war without loss of life."

"A bloodless war?"

"Well, bloodless for us," he said with a sneer.

The clerk's face must have twisted into such horror that the man became accusatory. "What? That's not good enough for you? You think lives should be lost on both sides? You think our men should die, don't you? See, that's why so many people need to be kept in the dark about this operation."

The mouse squeaked in the clerk's pocket, which seemed to cast a silence over the hangar.

"Wait, no, you've got it all wrong!" The clerk burst out. "I'm cool, I'm good. I am just in awe by the sheer power and impressiveness of the whole thing."

"Awe? You said awe?"

"Awe."

"Awe? That was the face of awe?"

"Yeah. Awe. Awe's all it was."

"It looked like awe to me," the senator added.

"Oh, well you're right to be in awe!" the military man said, his face lighting up again, which darkened the shadows in his hard, lined visage. "This here robot's pure awe-inspiring amazingness. It can fly faster than any animal or other machine. It's near silent as it cuts through the sky. The reflective coating makes it invisible from a thousand feet or more, and even if the enemy catches a photo of it, they can't tell it's not a raven in the distance. It does whatever we tell it, according to our specifications, and it's programmed with mock-intelligence to make the right decisions on its own in unexpected situations."

"It can think?" the clerk muttered.

"It can think what we tell it to think, yeah. And this whole underside is filled with smart bombs. Blows up whatever we want. Neutralizes our enemies before they can even think about hurting us. Before they can even have a hope of a hayseed in hell of getting close to us."

"Wow," the clerk said in a whisper.

"You're damn straight 'wow.'"

"So this is how—?" the clerk started, but his voice stopped.

"This is how what?"

"This is how wars are won, my friend. Now you've seen

firsthand what we're fighting for," the senator said.

Before long, the senator excused them and they reversed their route via the hand-cranked elevator and the maze of crawlspaces and hallways. They emerged out on the street in some sort of smokers' cove.

The senator began explaining some technical legislative details about votes in his favor and laws changed to reclassify civilians as enemies. "So you see, when I get this bill moving and blow this whole robot death strike thing out of the water, it's going to be bad news for our all-powerful Prime Minister. There's no way he can live down covering up all those civilian deaths. He promised us safety and security with those robots, but what he's doing is murdering children and innocents in lands we haven't even declared war on. Can you imagine that? Killing poor little ol' children just because they live in a different place? And it's downright the worst thing in the world that more children than ever are being killed in wars these days. The exact numbers are hard to get, but our government has been redefining 'civilian' and 'militant' to throw further smokescreens over just who we're blowing up. And you know, there's just something different about it when your name's on the bombs being dropped—and don't think we don't reap the benefits. You go up north to the war machine factories that are sustaining this economy and see what I'm talking about. I mean, it's still just as bad when other countries are out there committing these atrocities, but in that case we can debate about foreign policy and what can or should be done and all that—I personally subscribe to a philosophy of strong-armed pacifism. But when innocents are being killed in our names—yours and mine—that can't be allowed to happen. What we need to develop is a protection against such bombs from the sky. Is it not a matter of time before another nation replicates the technology and decides it is our citizens who should be obliterated?"

The clerk was bleary eyed, his skin clammy, sweaty, and itchy under his clothes. He had to get out of here, so he reached his feeble hand into his pocket, scooping up the coins that were now wet and slippery. With a shaky, moist hand, he held out the fistful of coins in the direction of the senator.

"Why thank you, my dear boy!" the senator exclaimed, his voice reanimating from the dark, brooding anger back into its usual joviality. "It's because of bog-standard citizens like you keeping their campaign promises that we're able to fight the good fight. We'll win this thing. We'll save the innocents. You'll see!" With a skip in his step as though he'd just been handed a trillion dollars, the senator made his way back toward the capitol building.

The clerk collapsed onto the ground, leaning his head back against the wall of the building. He took the little black mouse out of his pocket and held it in his palm. He gazed at it for a long moment. "I'm sorry I dropped the sandwich, Ellem. I'll have to find you something to eat soon." It squeaked quietly.

"Down on your luck too, my friend?" someone said to the clerk.

With a start, the clerk unceremoniously dropped the little mouse back into his pocket. He realized that the man who'd spoken was in a ragged coat, with messy gray straggles of hair escaping from beneath a wool cap and stretching down along his face. Before the clerk could respond, he noticed that there were many such people down here on the ground. He could see a sea of unkempt women and men stretched out along the sidewalk.

The man tried asking him another question. "Is there anything I could help you with?"

"Who are all you people?" the clerk uttered. He got a strong whiff of alcohol from the man's breath.

"Human beings, my friend," the man responded. "Citizens, my friend. We're all friends here. No need for labels."

"Oh," the clerk grunted.

"So you'll be bunking down here with us for the night, huh?"

"No, no," the clerk replied. "I need to get home."

"Home to your girl, huh?"

"Yeah."

"I could tell. I didn't find my girl yet. Not yet, not yet. Yeah, I did have a home once though. Yeah, I had a home once too, my friend. Not for me. Too restrictive. I felt trapped. What if I'm not there and it's time for bed? Why should I fight my way back? Why, I'd rather sleep wherever I happen to be. No, no. Homes. Jobs. Expectations. Not for me, my friend, not for me."

"Oh," the clerk grumbled.

"Anyway, why don't you just go home?"

"No money."

"Your own two feet don't cost no money."

"There's a river. It's far. I need a bus."

"Well a bus ain't too expensive, my friend. Just get some money."

"You can't just get money."

"Sure you can. You just do it like I do it. I do it every day. You just need one of these." He reached between two other people who were huddled on the ground nearby. His hand returned with a Styrofoam coffee cup. "The capitalists, they don't care about these, so you can just fish one out of a rubbish bin. And then you just keep it out in the general direction of the capitalists rushing by, and yeah, sure, most of them are rushing by trying to make money, not give it away, but there's so many people rushing by here, maybe every one in a hundred'll be a kindhearted capitalist and drop in a bit of change, and before long, you've got yourself enough for the bus."

"I can't do that," the clerk muttered.

"Sure you can. Anyone can. Why not?"

"It's panhandling."

"Yep. I 'spose it is."

"It's illegal."

"Living ain't illegal. Sure, sleeping outside is illegal, vagrancy is illegal, going to the bathroom out here is illegal, stripping down and washing off out here is illegal, and yeah, panhandling, that's illegal alright—but living? Living ain't illegal. So what's the problem?"

The clerk didn't respond. He just pouted, leaning his hands and chin on his knees and staring forward, ignoring the pungent smell of the hundred people huddled on the sidewalk with him.

"I tell ya what," the man said. "Here. Take mine. Go on. Go get your bus. You got some place to be, not me. So go get your bus and get back home to your home and your girl."

The clerk glanced over and saw the man was holding out a cupful of change.

"Wow, really? You mean it."

"Yeah. 'Course I meant it. Now go on. I know you can take it. It'll be easy enough for me to get more. I'm in no rush. I've got no place to be and no one waiting on me."

"Thanks so much! You're amazing!" the clerk cheered, life suddenly returning to his limbs. He grabbed the cup of change and hopped to his feet.

"Go on and enjoy your life, my friend! God bless!" the man said, waving him away.

Even at this late hour, the sidewalks were still stuffed

with harried business people. The clerk dropped the change into his pocket and ditched the cup. He struggled through the foot traffic in the direction of the river. He had no idea how to get back to the transit station, but the river—*that* he could find, and he followed it to the bridge. Once there, he leaned against the railing and watched the flow of cars and trucks in both directions. Whenever he saw a bus heading over the bridge, he would jump up and frantically wave his arms in an effort to get the driver's attention. "Luck is on my side!" he said as one finally opened its doors. It didn't fully stop moving forward, but he ran to catch up with it and jumped through the doors. "Can you take me to the small city?"

The driver responded affirmatively in the island language.

"Oh thank goodness," the clerk sighed, dropping into the nearest seat.

When he paid the fare as he exited the bus, he found that he had plenty of change to spare.

Despite the ordeals he'd undergone, the clerk arrived home the earliest that he had in some time, which was hours after his scheduled quitting time. Instead of taking advantage of this fortuitous opportunity to do something recreational and relaxing, his betrothed decided to set into him with one of those uncomfortable conversations prefaced with the phrase, "We have to talk."

The clerk's eyelids were heavy and his body quivering. He wanted to pay careful attention to the soliloquy, and he was struggling to recall the details of everything she'd told him the other night, but it was a losing battle.

His betrothed whispered, more to herself than to the clerk, "I thought you were someone with eyes that can see the infinite."

"I am," the clerk exclaimed, quick to defend himself.

"I'm the one who's seeing the big picture here! If I get that promotion— "

"Remember the life we used to dream of back when we were pen-pals, and you told me you'd move to the small city and we'd build our perfect life together? We spoke of animal conservation, betterment of society, attending art gatherings with the city's avant-garde—we were going to host dinner parties every weekend in our gorgeous loft apartment. Instead, we're trapped in here, a smaller surface area for ourselves than our pets have in their cages, and what progress are we making? I sit in here by myself all the time while you're gone, and I think of the life that's passing me by—of the days I'll never get back."

"Well that's why I'm trying to get a promotion. That way we can live our dream life."

"I thought we were supposed to already be living our perfect life. When you first moved into my room with me, you said you just had to land a full-time job and we'd be set."

"I did think that. Honestly, it's what I believed back then, when I first arrived in the city and didn't know how expensive and difficult it'd all be."

"That was years ago! We've made no progress at all."

"That's not true. I've almost landed this promotion— believe me! You don't know how much work has gone into this secret project. I've been busting myself every day to get it done in addition to my regular workload, and we're almost there! I know the director is happy with my work. I know I'll get that promotion!"

"I speak of progress and you speak of promotions. Didn't you say the same thing last time? You were hired as an assistant clerk, and it quickly became obvious that we had barely enough for food with the salary you made in that role. Before long, there was talk of an opening for a full clerk, and you were secretly put onto a special project for the manager of another department, which left you stuck doing double your regular job for more than a year—and you were right about one thing—because of the extra work, you did get a promotion. Yet we're still here. Now you work more than ever, I barely see you, and you're promising me that it's just one more promotion until our dream life. Where does it end? When you get enough promotions so that we can finally afford a tiny flat on our own? When you'll be stuck at the office 24/7, and maybe I'll see you on official holidays and days I steal some of your work time to bring you in lunch or dinner?"

The clerk's mouth was slightly agape, his lower lip quavering. He tried to twist his lips into a grin, to release a laugh or scoff and tell her that she was being ridiculous, but instead, a whimpering cry squeaked out of his mouth. He stuttered, attempting to say something. He could feel her eyes penetrating into his core. "I'm trying my best," he managed to whine in a whisper before sobs violently wracked his body, and he collapsed to the bed, shoving his face deep into a pillow.

"Oh, I didn't mean to make you cry!" his betrothed exclaimed with exasperation, rubbing her hand between his shoulder blades. "I know your job is putting all this pressure on you and taking advantage of you. But at a certain point, don't you have to say, 'I'm not going to put up with this anymore. I'm not going to be treated like this any longer.'?"

The clerk wanted to respond, but the cries leaping out of him were uncontrollable. He wanted to tell his betrothed that the only reason he put up with all of this was because he wanted to give her the life they'd always dreamed of, that he only came here to this city because of his love for her, but he couldn't bring himself to say it. He cried himself to sleep.

Sometime after two AM, the clerk was awoken by someone repeatedly shaking him by the hips. Three of the junior clerks were piled into his doorway, shoving paper and pens in his direction.

"What's going on?" his betrothed demanded, regaining consciousness more quickly than he did.

"We just need a higher ranking clerk to sign off on these documents."

"Get out of here!" his betrothed shouted. "He can sign them in the morning!"

"Begging your pardon, ma'am," one of the assistant clerks said, "but it is the morning, and if we wait until later in the morning to get these signed, we'll miss the deadline by far. It'll hold up all sorts of projects, and, well, it could very likely cost us our jobs."

"Just pass them over to me," the clerk said, grabbing the papers and a pen. "I'm already up. It will only take me a minute."

His betrothed sighed loudly and rolled over in bed.

* * * *

When the clerk returned home from work the next night, she was gone, along with all of the animals. The room was emptier, but it seemed smaller than ever. The clerk went out to the kitchen and asked the large men if they knew where his betrothed went, but they wouldn't say anything more specific than, "She moved out." They added that it seemed awkward for him to stay there on his own.

"Please, just—just give me a little bit of time to find somewhere to sleep. My betrothed is gone, I'm all alone. At least give me that much."

They obliged.

The clerk fell back onto the bed. "I lost my betrothed," he whispered. "Well, she's not my betrothed anymore. The world gained an artist."

Tears silently streamed down his face. The little mouse crawled out of his pocket and scurried all over his chest and legs. "Thanks buddy," he murmured.

The clerk didn't move all night, but he didn't sleep. At dawn, he rose to go to the office. He didn't bother changing his clothes. He shambled down the sidewalk unthinkingly, and the next thing he knew, he was sitting in the chair at his cubicle.

His rival's beady eyes appeared over the cubicle wall. "Haven't seen much of you lately. Yesterday you slipped out early and never came back. Seems like you've been doing that a lot. You must never finish any of your work!" The rival laughed as if he'd told a joke. "What have you, given up?"

"Maybe I have," the clerk whispered.

His rival popped his head back under the partition like a retreating turtle.

The clerk sat in his chair, staring at nothing all morning. No one else came and bothered him for hours.

Without warning, officers in riot gear hoisted him up by the armpits. The sore in his armpit caused him to wince involuntarily, but other than that, he made no reaction. The officers began dragging him down the hallway, his feet trailing along the carpet. His rival looked on with glee.

"What's this all about? Why are you dragging him away?" the clerk's manager said, emerging from her office.

"Ma'am, please stay out of this," the officers said in unison.

"I'm the manager of this department. I have a right to know exactly what's going on!"

"Ma'am, because you have such a high security clearance, I can tell you this, but it's regarding an ongoing investigation. The Technology Department alerted us that this clerk's computer has had an open connection to unfriendly countries all around the world. Now we're still in the process of investigating if they hacked in or if he let them in, but one thing is for certain: There's a file on this computer containing a list of coordinates of specific locations in two of the countries where there are active bombings occurring. Most of these coordinates indicated our most recent robot-plane bombing sites before they were bombed. Now we don't know why your clerk created this list or who's calling the shots here, but we're under orders to take him in."

"It can't be—" the manager whispered, clearly cowed.

"Just walk on your own from here," the pair of officers said in unison, letting go of the clerk.

He crumpled to the floor in a heap, the same as if they'd dropped an empty shirt. The clerk remained down there in his catatonic state.

"Look, we can't arrest this bloke. He's too sickly. His skin is clammy, pale, and green. He doesn't even look like he could make it from here to the bathroom."

"Which might explain the smell—"

They lifted him by the arms and feet and carried him into the cellar and outside the secret passageway to where their law enforcement tank was parked. The dropped him in back of the tank and drove to his address. Once there, they kicked in the door, to the shock of the two large men, and wordlessly carried him to his bedroom, where they dropped him in the bed.

"So here's my plan," one of the officers said. "I say we place him under arrest, but leave him be. Put him on three million bail so he can't leave this room—not that he can leave the room without the bail—and in the unlikely event that he does try to leave, we'll just revoke his passport and make him a stateless person. Bam. Problem solved."

"No problem."

"That way, even if he made a divinely miraculous recovery and managed to get away, he'll get his day in court. We'll get his day in court. Everybody's happy."

"But the warrant says—"

"Bah! I can interpret these things however I want."

"And there's that camera crew outside—"

"Bah! This'll give them a better story than they were hoping for."

On their way out, the officers said to the large men, "You should probably call that bloke a doctor."

The large men protested and asked for explanations, but the officers just left, and in their wake, they left behind a swarm of reporters with camera crews who were attempting to barge into the flat. The men barricaded the door with an armoire and called for a doctor. Then they searched for news about the catatonic man in the bedroom.

On the picture tube, they saw a woman reporting outside of their apartment building: "An unnamed government clerk has been placed under arrest today following revelations related to targeted robot death strikes in the nation's dual war. Sources say that the clerk was actually a quad-agent, holding high-ranking security clearance for this nation and three others. Evidently, he abused his authority to reroute the Prime Minister's official strike targets to coordinates that would result in massive civilian casualties."

A thick, bald man in a suit appeared on the picture tube descending a wide stone staircase. Reporters were surrounding him and shoving microphones into his face. He stopped walking momentarily and said, "As soon as our department became aware of the coordinate changes, we took immediate action to stop the individual. Our investigation is ongoing. No further comments."

"In light of these revelations, the senate has voted to veto a bill aimed at reigning in the Prime Minister's robotic war initiatives. The Prime Minister's cabinet declined to comment today."

The doctor arrived, pushing through the throng of reporters to get to the door and climbing over the armoire.

"He's right through there. In the bedroom," one of the men said.

The doctor disappeared into the bedroom. A few minutes later, she ran back out, shouting, "Get out of here! We all need to be sanitized immediately! We could have a medieval plague outbreak on our hands here!"

The men abandoned their flat, and when the doctor returned, she looked like an astronaut in her full hazmat suit, and she had a medical team with her who were all dressed the same way. They quarantined the apartment with a plastic barrier, and covered the clerk in wires, tubes, and beeping technology.

"My god, this infection's far advanced! It's a miracle this man could walk yesterday!"

Sitting on the sill outside of the window, a little black mouse was peering in. Its view was filtered by a pane of glass and the translucent quarantine wall, which caused some distortion. Its tiny, black, shiny eyes watched the humans buzzing about and causing a commotion. A long, high-pitched frequency entered its wide little ears. Then all at once, the humans stopped moving, staring down at the motionless body on the bed. The mouse turned away from the window and started down the brick wall. It deftly reached for little handholds in each individual brick. On an otherwise gray evening, a lone sunbeam reached through the buildings on the horizon and warmed the small animal. Before long, the mouse reached the grass and ran off into the bushes, its long tail following behind.

The following excerpt is a preview of
THE PROBLEM DEPARTMENT
A Novel About Problems—Not Solutions
Accurate Accounts of Office Work: Book 2

by
Joseph Patrick Pascale

Coming soon from Waldorf Publishing

THE PROBLEM DEPARTMENT

Savita was flipping through the huge backlog of Problem Reports that were stacked on her desk, looking for a few easy ones to get out of the way during this rare quiet moment. She read some of the summaries in an attempt to ascertain which problems to tackle.

"*Dulce de leche* spill in secure data-retrieval facility. Not sure if *dulce de leche*, but definitely something that shouldn't be in a secure data-retrieval facility." Savita squished up her face and moved onto the next paper.

"Rodent infestation in break room."

"People in this department keep brewing decaf coffee but putting it in the regular coffee pot."

"String cheese left on desk repeatedly."

"People in this department keep brewing caffeinated coffee but putting it in the decaf coffee pot."

One of Savita's interns climbed up the rope ladder into her office and dropped a paper into her inbox. As the girl was attempting to leave Savita said, "Hey! What's that?"

"Some guy just called. He wanted someone to go over to his office, but all of the Problem Specialists are busy right now, so I added a report for him."

Savita snatched up the paper and read it. "This guy just needs a piece of paper? That doesn't sound too bad."

* * * *

Savita poked her head into a cubicle and saw a guy with his office phone crooked on his shoulder. "Hi, Mr. Core? I'm Savita with the Problem Department. You called us about an issue you're having?"

His eyes lit up. "Oh great! You brought me a piece of paper?!"

"Well, no," she hedged. "I'm here to help with your problem."

"But my problem is that I need a piece of paper."

"So that's what I'm here to help with. Please understand that according to our department's policies, which you signed off on, we are able to provide you with guidance, but you must be the primary agent in any potential resolutions of your problem."

He made an exasperated grunt and took the phone away from his ear for a second. "You do realize that in this department each person only gets a ration of five pieces of paper per day?"

"Yes, I know. We're trying to be a green building."

"Important as that initiative may or may not be, it doesn't change the fact that I need one piece of paper right now. I have a mondo-important meeting with my supervisor and four contractors, and they each need a copy of my findings. I was already working short on paper as it is. I have my original that I'm abandoning to my supervisor, and then I put that document on the flatbed scanner of the copy machine and told it to make four copies. Copy one slides out like a fresh, warm pancake. Same for copies two and three as they stack on top of it—but copy four, that son of a—Copy four gets tangled up somewhere in the Industrial Revolution-era technology working the insides of that thing, and suddenly I'm taking the copy machine apart, I'm up to my wrists in black toner, and my paper's a crinkled mess that I'm tearing into pieces as I attempt to extract it from the jaws of the machine."

Savita's eyes were wide as she processed his disgruntled soliloquy. She took a deep breath and thought of positive reinforcement and optimism. "Is it possible you could send an electronic copy of your report to them?"

The look on his face plastered her to the cubicle wall.

"This is a sensitive document. I typed the original on an *Underwood*. Look, just get out of here—you're not helping. I'm on hold with the department in charge of extra paper."

Savita remained in place—eyes wide with a stunned expression.

She gulped and considered the grim possibility that this guy wasn't going to leave her a positive evaluation report. "Sir, sometimes it can be rather difficult to get them on the phone," she hazarded. "I've been down there before. I could take you—try to expedite the process."

He slammed the office phone down onto the hook. "Let's go."

As they exited the elevator on the 19th floor, a line of people stretching to the end of the hallway was all Savita could see. She had to admit to herself that this didn't look good, but she straightened her posture and began to walk forward with the client following behind her.

"Hey! Back of the line, you two!" someone shouted. Other people joined in and complained at them.

Savita looked behind herself and saw a conglomeration of people. "I don't even see the back of the line."

"Keep walking back there and you'll find it," a lady

nearby grumbled.

The client looked furious, but he walked with Savita. She realized that the door to the stairwell was open, and as they walked through it, she saw that the line stretched down the flight of stairs and wrapped around beyond her vision. She looked at the client, who was grinding his teeth as he gaped at the line.

"You didn't try asking anyone else in your office for a piece of paper, did you?" Savita asked.

"Do you really think that wasn't the first thing I tried?"

"Well, I don't—"

"Of course I asked. I stood in the hallway like a panhandling hobo, begging my colleagues for a slice of paper. No dice."

"Can you make the copy on the back of something else?"

"You really don't know the kind of people I'm dealing with here."

Savita trudged on toward the back of the line with the client in tow. A few flights down, she found it.

"So uh, what's this line for?" Savita asked a guy in an olive green suit who appeared to be the tail end of the queue.

"Extra paper. Don't worry. It moves faster than you'd expect."

* * * *

Hours later, they were within sight of the actual office, and not too long after that, they were face-to-face with a person behind a desk.

"Let me do the talking," Savita said to the client as they walked up. He rolled his eyes.

"Good afternoon. I'm Savita Alleyen, Problem Specialty Officer. I'm on a case here with my client. All we need is a good old fashioned piece of paper."

The lady at the desk had a grumpy slump to her lips. Her

eyes were hidden behind the reflections of her thick-rimmed glasses. "Who's the paper for? You or him?"

"Uh, him."

"Who are you?" she grunted at the client.

"Randal Core. I'm one of the assistant engineers."

"Engineering, I see. And how many pieces of paper did you use today, sir?"

He crumpled his face in disgust. "Four, I guess. The fifth was—"

"What happened to your daily allotment of five sheets of paper? We're not responsible for lost pieces of paper around here."

"But isn't this the Paper Products Supply Center?" he snapped. "If you're not responsible, who is?"

"You are. Each employee in your area can use their key-card to extract five pieces of paper per day. Didn't you extract your five already?"

"Yes, but the thing is—"

"We're not responsible for lost paper."

"It's not lost!" he shouted. "It's crumpled and ripped into a thousand shreds because of the worthless copy machines around here!"

"Well, why didn't you say so, honey?" she responded, her voice transforming into an understanding tone. "That's a maintenance issue. You're going to have to take it up with them."

"But I only used four sheets of paper yesterday—and two the day before that! Can't I just have one of those sheets of paper?"

"We have a no paper rollover policy."

"That's ridiculous!"

"Sir, we used to have a rollover policy and people were abusing it. People were hoarding paper—printing out a year's worth of documents in a single afternoon. There had to be changes."

The client's mouth emitted a loud, guttural burst of frustration that sounded as though his vocal cords were ripping to shreds.

Savita didn't like the look of this one bit. She wished she'd thought to contact maintenance first. There was no way he was going to leave a positive review on his evaluation of this session. In fact, he may be so frustrated that this becomes a worst-case scenario—he submits a complaint to the Complaint Department. Savita gulped and tried to force a smile. "C'mon now, let's not give up. There's still time before your meeting. I'll take you up to Maintenance."

* * * *

As they exited the elevator on the 91st floor, Savita took solace in the fact that the hallway wasn't mobbed. "I don't want to speak too soon, but there's not a huge line of people here," she said.

The client grunted.

They walked into the Maintenance Office and found it to be a large open area with people milling about. Savita noticed a circular desk toward the center of the room, so she walked up and asked the receptionist who she could speak with about a maintenance issue.

"If you just head over in that direction, you can take a ticket. One of our Maintenance Technicians will use the ticket to come help you in your department when your number comes up."

"About how long's the wait?" the client asked.

"Oh, it's tough to estimate. You have to describe the nature of your issue, and it gets prioritized in the queue."

"I don't like the sound of that," the client muttered under his breath.

He'd made it seem as though the ticket booth was nearby, but they walked for about twenty minutes until they found the thing. Once it was all settled and Savita's client was holding a ticket in his hands, he seemed more agitated. "What do we do now? Just stand around here and wait?"

"I think the point of the ticket is so you can go about your day without having to wait in line for hours. Don't you have any other tasks you'd like to take care of?"

"Other tasks?! Are you joking? Don't you realize that this meeting is all I've been working on for months? Don't you realize that if I make a poor showing at this meeting, it could cost me my job? I could be blacklisted from the field! I'll be on the streets shouting at invisible images of you and all the other worthless people populating the countless offices of all these damnable departments!"

"Uh," Savita muttered. She didn't feel prepared for such an irate client.

"Why don't you just steal me a piece of paper?" he asked. "Don't you have paper? Someone around here's got to have a fresh piece of paper we can steal."

"Sir, stealing's against our policies."

"*'Stealing's against our policies,'*" he mocked, stalking away.

Savita followed him around for a while. Maybe he was trying to find a piece of paper to steal, but he ended up slumped on the floor in his cubicle, complaining about the time. "Do you realize in an hour and fifteen minutes, I'm supposed to be in the conference room for this meeting? What am I going to do, show up with four copies of the report for five people? This is unbelievable!"

Savita chewed on the inside of her cheek and sat down next to him. Before long, it was only fifteen minutes to three and there was no sign of anyone from maintenance. The client got up. His hands were shaking and he was drenched in sweat. He wiped his hands on his trousers and picked up his four copies of the report. Shuffling slowly, he began to head in the direction of the conference room. Savita trailed behind him.

As if he lost his nerve, he dove behind a potted plant. "Stand in front of me!" he whisper-shouted. "I don't want my boss to see me."

"Uh."

"Go distract him! Tell him you're my secretary and I'm stuck in traffic, so I'll be a few minutes late."

"But lying's against our policies."

"Just do it!"

"I forgot your name!"

"Randal Core!"

Savita sidled up to the guy in the suit, who she assumed was the client's supervisor. "Excuse me sir, are you Randal Core's supervisor?"

He cleared his throat and peered down his long nose at her. "Yes. Why?"

"Well, I'm uh, assisting him, and he told me to tell you that he's been delayed in traffic."

"Traffic? Why wasn't he at his desk?"

"I uh. Well, the thing is, I think he was having some issues with the copier, so he went to try and resolve that."

"When you talk to him again, tell him he better get his butt in here five minutes ago."

"Righto," Savita said through clenched teeth that were supposed to be a smile.

She conferenced back with the client between the leaves of the plant. "What should our next step be?" she asked.

"We wait. We wait for Maintenance. I'm sure they'll be here any minute now."

She sat down next to him behind the plant. She tried not to make eye contact because he was so upset. At some point, three o'clock rolled around, and some executive-looking types walked into the conference room. The executives didn't notice Savita and her client in their botanical hiding spot. She could hear the client gently sobbing.

At five o'clock, Savita considered mentioning that her shift was over, but she decided against it. He was too upset and his problem wasn't resolved.

At eight o'clock, a cleaning crew watered them.

At midnight, the client said, "Well, I can get another five sheets of paper now." His knees cracked as he stood up. "What the?" He took the ticket out of his pocket. It was glowing and vibrating. Someone from Maintenance walked up holding a manila folder.

"Mr. Core? This is for you."

He opened it, finding one clean sheet of paper. He dropped the folder onto the gray carpet, and he screamed as he held the paper up over his head and ripped it in half. He tore and crumpled and stomped the paper before stalking off. The maintenance guy and Savita stood there in silence, listening to his curses fade into the distance.

"He's not going to be happy in the morning when he finds he's been written up for purposely destroying office supplies."

"That is against policy," Savita agreed.

* * * *

"My job is to run this branch's Problem Department," Savita explained, "a catchall band-aid to keep government workers contented. They come to us with all sorts of problems that we are ill-equipped to solve. We're kind of like an IT Helpdesk, except instead of fixing their computers, we have to fix their lives—whatever problems they have. And yeah, sometimes people come to us for help with their computer problems, and I could probably, technically send them up to the Helpdesk, but I don't dare do that—bad customer service."

"Ms. Alleyen, you do understand that speaking with us could potentially put you in a quite precarious situation, correct? While we will make every effort to maintain your anonymity, given the current governmental milieu and their harsh actions against leakers and whistleblowers, there's a possibility this could be tracked back to you. That would mean trouble."

"Yeah." Savita shrugged. "You don't have to warn me again." The group continued to stride down the alley, moving through the midnight shadows.

Acknowledgments

Thanks ever so much to my awesome wife, Suany, who always encourages my writing and was a fan of this novel from the first page. My parents instilled a love of reading and writing in me since I was a kid and scribbled them gibberish letters when I hadn't yet learned to write, so I can't thank them enough for all of their support. Thanks to my friend since third grade, TJ, who provided valuable feedback on the first draft of this book. Hugs to my mother-in-law, Liz, who accepted me as part of the family. And I'll thank my brother too, even though it's doubtful he'll ever read this page.

I express my sincere gratitude for my publisher Barbara Terry, my editor Carol McCrow, and the entire team at Waldorf Publishing who believed in my work and helped to make it the best it can be. I'm also grateful to the advance readers who provided early reviews of the novel. And thanks especially to you, reader! I hope you enjoyed the ride, and I'll catch you next time.

Author Bio

Joseph Patrick Pascale's short fiction has been published in *Birkensnake, Literary Orphans, Pidgeonholes, Spank the Carp, The American (Rome), The Apeiron Review, Off the Rocks, Instigatorzine, On a Narrow Windowsill: Fiction and Poetry Folded onto Twitter, Seven by Twenty, Cuento Magazine,* and other journals and anthologies.

He was part of the editorial team for *Drunken Boat*, an international online literary journal of the arts, and he contributes nonfiction to literary publications such as *Full Stop* or his personal blog, *Cryptomnesia*. Pascale studied under poet Mark Doty when he earned his Master of Arts in Literature from **Centenary University**. He worked as a farmhand, reporter, auto parts deliverer, executive recruiter, and reference book editor before becoming an educator. You can read more at his website: www.josephpatrickpascale.com.

CPSIA information can be obtained
at www.ICGtesting.com
Printed in the USA
BVHW032247190419
546078BV00001B/2/P

9 781641 368445